TAGA AND MAA:

A Novel

BY AMORET BUTLER

Order this book online at www.trafford.com/06-2394
or email orders@trafford.com

Most Trafford titles are also available at major online book retailers.

Note for Librarians: A cataloguing record for this book is available from Library and Archives Canada at www.collectionscanada.ca/amicus/index-e.html

ISBN: 978-1-4251-0636-2

We at Trafford believe that it is the responsibility of us all, as both individuals and corporations, to make choices that are environmentally and socially sound. You, in turn, are supporting this responsible conduct each time you purchase a Trafford book, or make use of our publishing services. To find out how you are helping, please visit www.trafford.com/responsiblepublishing.html

Our mission is to efficiently provide the world's finest, most comprehensive book publishing service, enabling every author to experience success. To find out how to publish your book, your way, and have it available worldwide, visit us online at www.trafford.com/10510

www.trafford.com

North America & international
toll-free: 1 888 232 4444 (USA & Canada)
phone: 250 383 6864 • fax: 250 383 6804 • email: info@trafford.com

The United Kingdom & Europe
phone: +44 (0)1865 722 113 • local rate: 0845 230 9601
facsimile: +44 (0)1865 722 868 • email: info.uk@trafford.com

10 9 8 7 6 5 4 3

To my fellow writer Richard Holtzin,
without whose encouragement this novel
would not have been possible.

CHAPTER
~1~

It was a gray cosmos of dirty sky and bleak tundra blending at a short distance into one: an empty universe of used matter now gathering blackness and threatening as if it all were a smoke full of the ash from a sacrifice to ancient gods. The frozen ground was solid under the hide-bound feet of small Tuit as he plodded behind the bear-like shapes of Taga and Maa. Hunger began to gnaw inside with a deep pain, so the little boy roared into the unpromising atmosphere a sudden, frenzied, impatient, uncompromising demand – a protest against the last mile of coldness and constant motion and against those consuming pangs. He stopped still and roared again in frustration.

Maa gave him a phlegmatic half-turn with her clumsy body, understanding as a mother does and weighing the chances of continuing on for another mile to the camp. Another roar disturbed Taga this time, and he nodded to Maa that they should halt.

She scuffled hack a few steps, her huge bootlings dragging, then stooped and pulled the boy into her ample fur wraps. She stuffed into his mouth a sagging nipple and held him close as his small body grew hot. Maa swung out toward home, a few steps behind her husband.

Their tundra was a part of the long reaches of today's Gobi Desert in Mongolia, but in their time of 25,500 B.C. these names had not yet been used, and the terrain was not desert but was a sometimes marshy, now wintry tundra south of the great ice mass which covered much of the northern hemisphere. At that time the area we call northern Europe was locked in an Ice Age, as was northern Siberia, Alaska, and northern Canada. This glacial period gave way about 23,000 B.C. to a warming, melting age lasting some eight thousand years, which in turn yielded to another glacial era called the Wisconsin Period in North America, lasting from 15,000 B.C. until somewhere around 10,000 B.C.

In the twenty-fifth millennium B.C. the earth was sparsely populated, but the caribou of this lonely region provided hunters with the incentive for living in the Gobi area, mostly in nomadic bands.

From time to time Taga glanced with satisfaction at the two ptarmigan hens in his fur-wrapped hand. The bright head feathers told him that his hunting luck had held, so now they would eat well tonight. He would make a drink also of dried berries and honey, and it would be good to share its sweetness with Maa and little Tuit. He smiled as he thought of Tuit dribbling the red juices as they were offered to him on a bone spoon.

A gust of wind, the *buran* of later millennia, brought a great, sweeping chill just as they came close to a gully beside a sharp hill; they were nearly home. Taga paused to look up, putting out his roughly wrapped hand to stop Maa while he examined the boiling sky. His outstretched arm was hit by a large, clear ball of ice from the clouds above.

At once a pelting rush of hail made them crouch down into the gully and crawl backward under a small overhang. There they bent low, with heads together, while the earth beyond their frail shelter went into a spin. A tornado passed close by with a drone and noise of confusion upon confusion; then it hailed again – those gigantic hailstones which rip the earth and all upon it. Their overhang was just wide enough; Maa moaned with awe, afraid to speak the name of the Storm God, not knowing what would come next. Whipped by wild winds, a blinding snow hit their gully. The sudden blizzard was so severe that they could only huddle where they were, now in darkness. After a short time, they yielded to sleep, keeping all three bodies close for warmth.

It was probably the middle of the night when Taga woke, stiff from the awkward position. He stood clumsily, orienting himself to their circumstances. Memory flooded into his brain and the fear returned, even though he could now see stars in a clear night sky overhead, a reassuring, blinking, beautiful universe of vast calm and cold. The snow was not deep; it lay with a gentle, tenderly close touch upon the earth, and he knew that the White Goddess of the Snow had calmed the Storm God. Taga bent down and rubbed Maa's nose with his until she roused with a sly smile at his mood. But as she stood up, shifting the little boy under the full wraps of her furs, she realized that they were not yet home, and a sudden longing to arrive there possessed her. She grunted and they moved, locked together in an urgent embrace on his part and a sort of pulling, enticing movement on hers; she was now intent upon reaching her own hearth in spite of everything. The man uttered some little grunts, small half-pleading noises to which she replied coyly. This was a game he would tolerate for a moment.

Her screams split his ear; they tore into his uxorious emotions like a splinter of ice, and he straightened up, reaching for his weapons as a reflex. Axe in hand, he surveyed the flat area just before them, then turned full circle to look for their danger, his eyes measuring and remembering contours above and under the snow. As he understood why his wife had cried out, wonder and fear bubbled up in his own throat and he gave voice to a harsh moaning complaint, "NO! NO!"

Where their hovel of brush and hides had stood there was a smoothly level area covered by a layer of pure virgin snow. The whirlwind had taken their hut away. The spirit of the Storm God had done his evil in the night.

CHAPTER
~2~

THE NEXT MORNING a broad stream of sunlight woke Taga. He realized that the small rocky overhang to which they had returned was facing the east. A blinding beam of light made him shift uncomfortably against his wife's leaning form. Maa had wept for most of the night, overcome by the abruptness of their loss and full of fears, so that now she slept heavily.

Stretching his feet outside the shelter, Taga cushioned his head upon Maa. She slept with rough breathing, perhaps because of the changeable weather. He closed his eyes lightly for a moment but did not drowse, for he thought of the pair of birds he had trapped during the previous afternoon. What had happened to them? He could not recall. Without moving, he opened his eyes and searched the tiny cave. In the dazzling light he saw something protruding from the rock sides – a rounded object like an egg but as wide as a man's two hands can cup. His trembling fingers found it was like stone – inedible. He easily dislodged it from the softer sandstone around it, using his stone axe. Was it a talisman left by the missing ptarmigan hens? He turned the fossil egg over and over: a perfect stone egg as long as his ample hand but more elongated than any bird's egg.

The rays of the sun picked out another oval on the wall, this time higher and with a complete crack in its shell. It appeared to him suddenly, just as if it had not been there a moment before. Working it free of the sandstone, he found a delicately made stone lizard head and two clawed front feet emerging from the cracked shell.

Maa awoke to see her husband contemplating a mystery beyond mysteries. She could not know that he had two pterodactyl eggs left in the sand here millennia before her age, from the time when Gobia, the central Asian continent, had teemed with reptilian life.

She murmured, "The East of the Dawn," for it seemed to her that Taga held two sun-gilded eggs. Truly the splendor of the Dawn Goddess transformed the fossil material for that moment.

Reverently, Taga placed the magically fashioned objects on the snow while he and Maa bent in adoration of East, the Golden Goddess of the Dawn. The long, brilliant rays of light beckoned to them in a personal revelation. They repeated the name of the Dawn Spirit over and over. Homeless, they had slept; fearful, they had awakened to a great Mystery in the dawning day – a goddess's gift, an inedible but imperishable sign.

Tuit awoke silently at that moment and stood. He stepped out in front of his kneeling parents and looked up to the sun before them. With a simple gesture, the child pointed toward the incandescence of the sun as its beams lit his face and his hand. Showered in gold, Tuit spoke as his parents listened in awe; he said, "East." It was not only the transfiguration by the golden light which held them silent. Their son had spoken a message and had made a gesture with authority.

Taga and his wife stood together. Their black eyes shone with an inner light, a depth of response which brought confidence, resilience, strength, giving their broad faces a singular beauty and vitality.

The two-year-old child seemed happy, too, and not yet remembering that he had not broken fast, for the time enjoyed the smiles on the faces of those two young parents who nourished him. What he had said seemed to have caused joy, and he felt that he had their attention.

He was happy. He waited quietly, solemnly, but with shining eyes.

Taga proclaimed it for the family: "We will go east." He picked up the two fossil eggs, wrapped them in a bit of fur and dropped them into a bag within his robe. Then he took the arm of his wife and held the hand of small Tuit as they walked eastward toward the sun.

This path brought them, of course, to the smoothed circle where their hearth fire had once been lighted, and the three paused.

Maa said a few words to take away the curse of emptiness from the hearth site – the same words she had heard from her mother. She wished to keep the favor of all the gods, and she must not make a mistake at this time. She murmured faintly, "Goddess of the Hearth, Spirit of the Family, I thank you for your favor on this our fire. Now accompany me as I go, and bless my family." She stood and made her sign in the lingering snow covering: she drew a round circle for the round stone pot used for cooking and then drew a smaller round circle underneath it for the rounded dried dung most often used as her fuel.

As she did so, she noticed that Taga had swept snow away from the spot where he had made tools. He picked up a few stones and she recognized the red of jasper and was glad, for he often made ornaments for her of this stone. To her surprise, Tuit picked up two smaller stones; he had recognized two bits of red carnelian. These he handed to Taga. How bright he was! But he had spent many hours squatting beside Taga as Taga worked stones carefully, making knives or tools from the colored stones as well as from gray flint. Stone working was Taga's special talent and vocation.

With no real final gesture, then, the three walked away, leaving behind the stony brook with its small copse of spindly birches a short distance away, the wide-sweeping view of the tundra, and the craggy hill behind.

She slipped to Tuit the last tiny piece of pemmican from the bag inside her robes, and he began to chew busily as they chose a barely-discernible path leading over a roll in the tundra floor, a trail leading into the sun.

A short walk brought them in sight of a low hut built at the foot of a small hill and burrowing into the hill. A door flap faced east.

Despite the whirlwind of the previous day, this hut of Tlan appeared to be mostly intact. Since it was made of brushwood, twigs, stones, and clay, it blended into the hillside in a cluttered way. A cave in the hill had been made habitable by homely additions, and the leather flap discouraged animals, while a large dried salt bush in front was a kind of camouflage. Tlan, who lived here, was an old one who only wished to talk endlessly about hunting the big game, the mammoth. He had been a master maker of stone points; it was he who had found for Taga the colored stones and had first shown him how to work them. Tlan also had become a shaman in his long and adventurous life.

As they pulled back the swinging hide door flap, they sang out the traditional greeting, but they saw no one in the dimness. A pile of ragged furs in the far corner got up, and a diminutive creature, bent nearly double, came toward them with arms outstretched in welcome.

"Old one, your fire is nearly out. Are you ill?" asked Taga kindly, but with tact.

"The fever in the joints is with me and I do not eat much. Therefore, I grow weak and sleep a lot," replied Tlan. "I am my own ancestor. I am aged."

As they talked, Maa drew out from her robes some dried dung she always collected as they walked over the tundra, and now she built up the fire upon the hearthstone. Its smoldering brightness changed the interior of the small room, while it improved the mood of the older man. Quietly Maa, after a nod from Tlan, investigated the store of food on a raised earthen shelf and began to prepare a meal. A few dried roots, some dried caribou meat, and a handful of dried berries went into a stone bowl with clear ice which she fetched from the frozen brook and allowed now to melt. When the cookstone grew very hot in the fire, she dumped it, hissing, into the bowl and let the ingredients stew.

As the men talked, Tuit hovered near them. Maa heard Tlan say, "You must stay with me." His voice had a flat authority. "We will eat the stew and I will hear your story. You will show me your miraculous objects. All in due time." And Taga did not dissent.

To the great delight of Tuit, as they waited for the stew to cook properly, Tlan went into his storeroom at the back – a well-hidden area set deepest into the hill—and brought out two handfuls of dried sweetberries in a second stone bowl. Maa washed the berries neatly, filled the bowl with clean water she had prepared, and forked in another large, hot cooking stone. Quickly the water began to boil, so she used a stick to mash the berries as they softened and plumped, staining the water a soft pink. However, as the water took a rolling boil, the color turned a deep, rich red and a flowery aroma filled the hut. When Tuit could hardly restrain his eagerness, the time had come to remove the cooking stone and to add a bit of wild honey. And then Tlan produced from a shelf behind his fur pallet four bone cups – each a rounded section of bone socket, smoothed and carved. Tuit's eyes widened when a wonderfully carved ladle, also of bone, was used to ceremoniously transfer the rich liquid into the cups, and each person received a cup. Motioning them to wait, Tlan dipped more of the liquid into the ladle and held it over a side section of his fire as he muttered an incantation and poured his libation so that it did not douse the fire but sent up a sweet odor. Then he lifted up his own cup to his forehead, then to his nose, and finally to his lips and took a sip. The other three drew a deep sigh of anticipation and sipped luxuriously of the wonderful brew. Maa made decorous little supping noises to show Tuit how to express his appreciation of this treat. And he did so timidly as she held a cup to his small mouth while his father smiled broadly.

When Maa was satisfied that the stew could be eaten, it was ladled into a broad trestle made of bone, and each person in turn bent over it to catch morsels in the fingers and greedily suck the food and their fingers. The meat still required thoughtful chewing, and Maa did much self-conscious wiping of her chin as the juices of the stew dribbled. Every now and then she removed bits of meat from her mouth and stuffed them into Tuit's moist mouth. The men showed how hungry they had been, and the trestle was soon empty. As Maa cleaned up, Tlan and Taga added fuel to the fire and settled down beside it in contentment.

CHAPTER
~3~

"YES, I HAVE heard much of the East. Far beyond the rising sun there is a great water, and before that there are two mountain chains to be crossed, as well as grasslands rich with animals to be hunted. And I have been there." Tlan was answering a question.

"We shall go to the east, far beyond our caribou herd. We are called by the mystery of the ptarmigan and the two eggs which turned to gold in the dawn's light. Here is the sign." Taga took from within his large fur garments the two fossilized pterodactyl eggs and set them before the fire. As the flames flickered, the tiny serpent atop one of them seemed to gain vivacity and color. It was curiously and perfectly life-like in its pert, questing head and its tiny forefeet planted upon the rounded shell. Wisely, Tlan said nothing but studied the two objects intently until the fire burned low. No one else moved until he sat back and sighed.

"The desert lizard has an egg which is elongated so. The size of a desert lizard's egg is small, very small. The lizard's egg is soft and leathery; it is not stone-like. This egg is wrought with such artistry that every detail is here. I myself work the stone, but I cannot reproduce details in stone with such skill. It came from a spirit; I am sure."

Staring into the fire, Tlan intoned an old chant:

Go toward the rising of the sun;
Follow the caribou.
The blazing round eye of the sun
Will give clear, distant sight,
Will let you see into the future,
While the triple-branching horns,
The horns of the prancing caribou,
Will give the hunter strong grace
And courage. These be your signs.

The people arose from the west.
They followed the caribou.
They moved over tundra and mountains,
Over tundra and mountains, ice and snow.
The people followed the herds
For many generations,
Fighting the dire wolf
And the great mammoth
And the sloth, heading toward the sun.

There was silence as the fire snapped about food scraps; then Tlan continued. "If you go to the east, you are to meet the Great Waters. There are no caribou in the deep waters. The lands to the east have mighty rivers. They must be crossed. There is marshy land in the valleys. There will be good deer hunting in the hills. I have heard of the giant ostrich seen in summer – the biggest, swiftest bird in the world of birds. A valley there is called the Valley of the Giant Sloth; avoid it. To the east also there is a giant mammoth with one broken tusk; it is as big as a mountain. I have heard it called Mountain One-Tusk. When I was your age, I wished to see these marvels. That was my great dream."

The fire was burning low but they were all warm and well-fed; misfortune which had seemed overwhelming earlier in the day had been forgotten. Little Tuit slept sweetly beside his mother with his head in her lap, and Maa gently swept back the thick black hair at his temples. The young couple smiled at each other, happy to hear the wise words of dear old Tlan. And they listened in respectful expectancy as he coughed a bit and resettled his thin body in his furs.

"To the north there is, of course, the great herd of your father Tzan. He has found his dream; he is powerful. He dominates many; no one opposes him in anything. Although he is my older brother, I cannot talk to him. I stay far away from him. And you, Taga, you stay far from him. He is your father and you keep far from him. When you chose your woman as a wife, you fled with her to save your lives. Is this not true, Taga? You fear your father more than you love him, so you took your Maa and slipped away into the night. Tzan is the leader of the people, husband of four wives, father of many, many sons. He had all his girl children drowned at birth. His many sons are bodyguards who protect him, who keep him in power. He is a bully; he is a despot who has harmed many people senselessly. If my father were alive, he would be proud of Tzan the Terrible. But you and I, we keep our distance from him and hope that he never thinks of us. Is that not true? You who once were the favorite son of Tzan – you whom he spoiled and allowed more freedom – you are now lost to him. And will be forever. For you cannot return to the people now. You look over your shoulder and move another distance away in order to keep room so as to stretch. But now the Storm God has touched you; he has driven you back to me. And I welcome you as if you were my son. It is good that you are with me. I am infirm and have felt life slipping away. Stay with me for a time, and we can talk about your past and your future. I have much to teach you. Indeed, I must burden you with knowledge I have accumulated, before it s lost, before I die. You know that I was once the shaman of the people, their prophet, their healer. Here, in my exile, I am less than nothing. But if you will hear, there is deep wisdom to be passed on to your generation—wisdom that is a source of great power, if you wish." He paused, and suddenly he seemed very, very old and tired. "I must sleep. You will find more furs in the corner. I am tired."

Despite his deep need for slumber, Taga pushed back furs and rose. Feeling an urgency stronger than the need for sleep, he stumbled to the door and went out into the cold. When he returned and was fastening the leather flap, he noted that his wife had spread furs upon the floor near the fire, with Tuit soundly asleep near the spot she had chosen for herself upon the pallet. With almost one motion he swept up covering furs and also swept up the woman into his own robes, with a single shudder shedding the cold from outside and welcoming the fragrant warmth of his wife.

CHAPTER ~4~

A MOON LATER, after a succession of bleak, cold days, Taga sat in the cave, pondering his latest lesson from the shaman. Over his head on an earthen shelf were set the two pterodactyl eggs, now betraying by their dusting of red ocher powder that they had been part of Tlan's ceremonies. They had now become holy relics to be cherished for many generations; one day they would be laid in a carved ivory chest – a mystery, an ancestral treasure within its ark.

Tlan rested or slept in his corner; Maa held a sleeping Tuit by the fire. Taga heard a faint sound, a human or animal cry from far across the tundra. He rose to investigate, slipping out noiselessly. Bringing his eyes to mere slits, he stared toward the north horizon and soon perceived a motion. Was it a wolf or another animal on the prowl for food? He dropped down to a crouch which he could have kept for hours, pressing against the side of the cave and intently watching the distance. Now he heard the cry again; it was a human cry of someone keening, someone wailing over human loss. In two years Taga had seen no other humans except his own family and Tlan; the circumstances of his departure from the clan ruled by his father had made him wish to avoid others. Now he waited with caution as a dark gray fur-clad figure emerged gradually from the white and gray landscape, toiling painfully along a course that would bring it near very soon. But as the figure grew close enough for Taga to discern that it was slight, too small to be a full-grown man, it stumbled; the creature stumbled, moaned heavily once, then lay still.

Taga slipped back inside the hut and whispered to his wife, "Keep Tuit quiet and stay here. Someone approaches from the north. The creature has fallen as if hurt, so I must go to it. I fear a trap. Yes, I will be cautious. Do not be afraid."

Outside, he listened, but there was no sound now. He felt his knife in its sheath; taking a long breath, he walked toward the crumpled body of furs on the ground, placing his feet carefully to make no sound.

As he stood over the sprawling figure, Taga lost his fear; it was unconscious and beyond power to hurt him. Nevertheless, he made a search and took away a crude knife before he lifted the young boy, probably about nine or ten years old and thin with malnutrition, and carried him back to the hut.

At the entrance, Maa waited, wide-eyed and fearful. She had covered both Tlan and Tuit with their furs, to hide them, and now she trembled as Taga brought in the young boy and dumped him near the fire. She helped unwrap his furs, frowning at the evidence of starvation and neglect. Who was this?

Maa saw what was to be done; she wet her hand and wiped his face. Then she poured water and dried meat into a bowl and put in a hissing cooking stone; this would make broth to feed the stranger when he opened his eyes. She realized that Taga was rubbing the boy's hands and wrists. This stimulation and the warmth of the fire began to work on the youngster and his eyes soon flickered but without interest at first. Then the heat seemed real to him; he saw the two people bending over him, and suddenly his eyes grew wide into a shocked stare full of fear, but he was too weak to pull away. Maa brought over a bowl of hot meat broth, while Taga lifted up the stranger's head and shoulders so that he could sip from it. This he did noisily, sputtering and slurping until the bowl was drained and he seemed ready to devour the stone bowl itself. As Maa retrieved the bowl, she noted some improvement in his eyes, but his body was still with a terrible languor and he did not seem able to speak yet. Taga lowered his head and let him rest by the fire, while Maa got ready a second bowl of broth.

During this activity, old Tlan had thrown back his furs and now he came to the lire. He quietly studied the resting boy, considering every detail from a short distance. When he was ready, he moved forward to touch the boy on the shoulder, murmuring, "You are from the clan of Tzan. Why are you here?"

The boy's eyes focused on the old man for a long moment; then his eyes went wild for a second before he shut them tightly against a searing memory and he gasped weakly, "Tzan…Dead. His sons…Dead."

The words, though soft, were like a thunderbolt in this room. Tlan reeled and sat suddenly, his head in his hands. Taga, his face stony with emotion held back, bent over the boy and heard a little more. "Wind storm. God of Winds killed village."

And then Taga buried his own face in his hands and sank down on the floor, for he suddenly knew that it was true; his father and his brothers had been killed in the giant tornado which had demolished his own small hut. Probably all the village had been wiped out by the windstorm, except for a few survivors like this youth.

He raised his head for a moment to stare keenly at the stranger as another thought came to him: what if this were an attempt to lure him and Tlan into danger? If that proved to be true, it would also offer danger to Maa and little Tuit, which was even more cause for concern. But then he shook his head and threw off this suspicion; the stranger really had almost come to his death and thus most likely had told the truth. It was hard, however, for Taga to believe that his father was dead – that most imperious, hard-willed personality, that huge, full-muscled, strong warrior. For a painful moment Taga saw in his mind the terrible Tzan. The tall, almost square figure swathed in furs seemed immense; the arms and legs were bulbous with muscles; the large, dark head was set upon an unusually thick neck; the features of the face were over-large: dark eyebrows, piercing eyes, big, high-bridged nose, great and lascivious mouth. And with the visual memory there came associations with the strong, violent smells and sounds which always surrounded the huge man. He felt again his father's big, rough hand on young Taga's small, bony shoulder in a hurt meant to be kind. This memory was at once supplanted by a rush of the keen anger they had both shared at times as Taga grew up.

CHAPTER
~5~

THERE WAS TIME to talk haltingly later with their visitor, Yun. Taqa wanted details, but he had already conceded to the reality of this calamity. Intuitively he knew that his father was dead. This knowledge brought him no feeling of security, however; it increased his fears for himself and his family. There was too much that he did not understand. Was the whole family of his huge, vital brothers wiped out? That seemed preposterous.

But here was Yun's story, still brief: Yun was near the herd of caribou almost two hills away when, out of a very dark sky, it began to hail, stampeding the animals. They chose an unfortunate course directly to the village of Tzan and his people. Yun was aghast at the scene. Howling winds and larger hail made the animals run faster. Rump to rump the mass of beasts moved as one, a terrified and senseless rolling wave of brown hide and branching horns. By the time the caribou herd reached the village, a great funnel cloud had already vacuumed up huts and people. An immense black cloud had boiled across the tundra with bushes, animals, rocks, and bones locked within its lethal embrace and spilling out at random. Some debris that kicked out of the cloud included half-clothed humans who then fell into the path of the sharp, thundering hoofs of the herd. Yun could see people lifted, whirled around, then tossed back onto the ground amid splintered debris, while the herd ran on through the seething confusion.

Yun said, “I threw myself flat on the ground with my robe over my head. I was on the far side of the stampede. I got bruises from that big hail, but I lived.”

Racing toward his village in the blizzard that followed, Yun, dazed and sobbing with disbelief, saw that all the dwellings were gone; all the people were gone. The herd was gone. Snow was covering scattered debris as deep darkness fell in a great empty silence.

Yun had cowered for hours in the dark until he knew that he himself would not suffer a similar fate; it was over. At last he had slept a fitful, cold sleep on the ground, dreaming again and again of roaring, whirling winds.

When bright sunlight wakened him early, he was chilled and sore. Amid the snow-covered debris on the village site there were a few horribly mangled bodies of those who had been caught under the herd of caribou. Nothing moved. No huts stood. He was alone. It was almost more than he could comprehend or bear.

He wandered over the area, examining each of the bodies; they were really dead, and he even felt dead himself with sorrow when he recognized three grown warriors as well as a cousin close to his own age. With a large bone he dug a shallow pit and, whimpering, dragged the dead ones into it, pushing some snowy soil over it all. To keep wild animals from the bodies, he piled stones over the place. It took a long while, for some of the stones were very heavy. Then he knelt for a long time, wailing for all his losses.

By this time he was hungry, for the sun was high. He was still alone in a place now vacant. He looked at the white landscape and the stone cairn as he chewed on a bit of pemmican, and then he began to move away toward the south, toward distant hills.

Tlan heard the entire story, overcome with the force of such a giant catastrophe. He was silent as Taga found voice: "But did you actually see the body of the great Tzan?" Yun shook his head to mean no; he was still full of emotion. Taga caught the eye of Tlan, and both had more questions. Could Tzan have lived, nevertheless, just as he had lived through many a tough battle? Could it be possible that some of the warrior princes had also survived? They asked, "Yun, did you search the ground in the direction in which the whirlwind went? Did you look for survivors who might have been carried off?"

But Yun grew uneasy and tearful as he admitted that he had only turned south and walked away from the grave he had made.

Taga said at length with deep feeling, "Tlan, I must go. There may be those who need my help." He rose to his feet.

"It will be a long and painful journey, but I, too, must go to help," said Tlan. "My medicines will be useful if there are survivors."

Maa spoke softly, "If Tlan and Tuit rode on a sled, we could all pull it. That would make a faster journey. I'll find hides, and you must look for sturdy side pieces of bone or wood to make the sled."

With surprise Tlan studied the shy face of this young woman; she was resourceful. He announced, "We shall all go on this journey to rescue the village people who may have survived. Let us prepare carefully and at once. Come with me, Maa, and I will find food and herbs to be packed." He was pleased to feel needed again.

CHAPTER
~6~

Taga was unable to sleep. They had planned to leave early in the morning to go to the site of Tzan's village. Memories flooded his mind, disturbing him and preventing sleep.

As long as he could remember, Tzan had ruled his world. The huge body of Tzan had been both fat and muscular, a powerful presence that had grown more demanding with each year. His voracious appetites were for more than food, and no one had dared to oppose him within his village. This village over the years had moved with the herd's necessity for new grazing land; it was Tzan who had learned to control the herd enough to call it his own and thus to stabilize the lives of their clan. The herd represented a vast wealth for Tzan and his family, an achievement bringing power and authority.

This last village had been Tzan's dream, his own design: a series of good-sized long-houses covered with skins weighted down to the earth by stones, the structures supported by wood or mammoth bones. Tzan's larger hut had two fire hearths like bowls hollowed out of the earthen floor and lined with rocks; one served for cooking and one for warmth. Tzan had directed his men to dig trenches intersecting at the fire-hearths so that air underneath could make fires burn brighter. At Tzan's long-house one stepped onto many luxurious hides carpeting the floor; in winter more hides were hung around the walls. Tzan kept this long-house for himself and two of his wives. His sons had several long-houses nearby – as barracks – but some of the young married men with children had built and styled their own houses. In addition to Tzan, his four wives, his fifteen sons and their families, there were in the village others more distantly related. The population had grown to about 150 people in all, before the cyclone.

Memories came to Taga of his childhood; he remembered sitting on the huge lap of Great Tzan at meals – so that choice morsels could be fed to him. Not only his father, but his giant brothers also, had been loud in their jocular teasing at the contrast of the small, thin boy and the grotesquely fat man. As little Taga's cheeks and chin collected grease, each tidbit was poked into his mouth with the command to grow fat! His brothers had laughed raucously.

Then Taga remembered bitterly the moment when he, at sixteen, had left the village with Maa, having betrayed his father's trust and knowing that to stay would mean a brutal death to both of them, for the Great Tzan would never forgive them.

Maa had lived in a small community of five skin tents two days' journey to the north of Tzan's village. A small herd of caribou served them well, and her parents were kind and generous to their three children, of whom Maa was the oldest. She was a strikingly beautiful and healthy fifteen-year-old when Tzan came by with a hunting party on the trail of mammoths. Taga was not there, but he heard later how Tzan had kidnapped Maa, leaving the skin tents afire and the villagers dead. His men had driven the small caribou herd with them as they returned home, abandoning the mammoth hunt.

Maa was held captive in a separate hut, her hands and feet tied, her face pale with terror and anger. Taga, at sixteen a tall, strong warrior, was one of the guards assigned to keep her from running away or killing herself. Told to sit inside the door and keep his eyes on her, Taga did so and lost his heart in one desperate day.

When a woman brought food, Maa pretended to be ill and refused to eat, trying to win a little time before being presented to Tzan. When night fell, Taga had already made his decision and had persuaded her. He turned away the second guard, saying that the captive had quieted. As the camp grew still after midnight, be loosed her bonds. They looked into each other's eyes and were committed to a dangerous course; then they slipped out the back of the hut and glided away toward the south. A windstorm in the night whisked away footprints; they had simply vanished.

During the first night they reached the distant hills to the south and beyond them found a series of gullies and dry streams. Their flight was sheltered in the day by the rough terrain as they ran on and on until a moonless night found them on the edge of a rolling tundra. Where the last gully split in two directions, a projecting wall hid them and they sank down to rest at last. Taga drew pemmican from a pocket and they ate, chewing slowly. Maa had followed him silently, obediently, with an unquestioning trust, and he had thought of her with each step. It had been only a night and a day since he had made the decision to take her away – to steal her from his lascivious father. His decision, he knew, was irrevocable. She was his, now. The girl understood that also. She was waiting now for him to touch her. He knew that she was quivering. He pulled her down beside him and parted her fur robes.

An intense, prolonged fear had, for Maa, become simply a prolonged physical struggle to keep up during their flight, because she understood fully the consequences to Taga as well as to herself if they were caught. He had run before her, fleet and unbelievably handsome; his firm hand had helped her cross boulders and small rifts without his spending strength on conversation. She had accepted this new destiny as he had accepted it. She had no parents or home to return to, so Taga was now her refuge. She had no tears but a tremendous wonder as she felt him roughly push furs aside and throw his own garments wide.

His smooth, hard body pressed upon her softness, and as his hands began a compass of discovery, he felt her round breasts lift and rise toward him, growing firmer. Her loins were growing warmer as his erection flared against her flesh and he found moist softness as he entered her; she gave a little cry and then he was the conqueror, ruler of their universe, lord of her body, her husband and lover. Their bonding was made complete, forever, sealed on the edge of the tundra in the rocky cleft where they lay.

When they had crossed the tundra, they found a line of low hills and a thin, rocky brooklet. But their entrance to this area was noted by unseen human eyes; Tlan lived nearby and shunned visitors. He had difficulty identifying his nephew Taga, but he recognized that this couple came from the clan of Tzan, so he risked meeting them face to face by the brook. He had stepped out before them, a very old and stooped man. He called, "Taga?" The pair of runaways had not wanted an encounter either, but fortunately Tlan was an ally who hid them safely for several weeks until Tzan, insane with anger and bewildered, called off his hunt.

CHAPTER
~7~

Maa woke first and shook Taga gently. "Today we begin our journey. Rise quickly while I wake Tlan and Yun."

Dawn on the tundra was bleak when they emerged from Tlan's hut. Tlan lay upon a sled improvised with runners of large mammoth leg bones bound to tough hides; he held Tuit beside him, though neither could be identified under the furs piled around them.

Taga had found two more salt bushes to hide the door flap, and as the sled left deep parallel tracks, he ordered Yun to erase their impression and all footprints made by their party. Taga pulled the sled, with Maa walking beside him. Yun, on all fours, rubbed out their tracks with much scurrying until they were well out of sight of the low hut built into the hill.

At first there was little talking; Tuit and Tlan slept a lot, although the bumping of the sled was very hard on the bones of the old one. Yun was at times playful, but when he was designated the hunter, he took this role very seriously, roaming sometimes out of sight but usually bringing back a small reptile or bird to supplement their traveling supply of pemmican and roots.

Taga was the navigator, having charted his course with Tlan the night before. The tundra stretched ahead, sometimes flat for miles and then again a rolling, low terrain. They did not expect to reach the rough hills on the first day, but in the afternoon of the second day they would come to the deep gully that marked the beginning of the rocky, almost mountainous area, and progress would be much slower. Taga expected to lift the front of the sled, with Maa holding up the other end, thus carrying the old one and little Tuit above the sharp rocks. They would ever seek the easiest way, and in the highest, craggiest section, Taga planned to bear Tlan on his own shoulders while Maa carried her son; then Yun would carry the sled and supplies until it became feasible once more to use the sled for riding. Midway through these hills they would make camp for the second night. Beyond the hills they would emerge into a higher, flat tableland, and they would know that they were a half day away from the camp of Tzan and his clan.

Encumbered with the sled, the party was at the mercy of marauders because of their slowness, but they saw only ravens that wheeled overhead to inspect them. Taga liked to be out in the open under the blue wide sky where he could see any animal approaching over the flat, reddish brown distances around them. He worried about the double trail made by the sled and thus took care to look back often to see if any animals followed.

The first day's walking brought them far across the tundra and when they rested a few hours that night, already they had seen far in the distance a misty, blue horizon where the rolling swells in the tundra preceded the even more distant hill country. On the second day the sun stood overhead in a hazy splendor when they first sighted the great split gully on the edge of the hills. They were then negotiating the gentle ups and downs of the swells, trudging up one side of a roll in the wasteland, pausing a moment at the crest, and then rushing downward as the sled pressed them forward.

Yun had disappeared, on the prowl for food. The wind, a constant force on the tundra, had become harder, sharper, so that it discouraged conversation. They walked in near silence, except for an occasional bark or howl carried on the wind from a distant fox or wolf. Suddenly they were startled by an enormous screeching from their left, and a huge bird appeared atop an adjacent hill, beating its gray wings and jumping into the air. Taga exclaimed, "It is an ostrich! Now we know where our Yun is!" And Maa was excited; she watched the strong, tall legs as the bird ran in circles and seemed to pounce with its beak at something on the far side of the hill. A volley of stones came from below, and the squawking bird began to run down the hill toward the south. With incredible swiftness the bird ran, its long legs stretching and propelling it while it continued to protest loudly. Soon it was gone in the hills, and there was silence again, except for the rush of the wind.

They had stopped still, amazed at the enormous bird's performance, and Taga and Maa waited, glad of a chance to rest a moment. Then Yun's head appeared as he climbed toward them; he wore a smile of triumph. As he came over the hill, they saw that he carried a giant egg. What a feast they would have now! Only Tlan had something to say as they found a sheltered nook in which to build a fire. "You know, boy, the power of those talons and that terrible beak! I've seen men who had lost an eye in an encounter with an ostrich." Yun merely grinned, pleased that he had been able to contribute a meal.

Having cleaned a large, flat stone found on the hill, Maa heated it in the fire. She brushed ashes off the top and motioned to her husband. Taga took out his stone knife and cut a neat hole in the top of the egg. Then, carefully, Maa poured the contents of the egg onto the heated rock, slowly so that as she poured, the egg began to cook and none was wasted. Each person reached in for a delicious handful, time and again, until they were very full, even little Tuit and old Tlan.

With new vigor they pushed on toward the great gully and the wall behind it. They stopped at that landmark only long enough to let

Tlan put his uncle on his shoulder, while Maa lifted up her son, and Yun carried the sled. Before it became dark, they intended to get as far as possible into the rugged country. Yun went first, finding footing like a gazelle and avoiding the most perilous rifts. It was hard work, but the good meal had given them the fortitude and strength they needed, and they all felt that they must get there as soon as possible. When they finally halted because the sun had set, they had traversed about half of the rough terrain bordering the high plateau of their destination. For safety they burned a fire throughout the night, and Taga rose often to make sure the small flame was still lit to frighten off animals.

As the sun rose through a mist, Taga woke the others and they left instantly; today they would arrive at the camp of Tzan. Finding gulleys heading north, they made good time and soon came out onto the level plateau in mid-morning. With Tlan and Tuit back on their sled, Yun was now free to scout this familiar territory, so he was with them off and on during this last leg of their trip. Tlan, worried about their reception if they should find that the camp was not deserted, warned Yun to stay near them, but he was so excited that he hardly heard. As they found their surroundings more and more familiar, they did not realize that he was not with them any more.

CHAPTER
~8~

WHILE THE SLED bumped along, Tlan fell into a drowsing state that became more and more emotional as he recognized passing landmarks. He seemed to be going back in time to a world ruled by his brother Tzan, a world where he had always felt uneasy and afraid.

As a boy Tlan had loved music, so he had made his first flute by the time he was old enough to help out with the caribou herd. On many nights he had played his flute to the accompaniment of the grunts made by the bulls or the softer sounds of caribou mothers conversing with their calves. An old herder, Tan, had taken an interest in him and had talked with him about the stars and their patterns in the sky, so that each period of tending the herd had became a session of learning more and more of the wide heavens above the tundra. A son of Tan was the clan's shaman, and he also was interested in the very intelligent boy who learned so eagerly. The shaman needed help; an apprentice who would be discreet, yet pliable, would be an advantage. So Tan's son, Jamus, began to teach Tlan the plants and mushrooms in his medicinal collection, and together they collected willow bark, pine tar and needles, and other simple remedies. When Jamus was called into a hut, often his medicine bag was carried by Tlan, the apprentice, while the shaman wore the mysterious regalia that signified his intimacy with the spirits of the other world. At first Tlan always stood quietly in a corner while the shaman ministered to the sick person, but he missed nothing of the performance by his mentor.

Then, one spring day Jamus was called to the long-house of Tzan, and twelve-year-old Tlan went as the helper. They stepped inside, noting at once that Tzan was not there. Two women were bending over a pallet on which lay a girl who was moaning. Stepping warily on the soft skins that lined the earthen floor of the hut, Jamus and Tlan went to the women, whom Tlan recognized as his brothers' wives, Kala and Zulga. Kala was Tzan's first wife; Zulga, at that time, was Tzan's third and newest wife. Tlan melted into the shadows as Jamus greeted the women and asked how he could help them.

Kala, always the passionate leader among the wives, tossed her black hair and said, "Tzan brought her here this morning. He means to make her his fourth wife, as if there are not enough women now to serve his needs. She is far too young, anyhow, just a child. Look." With her foot Kala prodded the naked, moaning figure on the pallet, and the girl wailed. The older woman flipped her hair again as she went on, "She gave him some opposition, it seems, and he was forceful." She arched her eyebrows. "I guess he beat her; you can see the bruises. Look at that dark spot at her right eye. We don't know if he broke any bones. We can't get close to her while she just screams. Terrified, we think." She punctuated this information with a jangling of bone bracelets.

Jamus nodded, assessing the situation. Then he turned and took his bag from Tlan, motioning his apprentice to leave. Tlan glided out at once, but the picture of the too-young girl and her suffering from shock, pain and anger was an indelible memory. He knew that she didn't have a chance; Jamus might give her something to ease the fear as well as the hurts today, but he could not prepare her for the inevitable blows to come in the future. This girl had spirit. Tzan would enjoy taming her.

Days later Tlan saw the girl being led across an open space in the compound of huts; she looked at him with an expression of stark pain. She seemed to be only about seven or eight years old, although she was so thin that she might have been several years older than that. Her dark hair had auburn tints in it as it flowed in large waves down over her shoulders. Tlan realized that he did not know her name.

Tlan felt that his heart had been cut into strips; his own older brother was responsible for this brutality, and Tzan ruled here. Nothing could be done to save her from this sad fate. But he was stricken with grief, and his heart went with her.

Half a moon later he was sitting behind the hut where he had his bed, resting after a morning of helping to slaughter a caribou for Tzan's huge appetite. He had leaned his head back and closed his eyes when a shadow fell over him. It was the girl; she had got away from her women keepers for the moment and was merely looking for a place to be out of sight. Recognizing him, she sat down, drawing herself up against the wall.

"Hello. You were with the shaman, weren't you?" At his shy nod, she went on. "My name is Passa. I shall be another wife to Tzan when I am older. He cannot stand me now because I am too thin and sad. What is your name?"

"Tlan. I am Tzan's younger brother. The shaman has been training me as his helper." He smiled self-consciously. "He told me to leave because you had no clothing on. Are you being treated better now? I felt sorry that my brother had been such a brute."

Passa gave him a rare, wide smile that transformed the little girl into a youngish woman of glowing beauty. "So. We shall be friends. Yes. While the other women are trying to gorge me with food to fatten me, I have found a little reprieve here with a friend. But they watch me every moment. I must not be seen talking to you." She started to slip away, then turned back and gave him a kiss on his forehead. "Friends," she said lightly and fled.

He put his hand to his forehead, which burned with brightness left from her dazzling smile. The moment flamed forever in his memory, for Passa was his first love – and a love that was forbidden.

The girl had been in his thoughts constantly before, but now Passa's wonderful smile lit every thought. His shaman mentor was puzzled that he had to wake Tlan out of a trance-like state too often. Inattention could not be tolerated, so he asked his young apprentice, "Who is she? What girl in the village have you seduced? She really has you in a dizzy mood. Who is she? Do I know her?"

Tlan stuttered as he denied that he had done anything wrong, but he knew that he could cause Passa more grief than she had ever had yet, so he was more careful to hide his private thoughts from others. The foolish grin that he had not previously been able to prevent became merely a happy attitude that came from a heart alight with love.

Passa, however, developed no good relationships within the circle of guards and women who watched her. The one friend she knew was the young man who was named Tlan, who said he was Tzan's brother. There was outright jealousy among the wives of the clan leader. Each wife wanted her sons to become favorites of Tzan, and Kala, the oldest of them, had borne the oldest son, Dono, the prospective heir.

Kala's other sons at that time included Undu, Alkun, and Tungun, all strong and stout men. They had better dispositions than Dono, the bully of the crowd. It was easy to despise Dono for his habit of teasing younger men.

Seldun, the second wife of Tzan, had grown a bit mousy after being humbled by Kala too often, and she kept to herself in her own hut most of the time, holding her two young sons near her, so that they were mostly courteous and helpful. Her sons were Bulun and Sanal, good-looking and open-faced, with the big legs characteristic of their father.

Tzan's third wife was Zulga, mother of Chun and Iruk. Not very tall, she made an impression on others with her good-tempered disposition; she always got along with everyone. She was not one to speak out against the bad behavior of others, for she had long before found it easier to accommodate and forget evil. Mostly it was not Zulga who had bad experiences; she was well-liked and avoided trouble. Kala worked well with Zulga.

Then Tlan's day-dreaming broke off, as he thought of the family which the Great Tzan had left now since fourteen of his fifteen sons had perished at once in the big whirlwind. He totaled them all up.

Now, he thought, Kala's sons had numbered six in all: Dono, Unda, Alkan, Tungun, Glun, and, finally, Taga. Seldun, the second wife, was mother to Bolun, Sanal, Bugun, and Muno; that made four more sons for Tzan. The third wife, Zulga, had four sons, Chun, Iruk, Fugun, and Tlog. The last of Tzan's wives was Passa, who bore only one child, a son named Alun. He mused, "And of them all, only Taga has survived, it seems."

Then his mind brought out yet another bit of curious information that must be confirmed: Zulga was the mother of Chun, who became the father of the boy Yun. Yes, that was what Yun had told them.

CHAPTER ~9~

TAGA WAS SURE that they had reached the site on which his father had built his long-house and the family compound. In the middle of the large open space there was only a stone cairn. The rest of the area was devoid of houses, people, and animals. Here there was once the happy confusion of many people of all ages. All were gone. Taga, Maa, and Tlan could only stand staring, full of perplexity. How could such a great calamity have come about? Apparently, it was just as Yun had reported. But where was Yun?

Then they heard a call from a short distance just as Tlan was making gestures to appease the angry gods who had wrought such destruction. Yun walked toward them, eating some food, and behind him trailed four men, identifiable as men of the clan of Tzan, the Caribou Clan. First, Yun shared his food with them, for they had not eaten all day. Then he told an exciting story, aided by the four men. They were hunters who had been on an expedition when the tornado came; they had returned to find everything destroyed. Soon, a few clan members from caves not far away had come fearfully to the scene and had rejoiced to find the hunters alive. This group, then, had gone to search the area to the east, the direction in which the tornado had carried its debris. They had found a number of dead bodies and some injured survivors. Among the survivors had been The Great Tzan himself, but he had been severely and painfully injured. In spite of their attention to his injuries, the Great Tzan had died. His body was now in one of the caves, and burial must be soon, for the smell was terrible.

As Yun had told, not only was Tzan dead, but of his sons, none had survived except Taga – that is, Taga and an unnamed baby boy. Of the caribou herd, some had been found, but most of them were gone.

One of the hunters, Beros, looked at Taga and said forthrightly, "Without a leader we are spiritless. There is a funeral to plan, for a great and powerful man. Most of us have no homes; many have lost families; and there are few caribou. You are the son and heir of the Great Tzan and you have come to help us. Will you lead us?"

The emotions that swirled inside Taga's head confused him. Taga knew well that he was the last person the Great Tzan would have chosen as a successor. Tzan had worn bitter revenge as a palpable garment, a fixture in his expression, and the wrong done by Taga in stealing a woman from Tzan had cut deeply. Taga did not feel any triumph in outlasting his father's revenge; he felt humble that he himself was alive when vital vengeful Tzan lay lifeless in a cave. "Give me some time for sorrow, my friend," said Taga. "The clan will survive, and we will have a leader. It is good that you have spoken to me."

With that, Taga turned to the tundra, away from the terrible body waiting in the cave, and he walked among the thin herd of caribou, alone with his thoughts.

Among the animals, he saw that a handful of the cows would soon have calves to increase the herd. That was a hopeful sign. Using his father's techniques to keep the herd nearby would surely mean that the clan would soon prosper and grow powerful as before. Having that much power centered in himself was a heady thought. Only a few days ago he had been stripped of his home and his possessions by the Great God of the Wind, and now, still the same person he had been then, he could replace the Great Tzan himself, with power and riches within easy reach. Self-doubt made him wish for the wise counsel of his uncle Tlan, and so he sought out the old one.

Maa, holding Tuit's hand, was standing near Tlan, who was sitting on the sled, weighted down by fur robes. Maa's eyes were wide with shock at the thought of her husband suddenly taking on a position of leadership and wealth; she had overheard the hunter's speech and was waiting now to know what future her little family would face. They had made this trip in order to aid Taga's relatives who might be dying – in order to help. And now their trip had not led them into danger but into the opportunity of having great power. She was surrounded by strangers – not unfriendly but at the same time those who had killed her own family cruelly. While she was excited, the situation was, to her, intimidating. Taga stopped by her to take little Tuit into his arms and to touch his woman caressingly on her shoulder. Just standing beside her was enough to convey to him her emotions; she was afraid. He, therefore, felt that he must be cautious.

Taga now spoke to the remnants of the clan who had surrounded them. "Let me get the old one to a fire where he can rest. I wish to talk with him alone because his words are wise. May we visit one of the caves where the fire is already warm?"

It was an older woman who stepped forward and beckoned them to follow her. Taga picked up his uncle and carried him as he had done during the trip, and they went to a cave between a gully and a hill very near the site of Tzan's camp. This cave belonged to the widow Elar.

Elar's cave was higher than the floor of the plateau, up a slight incline which widened into a shelf before the door of the cave. Two hide flaps hung before the wide door, and when Taga entered, he was surprised at the size of the one room within. While the roof was not high, men could stand easily; a fire burned on the bowl-like hearth in the center; around the two sides raised shelves formed beds. Most interesting was the carefully planned storage center at the back; this woman was uncommonly neat and had arranged a series of shelves and square-cut hollows so that all her household effects could be stored, leaving the rest of her cave for sitting and for walking traffic. Elar and her husband had used large stone knives and diggers to adapt this cave for living well. Now that he was dead, widow Elar lived alone here. She had led Taga's family to her cave because the boy Yun's parents had once been her friends.

As Tlan slumped down and fell into his furs, asleep already, Taga and Maa looked around. Maa shyly admired the convenient beds and the storage compartments, both new to her. Taga saw the effect on her and realized that this cave offered more than safety from the Terrible Winds; it allowed the hearth-wife to plan and create a home that was permanent and very liveable. If he were the leader of this clan, he would help every family to have such safe and attractive lodgings; he said as much in a low voice to Maa, whose wide smile showed him how important was this subject.

Elar took Tuit on her lap; he was very quiet and still for a bit, because he had never seen until today any people other than his family and, recently, Yun. Her gray hair and chubby body were not familiar, but her kind smile was reassuring, and there soon developed a mutual fondness between the two. The result was that Elar invited Taga and his entire party to stay in her cave as long as they needed. When Tlan awoke, this was welcome news for him. In a very formal manner, he thanked her for this generosity and promised her that the new leaders of the clan would not forget it

Taga felt that it was time for him to talk privately with Tlan, who was now rested. They walked together to the porch-like ledge outside the cave door, where they spoke in low voices. Tlan had been present when the hunter brought up the question of who would now lead the Caribou Clan, so he understood at once. Taga began to speak of his own lack of experience. Their relationship had always been that of respectful student and wise teacher. Taga had always listened instead of speaking. It still remained for Taga to test his unused abilities, to know that he could be a leader. And here Taga said plainly, "I need more time to learn and grow into leadership. In short, you must lead the clan for the time being." And at length Tlan agreed.

The most pressing business for the clan leader would be the respectful and impressive burial of the late Tzan. This was important to the status of the clan itself, for Tzan had been the most powerful leader of people that they had ever heard of. With limited resources and a small group to help, and with a need to get it done quickly, this project must be handled at once, obviously. What a relief it was to Taga to know that wise Tlan was even now beginning to think of the ceremony as one that carried on traditions as he remembered.

"Where is the body of my dead older brother?" asked Tlan, as he re-entered the cave of Elar. It was Elar herself who volunteered to guide them. Tlan stopped by the sled to get a skin of his shaman's supplies, and he spoke to one of the hunters to list other items needed for the burial. Elar then led them to the farthest cave set apart from any others; the body had been transferred here because of its offensive smell. Tlan considered the setting – a cave not very deep but with sheer, plain walls outside the round opening. "Here," said Tlan, "a kind of monument of stones could be constructed to seal the cave."

Inside, on a dark fur lay the body; Tlan pulled back a covering fur to reveal the bloated, gray face and wide-staring, open eyes. Then it was an effort to show the great arms where swelling had split the skin in huge, livid gashes and then the mountainous purple and red stomach where billows of fat oozed odorous brown liquid. With a shudder, Tlan ripped off the rest of the furs and stepped back from the sight of the magnificently contorted, varicolored genitals fringed in black hair. Below that, thick thighs ended in giant, hairy legs where fractures showed how roughly the whirlwind had thrown him out onto the ground, for whitish splinters of bone protruded from a number of festered, extruding wounds.

Tlan blanched and reeled. Taga stepped forward to steady him and felt the full impact of the corrupted, broken, smelly corpse that had been his father. They emerged from the cave and sat down abruptly.

They were still there when a hunter arrived with a skin of pulverized limestone which Tlan had ordered; this was sprinkled on the body to reduce the stench which now pervaded the area. Soon other supplies were brought, and all the clan gathered for the ceremony.

Tlan went into the cave with a handful of powdered red ochre, which he carefully sifted into the orifices of the head before tossing the rest upon the body. Onlookers knew that this symbolized blood, to give him health in the afterlife. Then, hurriedly, furs and robes covered and wrapped the gigantic body so that its dignity was somewhat restored when it resembled a rich mountain chain of furs.

Tlan spoke to the group. "Who among you have food for the Great Tzan to eat in the after-life?" At this, Elar and other women came forward with some wrapped packets of food, and they were encouraged to lay these next to the head of the corpse. When Tlan asked for weapons to protect the Great Tzan, Taga brought appropriately large stone axes, which he put down by the right hand of the dead.

Now Tlan, observing that his audience wished to move further away from the smell, began a short eulogy and then an invocation to all gods of the earth and heavens to receive the spirit of his brother. Here a commotion at the rear of the small group resolved into one woman, who stepped forward with the baby son of Tzan; it had been found on the ground near its father, tightly wrapped in furs and without injury. The woman who was caring for it did not really like the responsibility, and she was now offering the baby to be put into the cave with its father. There were strong murmurs from the clan – which Tlan could not interpret. This act of sacrificing the child was allowable in tradition. Else what could be done with it? Its mother was now dead also.

Taga held the baby for a moment, showing it to Maa; it was a pink, smiling little boy. He held the child up for all to see his little half-brother and then turned toward the cave. It was Elar who was so moved by the sight that she came up and silently took the child into her arms; with no words at all, she left, carrying the baby back to her own home. A great sigh went up from the clan – an approval of what had occurred, and general approval. Tlan was a good leader with dignity and ability. The ceremony ended as Tlan signaled the men to roll over their largest stone to cover the door to the cave. As the clan walked away, the men finished their work by piling many, many stones before the front of the cave. It was closed forever.

CHAPTER
~10~

Elar rose early every day. Her guests soon fell into the same pattern, a schedule dictated by the two children. She gave the tiny son of the late Tzan a pet name – Oola, and he received bountiful love and care. Elar said that she had never been so happy or so busy.

Both Tlan and Taga were giving their full attention to the management of the clan; Tlan initiated plans which were then carried out by Taga. Providing homes for those who had lost their huts in the windstorm was a priority. Both Taga and Maa were quick to praise Elar's enlarged and adapted cave; it was safe from windstorms; in winter it would be much warmer. The drawback was that it was not portable. Taga spoke up: "If the caribou are content to stay in this area, the Caribou Clan will not need portable homes."

Tlan's reply: "So the most pressing problems for the clan are interrelated, and both must be addressed at once: the herd and the new homes."

Yun took them to a line of caves a good distance away; there would be enough cave openings for fairly small shelters for all. Yun's surprise was that a larger cave central to these had in it a spring of cool, sweet water that formed a small pool and then disappeared underground.

Taking matters in hand at once, Tlan assigned a cave to each of the clan who needed a new home; this meant that without delay all could start the work of cleaning out, digging, and furnishing their new homes. The new setting of the village faced the tundra on which the small herd of caribou could graze. Taga saw a walled gully near by that might become a pen with the addition of some stonework.

Tlan named a herdsman whose responsibility was to keep the animals safe from marauding wild animals by remaining near them at all times. This was in the tradition of Tzan, so Gadu was honored to have this duty, for he knew there would be rewards for him if he was faithful. Other men of the clan relished the status of hunter, and they had already, indeed, been scouring the nearby hills for small animals and birds. They would organize hunts in more distant areas to get larger game, such as mammoths.

Yun also knew of a gully where huge old fossil bones were partly covered by stone rubble. This was exciting to some of the home builders, because they could see huge bones as uprights for temporary tents covered by hides. Uses of the bones offered many possibilities, as one man now planned to build an anteroom at the door of his cave; it would be an entrance as well as an extra room; his wife was interested and was exploring ways to light such a dwelling.

Then, as always, Tlan continued to teach Taga the ways of a shaman – the lore and mindset of a true shaman – and the practical area of medicine, for the shaman was both spiritual guide and physician for the clan.

Tlan proved to be a master at organizing. He said to Taga, "I have plans for a group of the strong young men to start a training program in two areas: first, as guards for the whole community and our herd; and second, as hunters, to increase their efficiency and prowess in that art." Taga, meanwhile, wanted to initiate some training also. His reply to Tlan was, "I must see that another generation of stone workers learn that craft." And a group of the young men were very eager to practice stone-knapping skills.

One clear night when the stars shone above with great clarity, Tlan led both Taga and Yun outside the cave and to a nearby hillside. The summer solstice had passed some time ago, and he had waited this night until the darkness contrasted with the gem-like stars. "What do you know of the gods of the night sky?" he asked. Surprisingly, it was Yun who spoke first, for he had often spent nights in the open near the caribou herd, and he had studied patterns in the sky. "There. That one is bright; it points always toward the great ice wall in the north. By this Weapon I can find my way. Many who work with the caribou and those who hunt look to find the strange star which does not move. Look there." And he pointed to the star which in later generations was called Thuban, in the sprawling figure of the Dragon; it was the Pole Star of Yun's lifetime.

Producing a bone slab, Tlan suggested that Yun use the blade of his stone axe to incise on the bone the pattern of stars around this important god of the sky, a special friendly spirit for Yun, because Yun felt close to this Weapon in the Sky. Trembling at the importance of his commission, Yun went inside their cave to kneel by the small fire and begin his work.

Continuing the lesson with Taga, Tlan reviewed with him several important arrangements of stars which he himself had been taught by others. There was the great animal figure near the Weapon, with head, body, and legs; Tlan called it the Caribou, but of course in modern times its name is Ursa Major. Tlan recounted a story to explain why the Caribou had no branching horns in its place in the sky. He said, "You can see its horns are beneath the animal. There, those three stars. They are the horns which were wrested off during a fight." Taga had heard this many times, but he understood that such information had to be repeated many times so that it could be remembered accurately and passed on to another generation. If asked to, Taga could incise on a bone slab many, many named figures of gods in the sky and tell their stories. This had been part of the education his mentor, Tlan, was giving him. Taga had been chosen by the constellation which Tlan called the Spoon, known to moderns as Ursa Minor. Tlan himself had been chosen in his youth by a tall god in the sky, the Hunter, and he had always identified with this god.

Another aspect of astronomy which Taga was coming to understand concerned the recording of passing time as evidenced by the moon and by the sun. Each morning he accompanied Tlan as he performed a ceremony of incising a mark on a large bone slab, the mark representing the reappearance of the sun for another day. Then Tlan made another mark to record the place where he had seen the sun rise over a horizon he had drawn on the bone. At sundown Tlan watched the west to be able to record the location of the sun's disappearance, again on a bone slab. The day of Tzan's funeral had been circled on a bone slab as an event to remember, as had the day of the Great Wind.

The lunar observations recorded by Tlan had to do with the phases of the moon and were especially important because his records covered a lifetime of passing moons. With Tlan this was serious; he continued work carried on by his old mentor, Jamus, and shamans before him. Tlan had a reputation for predicting weather for hunters of the clan, as well as for clan celebrations. This accumulated wisdom and honed common sense made Tlan a very wise leader, and his passion for gathering detailed information had made him an exceptionally well-educated and gifted shaman.

CHAPTER
~11~

IT WAS SUMMER and the tundra's blossoming plants, in their quick seasonal display, gave cheer to all until the combination of drought and burning sun dried up any flowers. While the plants could be identified readily, Tlan walked out to gather those he might use as medicine to dose colds, to relieve pain, or to soothe stomach aches. He had found a relative of the hyssop which, with its pungent taste, helped to cure chest colds as a tea made with it would loosen the mucous in the throat and chest. The stem of this plant had hairs that could help prevent the clotting of blood. There was a wild mint which he used for patients complaining of digestive upsets; because it was soothing to all kinds of cramps and spasms, he gave it for headaches, fevers, nausea — except for pregnant women; because mint could stimulate the menstrual flow, he never prescribed it for morning sickness. Wild sweetberries were easy to see amid other greenery; the enticing little red berries appeared early and lasted all season, and while they were tasty morsels, the medicine man gathered them to use for patients who had trouble urinating. The wild horseradish he found was good for that ailment, also. A small wild version of burdock, which in warmer climates grows very rank and tall, was very good as a poultice on infections or abscesses. When he found a little relative of the modern gentian, he recognized in the little blue flowers a source of help for those who pass stones – in modern terms, gallbladder sufferers. The milk of the wild dandelion could remove warts, he knew, while a paste of the leaves helped bone fractures cure more quickly. He always looked for wild boneset also as an aid for broken bones and as a tea for aching bones. When he found wild meadow buttercups, he thought of using them, cooked and mashed into a paste, as a remedy for his own arthritis.

Tired of walking, Tlan sat down to rest, and the deep quiet around him, the wide skies above, and his own lassitude led him into a daydream. He was fifteen years old again and proud of his muscles, straight in carriage, and very physical in his outlook on life.

He knew that he was handsome. He was the younger brother of the Great Tzan. He walked with a slight strut. He was careful to obey orders and cause no problems, for he had a great secret: he had been in love with Passa for a very long time and this year Passa was old enough in the eyes of the other wives to become the fourth wife of Tzan. In private, when they could get away from others, their young love burned fiercely and they clung to each other. She was not happy with her station in life, but it could have been worse, she thought. Tlan was her only love, her source of happiness, and she could stand anything, she said, rather than be parted from him. When Tlan went on hunts for large animals with Tzan's trained army of hunters, he was away for several moons at a time, and she wept with loneliness even while surrounded by the lively family of wives and children. When the hunters returned laden with fresh meat, there were feasts and celebrations, and everyone laughed easily. The brightness in Passa's eyes was all for Tlan's return, and when they met in the dark behind her hut, she refused to hold back any of her love.

When Tlan was sixteen, Passa was a stunning beauty with adult status in the clan; her only worry was the jealousy of the other wives. Her long, wavy brown hair and her dazzling smile had long ago won the heart of her husband, Tzan, who pampered her to an extreme. She understood her position as a favorite and made the most of it. The moments with Tlan were never long enough, and now that she was married, she no longer felt that pregnancy would be a problem. While they were careful, their intimacy became deeper and more tender all the time.

Tlan was seventeen years old when he began to feel that the situation was not tenable for him. He asked Passa to elope with him. Her fear of Tzan made her tremble so that she could not think of running away. It would mean death for both of them; Tzan would kill them without mercy. Then she revealed that she was pregnant. She had to think of the baby. He asked if it was his baby. She did not know.

And so he left, making an explanation to Tzan that he wished to learn more of the world and more of the role of a shaman. His plans seemed grandiose, but Tzan was much less aware of the men around him than he was of his darling wife who finally was with child. Kala remained as mistress of his long-house, but Zulga moved out so that Passa could live in the luxury of the long-house for an indefinite time, near Tzan.

There was no more opportunity for Tlan to be alone with Passa, so he left without further goodbyes. He knew that he wished to visit the great lakes to the north, one of which was said to be bottomless and ancient, and his spirit of adventure took over as he left with two companions who would accompany him for two days before returning home. The weather was warm and their leavetaking was short. Tlan did not realize that he would be away for eight years, during which time he went north to the great body of water today called Lake Baikal. He learned some of the deep secrets of the lake as he visited with a clan who lived on the north shore. He ate fish he had never heard of before and found that the large game that ate grasses could be found more easily there. After spring melted the terrible ice, a party of the clan people departed toward the northeast, where they expected to follow a huge river into more grasslands to the east. Tlan went with them.

He went only a part of the way, for the terrain was difficult; he then doubled back south through eastern mountains to the ocean. Here he felt the power of the seas of the world and had an out-of-body experience which let him float for an infinite amount of time over nothing but giant waves. He toured a part of the interior, meeting dangerous animals and fierce tribes. Somehow his status as a shaman helped to protect him in most situations. He came back from the south into the desert land, entering from the western side of the great desert and traversing the mountains of birch and pine, with their cooling rivers and caves, before coming again to his home village eight years later.

Tlan was then twenty-five, a full shaman with a marvelous knowledge of plants and medicines, geography, music, and the stars. He was a very learned man at the height of his ability. He was also exceptionally attractive.

Jamus, the old shaman of the Caribou Clan, was old and sick, so when Jamus decreed that Tlan would be his successor, Tlan agreed. After eight years of traveling, he wished to be comfortable again.

He quickly found that Passa still burned for him with a fretful, anxious passion. She was even more beautiful. His feeling for her was doubled when he saw her eight-year-old son, Alun, for he knew at once that Alun was his son, and he regretted that he had missed any time at all with this grave, brilliant, and handsome boy. Alun was the main reason that Tlan served the Caribou Clan as its shaman for ten years, until he was thirty-five years old. During that time Alun was known as the adored son of powerful Tzan, but Alun became a very special friend to Tlan. That life was very full for Tlan, even though his devotion to Passa and her son had to be a secret.

With a sigh, the old shaman left his dreams of the past and shuffled across the tundra toward the home which he shared with Taga, Maa, Yun and Elar.

CHAPTER
~12~

While it was still early, Elar prepared both little children for a day outside, and she soon was gone, holding Tuit's hand and cuddling little Oola in her arms. Both Taga and his wife Maa had announced that they would be helping to renovate a cave, and Yun, as usual, was not around. Tlan enjoyed the calm and quiet as he sat alone near the fire.

His reverie was interrupted by a child's crying. Elar burst in with Tuit in her arms. His sobs grew louder when he saw Tlan, as if he could get more sympathy for his pain. And Tlan quickly saw that Tuit's dimpled pink hand was marked with an angry burn.

An explanation was quick to come. Elar described Tuit's mischievous reach for a stone bowl at the neighbor's fire. She said, "There was a fire stone in the bowl, and it had heated the surface of the bowl as hot as the stew inside. Ordinarily Tuit would have been nowhere near the fire, but Troz and I were enjoying the good humor of little Oola. He is such a sweet baby, laughing all the while. I jumped to rescue Tuit and got burned too for my efforts." She showed the fiery mark on her right hand.

Taking the howling youngster into his arms, Tlan got his attention and then held the little hand up to inspect it. He put his lips close to the red area of the burn and began to blow upon it softly. Tuit, fascinated, had already ceased to cry. Then Tlan began to suck in as he made a sweeping movement across the little hand, as if to draw the extra heat into his own mouth. He alternated blowing and drawing in his breath in a soothing manner for a few minutes. Then he said calmly, "It will not hurt you any more, Tuit." And the child smiled, charmed at the ceremony of the cure.

Tlan now turned to Elar. "You were burned also? Let me talk the fire out of your burn." Blushing and holding her hand behind her back, Elar was a reluctant patient. But Tlan took up the well-rounded, weathered hand of the woman and blew upon the wound as he had done for the child. He was very gentle, and soon the hand did not smart at all. Before he let her hand go, Tlan kissed it lightly and then turned back to sit down again. He did not see the confusion in her face.

In another minute, Elar and the child had gone. He sat again in quiet and after a short while he reached for his shaman's bag. He rustled inside until he found a hollow leg bone twice as long as his hand. Then he searched until he found his bone drill and began the patient work of making two small holes along one side of the bone, aligned three fingers apart. Every now and then he paused to blow into one end of the hollow bone, shaping his lips in a practiced, careful manner so as to produce clear, musical tones. When he had two holes completed, he used a finger to cover one hole at a time as he blew, and with a little more adjustment with the drill, he played a sequence of three whole notes on his bone flute.

Pleased at this success, he launched into a repetitive melody of three ascending notes followed by one note back, then a pause before repeating. It was soon clear through the expressive, nuanced arch of the melodic line that this was a gifted musician, for as the music lifted and descended, it seemed to be his inner life which was emerging in the sounds. Tlan played on and on, losing himself completely for a time.

Elar paused at the door of the cave; she had returned alone and could not believe her ears. She had never heard music like this before, and it was sweetly compelling. She sank down silently just inside her threshold and did not move. She was enchanted.

At last, his musical reverie over, Tlan ceased playing. He was completely startled to hear Elar's voice saying, "No! No!" Putting away his flute, he rose slowly and went to the woman. Was she in distress? She seemed to be in a trance, with her eyes unnaturally fixed and wide.

"Elar, is something wrong?" he asked as he helped her to rise; they moved toward the fire.

"Do not stop. Do not stop." Her wide eyes were on him as her stout body sat clumsily, and she continued to stare at him.

Uneasily, Tlan resumed his seat and took up the flute. He paused for a moment and looked questioningly at Elar to see if he had understood her request. But she nodded and continued to stare at him. He closed his eyes and slipped into the same melody repeated again and again but new each time. Elar did not move. The melody swirled, lifted and fell around them, then lifted and fell again, over and over. Tlan, his eyes still shut, wove the spell more and more tightly, playing on and on. When he stopped at last, they sat on in the unfinished spell, with neither moving.

In mid-afternoon the cave family began to drift in, eager to rest, and they broke in upon the utter stillness. Maa felt forced to begin preparations at once for a meal, but Elar remained in her trance, as if she did not hear. The children climbed upon her, expecting her welcoming smiles and hugs, but she was not responsive until Maa spoke loudly to her, "Elar, is something wrong? Are you ill?"

But Elar had changed. For days she exhibited strange lapses of attention, sitting in a preoccupied silence as if she heard something the others could not hear. Tlan, too, became moody and more often than not chose to sit by the fire all day. Daily life went on busily around them, without much attention to the pair.

However, only a few days had passed when Tlan made his move. As the adults prepared for sleep, Tlan stepped over to Elar's pallet of skins atop one of the built-in beds.

She lifted her head and melted into his embrace as he pulled her onto his pallet of skins on the floor. She had been waiting.

CHAPTER ~13~

YUN WORKED FURIOUSLY at his skills as a hunter, and he intermittently took classes in astronomy and stone-knapping, as well as other practical matters. One project which he was doing for Tlan was very practical indeed: he was systematically counting the caribou. He had gathered a pile of stone pebbles, each about the same size. Maa had made him a pouch out of a small animal hide. With the help of Gadu, guardian of the herd, Yun carefully put into the pouch one pebble for each caribou. Then, seeking a sandy spot, Yun put one hand down and drew a mark on the sand for each finger; beside that he laid his other hand down and added a mark for each additional finger. Now he arranged the pebbles, one by one, along the ten marks; when he saw that he had more pebbles, he put two pebbles for each "finger mark." There were still more pebbles, enough for three pebbles for each mark. Again there were more pebbles, and Yun and Gadu concluded that they could account for four double hands full of pebbles representing caribou which were full grown, plus many small calves just born two moons earlier.

The pen was crowded with the huge antlers borne by both males and females; many of the male animals had a span of branched horns almost as wide as Yun was tall. These antlers, which would be shed after rutting season in a few moons, were flattened as each main antler divided into three branches and curved to project forward. Then at the brow another curiously awkward horn, a flattened brow tine, jutted forward over the large snout. The shaggy brown fur was touched with white at the throat and on the short, furry tail and rump. A bit of white was on each ankle above the hoof, and these hooves were very large and round, cupped and well padded in summer, when they handled the softening, boggy tundra well. In winter the hooves grew sharp and were hardened to handle ice.

Gadu was unhappy when fights broke out. He opened the pen and let every animal out as much as possible in the summer months, aware that flies could be terribly annoying to the shaggy caribou. They often sought the tundra as a foraging ground just because of the strong winds that gave them relief from flies. Gadu tried hard to keep them from scattering too far.

Gadu knew also that when nights grew cold again, the bulls would rival each other as the mating season would begin. Gadu had learned that he was dealing with animals who recognized only one master, the head caribou, a wily and powerful bull. Gadu kept his eyes on this key figure, gaining all the knowledge he could about his instincts and reactions. If the bull moved at night, Gadu could discover him by the "click" made curiously by a tendon which slipped over the sesamoid bone in the foot, or by his pig-like snort or grunt, or especially by his fiercely rank male scent.

Gadu wished to control the movements of the herd in a loose way, by understanding and controlling this giant bull. While the herd was so small, it might be possible.

The instinctive movements of a herd of caribou are southward to a winter range after the fall rut, and then northward in the spring as cows start toward their calving grounds. Crucial in this seasonal migration is the cows' choice of a calving site, often beside water with an accessible beach. The cows seem to have a homing device much like that of birds, and they start the race toward a traditional site, followed by juveniles and adult bulls. They are impelled by some inner knowledge of their 230 days gestation period and by the ungainly, heavy little animal within, which will weigh about thirteen solid, lively pounds and be well-developed at birth, able to stand up in half an hour and to run about in an hour and a half.

When the Great Wind hit the herd of the Caribou Clan, the cows had not yet left, but the bulls and juveniles had gathered around them and soon the great mass of caribou would have begun a forced march to the northwest, to an icy lake formed long ago by run-off from the great glacier to the north. In the aftermath of the wind's destruction, however, the part of the herd that was left took time to gather again. Gadu, in his new role, observed the fawning in the new pen while the males milled about outside. For weeks Gadu was a careful guardian, for the small calves could attract gray wolves at such a time. The cows would be fiercely protective, but they did not have at any time the huge antlers which decorated the bulls.

One early evening while it was still light, Gadu saw a movement among the rocks circling his pen, almost as if a rock glided along. He was ready. In his hands he held a primitive sling, the weapon of his choice during his youth, and a stone half the size of his mighty fist. The sling, though made of a length of caribou hide, was worn into a hairless, smooth and supple gray now, and Gadu's aim was deadly. His right arm moved swiftly, fluently, and the wolf made no sound or movement. Gadu waited so that the cows would not panic, although he knew that their sense of smell might tell them what had occurred. Later, he threw the dead animal among the herd of bulls, where the reaction was amazing; the hated enemy was reduced to shreds by their sharp hooves and antlers. Then Gadu sat up all night, calling for two other men to help keep vigil over the entire herd, lest there be other wolves near. His action of tossing the dead wolf to them had warned the great males that wolves were in the vicinity, and they planted themselves in a circular pattern, facing outward toward the enemy with nostrils flaring. Snorts echoed among them for hours, angry grunts.

Within the pen, cows and calves continued their grunting communication in calmer tones: the usual questions and reassurances. The cows, who had dropped their antlers, sometimes chewed on them, for the calcium they contained was needed as calves continued to nurse.

CHAPTER ~14~

As the summer progressed and the tundra was moist, flowers sprouted, then bloomed. The caribou found much to eat: grass, green plants, sedge, mushrooms, as well as their staple, lichens. Both bulls and cows had good reason to eat voraciously while there was plenty. The cows, who had lost weight after the long winter followed by the spring calving, were eager to prepare for another winter and spring of similar rigors. When the mating season was begun, a cow in poor health or underweight was prevented by nature from conceiving and had to wait until the next year to have another calf.

As for the bulls, they had to eat to gain weight also, for the rutting season of the fall required much strength, and they would not eat much then or during the winter. In late summer and very early autumn, they lost the velvet covering of their horns and, of course, the antlers would be shed after the rutting season was over. Each bull gained as much as three inches of fat on his back and on his rump during late summer. Then their necks grew extremely large as hormones such as testosterone were produced in the body of the adult bull, and he started to become more contentious than usual. Many small fights were not really in earnest, for all this was preliminary to major skirmishes later on. However, the sharp cups of the hooves and the huge rack of tri-pronged antlers both could damage an opponent, leaving a wounded caribou vulnerable to attack by wolves or bears.

The caribou had remained on the tundra nearby as cold arrived, and they had been content to stay and eat, since the herd was small enough for the food supply to be ample. As the cold increased, mating began. A bull singled out several cows which he watched, and as they became receptive to him or other males, his task was to keep other males away. The cows at first ran away from him, but they knew that the fleeing was part of the game. Soon he was able to mount a cow successfully, to the satisfaction of both, and with some swagger of his handsome fat flanks, the bull was off to breed with another cow. If another bull got in his way and he had sufficiently large antlers and physique, his tyranny among the cows went unchallenged. A direct match between two equally powerful males was an exciting, virile fight to the finish.

Gadu, jealous of losing any of his animals, saw that they all had plenty of room on the tundra. It was dangerous to interfere with rutting rivals.

When the weather grew very cold, the bulls lost their antlers. Those proud symbols of male strength were nearly as wide as the animal was tall. The horns would re-grow in late winter or earliest spring.

The pads of the caribou's hooves shrank and hardened in winter, and they were covered with tufts of hair. The sharp-edged hooves could then bite into ice or hardened snow without slipping. The cup-like hooves also had the advantage of supporting the creature in snow or melting tundra, for they could spread widely. All the caribou used their hooves to dig for lichens under ice or snow when their keen sense of smell had detected them.

One crisp autumn night Tlan emerged from the warm, stuffy cave into a spectacular desert night. Looking toward the east, he saw with stunning clarity the orange-gold sphere of the moon, which had just risen. It hung in a deep blue, velvety sky. Dramatic markings and shadings indicated the vague features of a head; Tlan was troubled at this aspect; if the Goddess of the Moon showed her face so clearly, what could that mean for his clan? The level black horizon was typical of eastern tundra at night. What was so startling was the size of the brilliant orb, the full moon. Its beauty arrested him; it brought tears to his eyes that so wonderful a night might be revealed to him here, at his new home.

The hills behind him stretched to the west, awkward and uneven in silhouette. Here the clan had found caves to shelter most of the families. The caribou herd had increased and Gadu had become a perceptive manager for the animals. With so much improvement in the condition of his clan, Tlan felt satisfaction that his leadership had been good. But tonight he felt, in addition to his awe at the beauty of the scene before him, an uneasiness. When the gods of nature appeared most beneficent in aspect, the most kind and generous, sometimes treachery was closest. With a shiver he turned his back on the remarkable moon and went in to the fire.

There followed several days of unseasonably warm, clear weather. Men laboring at various projects complained of the heat at midday and everyone laid aside hide coverings in a general feeling of freedom. Taga emerged from his cave wearing only his thong; he was taller than average for his time and well-muscled. As he strode toward the herding grounds out on the tundra, many of the women admired his appearance. His black hair had been cut that very morning by his wife, Maa, as she knelt behind him in the cave, patiently using a newly edged stone knife. He had refused to let her use a comb made of bone, and he had insisted that in the back the length must be the width of her hand, so her task had been to shape his hair as she cut, giving it an attractive rounded effect. No one had touched his black beard, but it was not too long. His body, bronzed by the summer sun, shone with good health; the demarcation of heavy muscle groups on his arms, chest, and legs were clear despite his leanness and fitness. Most attractive of all was his countenance; his dark eyes sparkled with intelligence and initiative and his teeth were strong, even and white. He held himself tall, for he had developed as a leader, the role to which he was clearly born.

CHAPTER ~15~

Tlan had been watching Taga as he went by, and the beauty of the young man reminded him sharply of the son he had enjoyed – Alun, his son with Passa. He closed his eyes as he remembered what a handsome and brilliant young man Alun had been as he approached his eighteenth year, in love with life and adventure.

He himself had been thirty-five then, after ten years as the shaman of the Caribou Clan. The time had gone well for him only because he saw Passa every day, and their son Alun was his constant companion. Alun's quickness at learning was his great joy, and he spent much of his time imparting his own rich background to the younger man.

Then when he was thirty-five, he sensed a restlessness in Alun, the handsome young man. Alun wanted real adventure and would have struck out on his own if Tlan had not invented the greatest of travels for them both – a tour to the west, to the highest mountains of all. His own reason for this trip was to acquire stones with unique properties which were not available anywhere else. On the way he would replenish his supply of red ocher and perhaps acquire some rock crystals and lapis. Alun was inexpressibly eager for the opportunity to travel for the first time. His mother was reluctant, and so was Tzan.

In time Alun wore down all the opposition to this trip, and he was allowed to go. Four hunters accompanied them for three days; when the hunters turned back to the village, Alun looked at the tall mountains in the distance and cried out, "We shall climb them all!"

He was right; they did climb many mountains, straining to breathe in the thin air at high altitudes, surviving the cold of snow and ice, and enjoying the test of the spirit each day. They met humans unlike any they had ever known, and they lived among villagers for months as they waited for the opening of trails that were not negotiable because of extreme weather.

They had been traveling for over three years when Alun was lost. Never would Tlan forget the scene. They were surrounded by whiteness on a high pass which was perilously close to a crevasse. One moment they were talking and the next moment Alun was gone. There was no one close to help look for him, so Tlan called and tramped the snow in all directions until he had to camp for the night. The next day he searched until a group of travelers came by going down to a village below, where he had to be restrained while they reasoned with him that no one could have survived in that snow for long.

He stayed with the villagers there for a year before he had the courage to start the long walk back to the Caribou Clan's village. He was forty years old when he showed up with long white hair and white beard, stooped and old, and with news he could not bear to deliver to Passa and Tzan. Instead of telling of glorious adventure, he had to tell them that their wonderful son was lost. Passa was crushed, unbelieving. She could not weep. She never forgave Tlan. She would not even speak to him. Tzan had only one emotion for every situation now: anger consumed him. Tlan fled into exile, choosing life in the desert to the south.

When Taga and his bride, Maa, fled from Tzan and also went south, Tlan learned from them that his love, Passa, had died. Tzan knew that the cause was her broken heart. He had felt inexpressible guilt.

CHAPTER ~16~

THE HOT DAYS on the tundra had been deceptive; clouds gathered and boiled overhead, turning ominously dark. Women and children hovered in the caves. Gadu, studying the sky, believed that the caribou calves would be vulnerable in the flash flooding that was imminent. He began working on a plan to save them. First, he rounded up a team of men to walk behind the herd, helping to drive them in the direction of higher ground. Then he worked on the gigantic bull that was leader of the herd. He laid a path of freshly dug lichens and the bull ate his way up an incline exactly as Gadu desired, with the entire herd ambling along behind him, bulls ahead of cows and calves.

Gadu was able to lead the bull to the upper plateau where the herd would be safe, but now the first raindrops were falling while the herd was still ambling along the rocky defile. If the flood waters caught them in this ditch-like site, they would all be swirled against rocks and under water. The animals were skittish but were still taking their time. Gadu gave a snorting grunt, a good imitation of the lead bull. The bull himself snorted, although not in his usual fierce voice. Picking up their pace, the group snorted, a community of grunting sounds. It rained hard now, making their footing less certain. In a downpour, the cows and calves, with men following them, emerged on the higher plateau, safe. By this time the cows and calves began gathering into the middle of a circle, with the bulls guarding them.

Gadu and his men saw the flood waters begin their rush down the path the animals had been on. Looking around, they saw the hills around them channeling streams of roiling water, and out on the lower ground of the tundra, flood waters became a lake. A swiftly moving chain of lightning strikes frightened them as it passed by, but the center of the terrible thunder and lightning seemed to be further west, where the hills echoed with the rolling of heavy thunder. Men and caribou stood, staunchly defying the heavy deluge.

Then, the rain became gentler and began to taper off. The herd did not move. Gadu was at once concerned with the safety of the calves. The bulls faced him as Gadu walked around the herd, peering into its middle where calves huddled close to cows, all in a sea of shallow water but all safe.

It was some time before Gadu and the men could return to their homes, to assure themselves that their families were safe, for there was water everywhere.

The air, saturated with water, immediately took on a chill and the temperature began to rocket downward. Next, the water-soaked landscape would become coated with ice, every surface slippery. Although the next morning's sun shone upon a crystal world of unearthly beauty, nature's glory was treacherous.

Gadu saw his herd fanning out onto the tundra more distantly than he wished; the area near the craggy hills was now covered with thick ice, and the herd was looking for foraging grounds that did not require so much effort, although their hooves could dig holes in the crystal covering of the tundra to get to the lichen.

While older people worried about falling on icy paths, the younger ones ran out on the thick sheet of ice below, throwing themselves down with enough momentum to carry them far, far across the surface. Then, rising, they would take another swift ride. Tlan, coming to his cave door, watched them and proclaimed that he, his wife, and children would not venture outside the cave on this day; besides, the cold and wet weather had brought on a bout of joint fever. He headed for his pile of furs.

Elar was happy to see Yun come in, bearing in his hands a couple of icycles for the little ones. Oola and Tuit happily sucked on their deliciously cold treats, as Elar ran over to wipe away some of the baby's slobbering. She knew it would be a long day, as she would be trapped in the cave with two little ones and an ailing old one.

Taga and Maa had begun the task of visiting every home of the clan to see that all had survived the flood. It was hard to keep their footing, as their feet were bound with furry hides, but they went from cave to cave, giving a cheery greeting to young and old. Taga had just decided that all were well, when they came to the last cave, where Tol had chosen to build an anteroom at his entrance to increase the size of his cave. He had at first planned to use only the large old bones they had found, but there were loose stones of some size around his cave, and they were easier to stack to form walls. He had ended with a combination of large bones and stones, and Tol had been so pleased that he could not stop building. As the terrain outside his entrance led uphill, he laid stones to follow the upward curve. In fact, he had not finished, and the end of this passage was still open. Tol had planned to use hides for the roofing, but he had not yet done so.

Taga climbed alone to this cave, feeling that something was amiss. And indeed a calamity had come to Tol and his family. Wading in as the icy water was receding through holes in the new stone walls, Taga saw that flood waters had entered the passage curving downward and filled Tol's small cave so rapidly that they had no chance to escape. The three bodies of Tol, his wife, and a small girl lay amid sodden robes and furs, under water that was still as high as half up a leg. And all was crusted with skim ice.

Shaking his head in sad disbelief, Taga gingerly climbed back down to tell his wife. These were the first deaths to members of the clan since they had moved to this location, and they would miss Tol and his family, because the community was still small. How pitiful it was that these deaths could have been avoided.

They sought help from men who lived near. Taga, Maa, and the neighbors removed stones from the lower part of the anteroom so that the remaining water could run out. Sadly they laid the bodies on robes and arranged them for a burial to be held at this cave. More stones were removed and set to one side, leaving the entrance of the cave open once more. The stage was set for the clan to gather down below, with a view into the cave. When the public ceremony was over, men would use Tol's building stones to seal this cave forever.

As they worked at Tol's cave, Taga and Maa felt the heat of a bright sun, even though the weather remained cold. The rays of the sun melted ice on the rocky paths, to their relief, and by afternoon the paths and rocky ledges were dry and safe underfoot.

Taga was mournful as he returned home to tell Tlan the dreadful news. His face gave away half the story before he spoke. Tlan frowned to hear how Tol's misplaced pride in his building had brought misfortune upon his family.

They sat for a time in silence, then Tlan said, "You will help me with this burial, for the fever in my joints pains me. We must provide music and dance as evidence of the spirit that lives on in the clan despite death. I will play my flute, but you will be there to play the drum. We have time to prepare spirit masks also. In the grave, we will place food and Tol's weapons, and a doll for the little girl. After this burial I shall require more red ocher, and perhaps other shaman's supplies. And the clan will expect a feast, so some of the caribou must be sacrificed if the hunters do not bring in big animals. Tell Gadu and prepare for the meat to be roasted. The very smell of the roast will drive everyone wild with hunger, and that is what they will remember most."

Tlan asked for Elar's help in preparing the two masks, which needed to be outsized, with holes for eyes and mouth; Tlan found two very stiff hides from which to cut them. He decided to cut two enormous triangles with triangular eye and mouth holes. Some red ocher powder was mixed with water, and with his finger he painted on lurid designs. Elar managed the business of running leather cords through holes at the side to tie the masks behind the head. Then Elar brought in bright ptarmigan head feathers and tucked them into little slits at the top; this was so good an effect that ostrich feathers and a few bear claws were added to the design. Tlan confessed to the others that the idea was to make the two performers look "otherworldly." They did.

The doll was made from small reeds tied into a bundle with more reeds tucked in crosswise to serve as arms, and a head was created by tying off a smaller round section at the top. Oola found this toy so delightful that it was difficult to give it up for the burial, until Elar made him one of his own.

The most difficult item was the drum. Tlan had set aside a large round hollow fossil bone of the right diameter and length, and now he stretched a skin over it to cover both ends, securing it in the middle by a leather cord laced through holes in the skin. By pulling the cord tight, he was able to make the skin taut at the ends, and the drum gave forth a hollow, mournful sound when hit with the hand.

CHAPTER ~17~

As Tlan had foretold, the day of the burial of Tol and his family was memorable for the voluptuous smell of meat that wafted through the area. Whole carcasses were wrapped in water-soaked hides and buried in the coals of a huge fire, where they smoldered all day.

The clan gathered at the burial site when they heard music just before dusk. In front of Tol's cave there burned a dancing fire; the clan members knew that the cave behind it held the bodies. At one side sat Tlan, playing on his flute, and Taga, holding the cylindrical drum. The fire illuminated the grotesque masks they wore; they sat still as they played, but the flickering flames gave drama to the scene. Their music consisted of the flute's melody of three ascending whole notes, followed by one whole note down; at the pause here the drum gave three hollow, desolate beats. Then the entire musical phrase was repeated, all with much sensitivity and dignity. The listening clan members were deeply moved.

After a hypnotically long period of this musical repetition, Tlan laid down his flute and stood while the drum beat became regular, constant but slow. Moving slowly to the hollow beats, Tlan moved around the fire as his hands, lifted high, told a story. The clan knew the story; it was about the lives of the three who had died. They had lived; they had been loved; they had died; their spirits had ascended to the sky. Again, the clan members were all lifted out of themselves by a sense of the significance of these lives and by the survival of their spirits.

As the drum ceased, Tlan came forward and took a commanding stance; then he began to recite:

The people arose from the west,
They followed the caribou.
They moved over tundra and mountains,
Over tundra and mountains, ice and snow.
The people followed the herds.
The people are strong in life and death.
The people move toward the next dawn.

Tlan was growing tired now. He came to sit down while Taga began again the slow beat of the funeral drum. The clan remained quiet, their appreciation evident.

Tlan arose and went into the burial chamber, still wearing his mask. With great ceremony, he sifted red ocher into the orifices of the head for each body and continued a sort of pantomime of the spirit escaping from each corpse. Finally he came to the fire and asked of the crowd, "Who among you have food for Tol and his family to eat in the afterlife?" At this, many of the women brought packets of food, and Taga descended to take the food, which he placed by the heads of Tol and his family.

Again Tlan faced the clan, asking, "Where are the weapons that will protect Tol and his family?" Taga placed several axes by the right hand of Tol.

When Tlan asked for a parting gift for the little girl, and Taga brought out the reed doll, the clan gasped; this was a special and cunning bit of planning on the part of Tlan.

Now Tlan approached the fire and put it out. It was the symbolic end of the burial ceremony. Men came up to seal the cave with the many stones near its entrance, and the crowd finally responded to their yearning for the roast meat, which now smelled even more enticing. They were gone quickly into the shadows of the night.

CHAPTER ~18~

Tlan stirred restlessly as he sat by the fire in the early morning. At length he spoke directly to Taga, "Alas. My bag of shaman's supplies is running low. Now there are some items I cannot replace myself. My usefulness to the clan will be limited without the red ocher. We've had too many burials. And there are crystals that I need also."

Taga was at once alert. "I understand. We have a great need for good chunks of hard stone for making tools and weapons. It is time for me to journey toward the mountains where the best chert and flint can be found."

"You cannot go alone. To be safer you should take two other men who are skilled hunters and who are trustworthy. May I suggest that a shorter journey might be to the south where I used to gather chalcedony and red jasper from the limestone-floored valleys. The red cliffs that I remember are not far from the sand dunes that are covered with salt bushes. You might be lucky to encounter someone who could trade with you. What would you have to trade?"

"My finished tools and weapons, I think."

"And what if you meet men who have better skills than you at this stone work?"

Taga looked down. This had not occurred to him. "Food is too scarce for me to use for trade. Hides would be too heavy to carry any distance. The stone bowls would be very good if they did not have to be carried." Taga rose and looked around his cave environment to discover any item which would be easy to carry and also would be attractive for barter.

On display were several bone cups belonging to Tlan; Elar had found them very beautiful because of their handsome carving. Indeed, they were old and prized by the shaman, gifts that represented his adventurous past. Taga picked one of them up and admired it. "These are crafted well. If I had time, I could make the tools needed for this kind of carving."

"And you would meet a man who has more chert than he needs but who does not need a cup because he bends to drink from a stream."

Again Taga looked down. "I will think about this, and later we shall talk again." He turned to leave and at the door called back, "Don't worry. We will get your new supplies."

Outside his cave he met Beros, the skilled hunter who would probably be one of those to accompany him on this trip. As they walked together down toward the tundra, Taga mentioned that Tlan, their leader, needed supplies for his shaman's duties, supplies that might come from far away. Also, he himself needed to replenish his supply of good hard stone used to make tools and weapons.

"One of his most difficult requests is a clear crystal stone. Also red ocher. What do you know of the sources of these, Beros?"

"There are mountains far to the west that are higher and higher; there one can find many such special stones as obsidian, chalcedony, lapis, quartz crystals, and many other kinds of stones. A trip to those mountains would be long; preparing for such a trip would take much time. Already those high mountains are covered with deep snow and ice."

"Tlan has suggested that a short trip might be to the south where the red hills overlook small valleys floored with limestone that has beds of red jasper and other hard stones. These red hills are near the sand dunes with green salt bushes. In that area we might find chalcedony and slate, as well as red jasper."

"I will be glad to go with you on this shorter journey. My brother Ino would be a good companion, strong and careful; he might also know the path to the salt bush region."

"We should make such a journey in the next few days, while the weather is cold but not too much a burden to travelers. Let us take two days to prepare and leave on the third morning. Tlan and I discussed our taking goods to barter, in case we meet people with some stones that are hard to find. I have no goods to trade with others."

"The mountains to the northwest are forested; wood is very important. We might next take a larger number of men on an expedition to the forests. Wood can be made into many useful items to be used for barter."

When Tlan was told of this conversation later, he heartily concurred with the idea of a second trip, to secure wood from the mountain forests. He also agreed that these two men would be strong, alert, and companionable, and thus would be good choices for any trip. Tlan knew that the short trip to the south would yield lots of chalcedony and red jasper, perhaps enough to last for a long while, and this would be very profitable for Taga. He thus urged Taga to go as he had planned, taking Beros and Ino along. They would take food to last for at least a week but would hope to be back within that time.

Early on the third day, Taga, Beros, and Ino took a trail that first led out on the frozen tundra as they circled the last outcroppings of the hills in which were their caves. Then their course was due south, with the rising sun on their left. They ran with a loping, easy stride, almost joyfully because this trip was a release from daily responsibilities, as well as an adventure.

All three men were fairly tall and superbly built, trained to defend themselves and fearless in doing so. The frozen ground underneath their feet sometimes became treacherous, but they were sure-footed and agile. A strong, chilling wind came from the west all the while; therefore, Taga, in the lead, constantly watched the sun to correct their course if the wind affected their heading.

As they reached the open, flat tundra and sped across its vast brownish expanse, they were aware that they could be seen from a great distance, a line of three men in single file, with Taga in the lead. As long as they were on the open, treeless tundra, they, too, could see any approaching enemy, but as they drew near hills, they would have to be aware that they had already been seen by wolves, bears, lions, or unfriendly warriors long before they themselves could become aware of watching eyes.

They stopped only for water or pemmican. In mid-afternoon Ino, taking careful sighting of the sun, indicated that they must veer to the southwest. They did this without having encountered any animals, although flocks of ravens flew high above them.

They slept on the tundra, awakening to the sun's piercing but cold light. Conferring about their directions, they were relieved when Ino showed them how he had, immediately when they had stopped for the night, drawn a long directional line to show them their course. So they trotted off confidently, now partly facing the invigorating cold wind. Now, too, each man wore an eye covering with small horizontal slits, protection against both sun and wind. These items had been contributions from clever Elar.

About noon they arrived at the low hills which they had sighted first from a distance. Ino confirmed that this was exactly right. For the rest of the day, then, they followed the edge of those hills. By nightfall Ino, watching the last rays of the sun, said that they must go south, so another night was spent on the tundra; this time they took turns staying awake to watch for predatory wolves.

On the morning of the third day, Ino advised them that across a stretch of flat tundra they would find several low mountains covered with jagged rocks, where there were dry, sandy valleys. The sharp rocks slowed their progress, but beyond the mountains they found another flat tundra and soon they came upon a sluggish river that was nearly dry. Ino cheered them on; they were nearing their destination.

The grassland near the river became a sandy waste punctuated by thorny salt bushes; soon sand dunes were topped by these bushes. The extraordinary long roots of the bushes found water deep below the sand and gravel, so that some areas were green with a forest of the tough, thorny growth. Then Ino stopped and pointed to a rise of jagged red cliffs in the distance. He said, "There."

Beyond the cliffs there was another mountain range, but it was evident now that they were going to those red cliffs.

Soon they were clambering among them, searching the valleys where the limestone floor was often swept clear of sand by the incessant winds. This was where they might find embedded red jasper or other stone which had forced itself to the surface in molten form and then hardened. Unlike the soft limestone around it, jasper could be worked so that the resulting knife would have an extremely fine and long-lasting blade. Taga was delighted with their find and greedy to carry back as much as the three of them could transport. It was his plan to dig out chunks and then refine them as much as possible right there, so that they would carry no waste stone. One valley was soon littered with sharp flakes as they worked industriously. Taga was the one who handled each piece of stone which was packed into their hide bags, and he accepted only the best quality. The result was a valuable haul of excellent hard stone, and Taga was very, very pleased. They worked the rest of that day, slept briefly, and began again early on the next day.

Ino, who had been to the Cliffs of Red Fire before, wandered off as he saw that their work was ending. He was over in the next valley, scanning the rocky floor, when the sun glinted off something in his peripheral vision – off to the left. Investigating, Ino saw lying on top of a pile of sand a clear quartz crystal as long as his large middle finger. It did not seem to have any relationship to its surroundings. Rather, it was as if someone might have laid it there on the pile of sand. It was incredibly beautiful and pure. In the sun it created a wave of prismatic color. He was fascinated. He wanted it for his own. He knew that this was one of the items which Tlan had specified that he needed for his work as a shaman: a crystal. He also knew that there was a very special relationship between a shaman and the beautiful crystal which he might use for healing or for spiritual ceremonies.

Ino played with it for a long time, enjoying the rainbow of colors which splashed out upon his brown hand. The magic of this crystal was impelling. At length he dropped it into a bag within his wraps and slowly returned to the others. He would not tell them what he had found. By sheer luck it was his alone.

Taga and Beros were resting beside the three bags of raw stones; they chewed slowly on some pemmican as they planned for their departure. Taga's face showed his happiness over their success. Ino joined them, sinking down on a rock to rest, and he did not say a word about his find of the crystal stone.

It was about the middle of the afternoon as they slung their bags of stones upon their broad shoulders and emerged from the Cliffs of Red Fire. Before them was the area of the sand dunes covered with low salt bushes. They swung out briskly, handling well the precious burdens on their shoulders. Behind them was the rugged line of red cliffs and far ahead of them was home.

CHAPTER
~19~

AMID THE JOYFUL homecoming of the trio of hunters who had gone to the Red Cliffs, nobody noticed the silence of Ino.

The large amount of valuable stones made the clan wealthy in a way and more independent, too. It was all carefully chosen, and each chunk of red jasper was now ready to yield many sharp, strong tools or weapons. All the young men who wanted to learn stone-knapping could join Taga's classes. Taga was elated at the great success of his mission. It had been a test of his ability to lead men in a situation beyond their home environment, and he felt that he had performed brilliantly.

Maa was too happy for words. She was expecting her second child, and now she had her husband back safely just in time for the event. Elar was planning to be the mid-wife, a role she played most often for the women of the clan, and this birth would be in her own new family.

Yun, realizing that soon there would be three little children in this one small cave, had been doing some thinking. He loved all the little ones and helped to take care of them, but the noise level would now increase a lot, and the two women would be busy with all the children. They needed more space. And Yun thought also of the brown-eyed beauty of his own age who had stood beside him at the burial of Tol's family and who had afterward shared food with him at the feasting; her brown eyes followed him everywhere. Lin and her mother had a hut near the tundra, where a handful of families had chosen to live. The father had perished in the Great Wind, so they had no man in the home. Yun was young still, but they would welcome him into their home as a future husband to Lin. The more he thought of this plan, the more it delighted him. He resolved to speak to Lin and her mother about it first, before he told Elar.

Tlan, sitting by his fire much of the day, was often lost in thought even as he appeared to be drowsing. There came to him a project which he pictured in his mind as if it already existed, and he began to think of it as necessary for the clan. He wished to have a circle of huge stones from the hills behind them ringing the site of the old village of the clan, where Tzan had ruled with such a heavy hand. It had remained a blank space with only the cairn of stones covering the grave of those lost in the Great Wind. Now Tlan felt that the sanctity of the area should be guaranteed by a larger memorial. All the people still alive had lost close relatives in the disaster, and Tlan knew that they would all be gratified to have a monument built to help them remember those who were gone. This monument would be circular, and he would explain to the clan that the circle had no beginning or end; the symbolism would have great meaning for them. Within the circle there would be no homes built, and the area would remain an outdoor area for clan gatherings. He began to plan the number of stones and the placement of each, with about the length of two caribou between each two stones and each stone to be about the height of a female caribou.

This project was accomplished with great enthusiasm by all members of the clan, for they missed their relatives and wished to memorialize them. Also, the prospect of having a special meeting place that could accommodate crowds in the future seemed good. The men looked far and found twenty-one stones of good size and height; bringing them to the circle was not easy; here the sled Taga had made for his family's trip to the site of the Great Wind disaster gave them inspiration to make a stronger one, and the stones were set up, one by one, to form a large circle.

Tlan was the engineer, overseeing carefully the planting of each large stone. Members of the clan stood by in awe to see the magic of this ring of huge stones as it appeared more complete as each moon passed. They did not know that each stone had a special meaning for Tlan; as an astronomer he had spent hours and hours to ensure that the stones marked the spring and autumnal equinoxes, the important times for the caribou herd's fall rutting season and spring calving, as well as other seasonal times for the clan. When the stones were all in place, the plaza area thus created seemed holy, set apart, and a place for contemplation as well as for group activities. It had taken the clan a year and a half to accomplish the task.

Tlan had to think then about the dedication ceremony which would establish this area as a special and sanctified site. He got out the trappings that he and Taga had used for the funeral of Tol's family. The musical instruments would be an asset; the masks would be good with additional decorations. Something more was needed for this ceremony. Then it came to him that Taga needed to be initiated as a shaman, since at any time Taga might have to succeed him, should he die or have an incapacitating illness. Now was the right time for an elaborate display of psychic energy and power by the shamans.

The time that had passed had allowed for the clan to grow in their ability to work together without quarrels. The young men of the clan had advanced in their chosen skills through the education provided by Taga and Tlan, and this had increased their self-confidence, as it had benefited the whole clan.

Tlan and his wife Elar had moved into their new long-house by the tundra, where the many hides wrapping the building had made it warmer for the arthritic old man. On the floor were also skins that were soft and warm underfoot. Tlan always had the two fires burning, as in the old days of the Great Tzan, and his house was cheerful and neat, thanks to the good woman who had become his mate. Little Oola bubbled over with genial laughter all the time; his good nature was remarkable and made him popular with everyone. Tlan foresaw for him a continuation of this happy disposition; with his inheritance in the minds of the people, he could become a leader of immense following with great persuasive power. Tlan, thinking of this, talked with Elar about the future of this little foundling who almost had died in the tomb of his father.

Tlan said to his wife, "With his prospects, Oola must be given good guidance and training in morality, for people will always tend to let him have his way."

And Elar agreed, for she intended to see that he knew right from wrong and to care about others unselfishly.

The second child of Taga and Maa was named Tor, at the insistence of Maa, who remembered that it had been her father's name. The family continued to live in the roomy, well-ordered cave which had once been Elar's home. Maa often said that she had learned much from Elar about keeping the greater part of the cave free so that people moving about found it comfortable. She had really learned much more than that. Elar's gentle, industrious, and inventive spirit had spread to all the housewives in the clan, and as a result all the wives had more harmony and goodwill in their homes.

Taga was busy much of the time with tasks that had to do with the welfare of the clan. He now was indispensable to Tlan. When Tlan discussed with him the responsibilities of a shaman, Taga understood very well the skills involved in serving as an intermediary between the world of the spirit and the practical world of daily struggle. Taga sometimes now visited a person who was ill, doing his best to find an effective cure in imitation of Tlan. He studied the herbs and powders in the shaman's bag and learned about their powers and where they could be obtained. He spent many nights and days gazing at the sun and the moon. He practiced on the drum to learn rhythms which would enhance different moods for the ceremonies of a shaman. The flute was much harder to learn, until Tlan encouraged him to make his own bone flute and master it enough to produce a tonal quality that was less breathy as time went on. One area of the shaman's responsibility was hardest of all; that was the great reach into the unknown of the spirit.. Tlan kept reassuring him that this would develop in time.

Tlan said casually, "Have you considered taking a few days and nights to go away into solitude where you can confront yourself and then go beyond yourself?"

Taga agreed that this would be a maturing experience. "It could even be risky. That sounds exciting."

But because Taga was needed so much every day, they did not find the right time for him to go off by himself to contemplate. In his cave, however, Taga occasionally took from their shelf the two fossil eggs which he had found, and he thought deeply about the mystery they represented for him and how brightly the sun had shone on his family that morning, turning Tuit and the eggs to gold as Tuit pointed and said, "East." This mystery held so much emotion for him that he was still awed by the memory.

CHAPTER
~20~

TAGA COULD NOT sleep because the baby was crying incessantly; Tor was cutting teeth and letting everyone know about his feverish discomfort. Maa held him, made rocking motions with her arms, and uttered cooing sounds, but nothing soothed him.

How relieved, then, were they all when in came Tlan with his wife Elar. Both knew that little Tor was in pain, and either one could deal with this situation – the shaman or the mid-wife. Tlan drew some herbs out of his bag and handed them to Elar, who at once made a little concoction in a stone bowl. She put her finger into the bowl and rubbed the child's inflamed gums, and in a few moments he fell asleep, exhausted by a long session of crying. Maa laid Tor down tenderly on his own pallet and looked at him; he was so innocent and beautiful that it was as if this was a different baby.

Taga made a proposal that they all enjoy some herbal tea, and the older couple agreed. However, first they wanted to tell about the special errand they were on tonight. Tlan said, with some excitement, "Taga, a meteor shower is filling the whole sky. Stars are raining down from all parts of the heavens. This is a phenomenon so rare that I cannot remember having ever seen so many stars falling at once."

Said Maa, "This makes me a little fearful."

Forgetting the tea, they all stepped out on the terrace outside the door. They were met by a flood of light from overhead and from horizon to horizon as a vast panorama of falling stars covered the night sky. The four of them were just high enough to appreciate fully this awe-inspiring light-show, and there was no need for words as they gazed raptly above and all around them.

Elar's uplifted face glowed with light reflected from the dazzling sky and from her own keen inner response to this unearthly beauty; she yielded to the moment and was wrapped in her sense of wonderment. Maa, too, responded with awe; to her these were the gods and goddesses of the sky visiting the earth in myriad numbers, showing their beauty and power and bringing light. She felt fear in her heart when she thought of such vast power all in continuous movement; she was dizzy with the fear and the other strange emotions rushing to her head.

Taga and Tlan, men who were trying to understand the gods of the heavens, looked at each other. There was no possible explanation for this rain of stars coming from all directions; the grandeur of the exhibition and its awesome beauty moved them tremendously, and they wanted desperately to know what it meant. If the stars were everywhere, turning the night into day, was this an omen of good for their clan, or did this portend tragedy such as they had suffered from the gigantic force of the Great Wind?

Tlan remembered the night when he had looked long at the huge autumn moon which had hung in a velvet sky, orange-gold and terribly near the earth. It had been so brilliant and close that its beauty had brought him to tears, but he had felt, too, a sense of uneasiness that the Goddess of the Moon should show her face so clearly to men on the earth. Then the treachery he feared had come about; an intense rain had brought flooding and the result had meant death for three members of their clan. Tlan searched his memory for enlightenment, and finding none, he sank on his knees and bowed his head to the stony floor of the terrace.

Seeing a few members of the Caribou Clan below, and realizing that they were terrified, Taga slowly descended to meet them, trying to give an appearance of calmness. "We have been given a gift of great beauty. The gods have given us a shining sky full of streaming stars. You want to know what it means, don't you? I cannot tell you, but it must be good because no stars are falling on us; no one has been harmed. Perhaps the gods are thanking us for building our Circle of Stones. You must put aside your fear and enjoy this wonderful gift of many, many stars." And with his natural optimism, he gave a positive explanation that made good sense to these worried members of the clan, and they smiled to hear that their hard work in making the stone circle was being rewarded so spectacularly. Beros and others hurried off to let their families know that they need not fear.

Taga returned to his family on the terrace and repeated what he had just told Beros and the others – that the gods were rewarding this clan for building the Circle of Stones. The women saw that this was a perfect explanation and continued to stare at the sky for a long time. Tlan kept to himself his thoughts, but he was glad that Taga had drawn a positive and reasonable conclusion from the phenomenon.

As dusk drew near the next day, everyone watched the sky intently, for only at dawn had the shooting stars been dimmed by daylight. And, to their amazement, only a brief rosiness accompanied the sunset in the western sky before the streaming of the glowing, burning cinders filled the entire dome of the heavens. Their splendid and fearful stars had never stopped falling, and they shone just as brightly for all the second night.

There was a chill in the air, cold for the last days of spring, for the usually warmer days of summer had just been felt a few days earlier. The caribou had calved a moon before, bringing an increase in the herd which had good implications for all. They were dependent upon these animals for food and clothing.

It grew colder during the day, and in the afternoon a light snow began to fall.

As dusk came on the third night, the quiet snow cleared, leaving a white landscape which reflected and multiplied the effect of the falling stars. It was an eerily lovely world, pure and glowing with dancing light from above.

All human activity ceased as the clan gathered to huddle within the great ring of stones. They were seeking the company of others, and this coming together had simply happened naturally. Men, women, and children could no longer bear this bright movement in the skies of the light-gods; it was incomprehensible.

Taga went to the long-house, where Tlan was meditating, still full of perplexity and fear of doom. "The entire clan has come to the ring of stones, old one. They wish to be given guidance and reassurance. You must come. They need you."

Tlan was very slow in replying, for he had been far away in his thoughts. When he stood up, he said, "I will quiet them with my music, Taga. That is all I have. The gods have not spoken to me." As Taga watched him, he found his flute and long winter cape of skins and prepared to go.

Coming through the door-flap of his home, Tlan gasped at the scene of the falling stars as they were reflected on the light snow covering the tundra and the hills behind. It was mind-bending, more than ever before. Was the world henceforth to be this wondrous white?

Led by Taga, the old shaman shuffled a bit but then began to assume the character which the clan expected of him. By the time he reached the ring of stones and stood facing the group of family and friends for which he served as leader, he was able to lift his head and raise his right hand as he declared in a clear, strong voice, "People of my people, my clan, you must not be afraid. The gods have given this enchantment to bless this monument which you have built, this ring of stones. In this moment, then, it is being sanctified and made holy by the purity of the snow. The gods are participating in this ceremony, as you see, because they are pleased with your wish to honor those who have died here. Think of those relatives who have gone and who will not return to us, for in that way they will remain here forever in your memory."

Then, in the silence that followed, Tlan raised his flute to his lips and its clear, poignant voice lifted and swelled over and over, with a sweetly haunting sadness that reminded them of the dead who were being honored. The mingling of their grief with their individual emotions about their achievement of raising this monument of stones, and their awareness of the grandeur in the heavens became as one with the tones of the flute, and their hearts were released from the grip of fear.

As the notes of the flute ended, Taga stood beside the old shaman and said, "You may now return to your homes without fear tonight. Sleep well, my friends."

Taga led the old man back to his home, worrying about his cold hands but pleased at the simple ceremony that had met the needs of the clan. The crowd, chilled because they had stood still for a long time, quickly went back to their warm hearths.

CHAPTER
~21~

THE SNOW AND cold had left Tlan with some pain, so he sat up, as near the fire as possible, after Elar and the child were asleep. His mind turned over and over this great enigma of three nights of stars falling from all points of the sky without reason; finally, to highlight and emphasize the grandeur of this scene, an unseasonable light snow had come suddenly, leaving the white ground to reflect and multiply the light of the myriad falling stars. There had to be significance in these phenomena, and this meaning must be for himself, the shaman.

He became aware of a dark shape entering his door. It was very late for any visitor, for any reason. Nearing the fire, the shape became Inos, the tall and handsome hunter friend of Taga. He seemed very nervous; his eycs shifted alarmingly. In his winter clothing Inos looked large and possibly threatening.

Keeping his voice calm, Tlan spoke to him, "My friend, sit down by the fire. What brings you here so late?"

Inos made no effort at calmness and refused to sit; he was on an errand that had turned his soul inside out. During the speech and the music at the ceremony earlier, his conscience had come alive; he knew that Tlan needed a quartz crystal just like the one that burned like a flame within his robe. He had kept it in secret for this long time, looking at it in secret, and gloating over it in secret. But tonight his heart had undergone a change as the unearthly light, the memories of his lost family, and the plaintive music combined to force a difficult decision. He needed to give his prized crystal to the old shaman.

Inos held out his hand. At first Tlan could not discern what Inos had in the hand. When it began to catch light from the dim fire, the crystal flashed like magic from the gods. It was unnerving. Inos finally found the words to explain himself. “You, shaman, need this clear stone. I found it. I want to give it to you. Take it.”

As he gingerly took the sparkling stone, Tlan realized a purpose for himself in the past three nights. He was completely caught by surprise. His mood lifted; after all, the gods had planned for him an incredible gift, and one of his own clan had been the go-between to see that he received a crystal to help him know divine decisions about the fates of humans. This crystal would be instrumental in healing the sick, first of all. It would be powerful in helping him to penetrate the curtain to the spirit world, a curtain that had grown too dark for him recently.

He began, “Inos! My friend, this is a very important link to the gods themselves. May you find blessings because of this generosity. I thank you, Inos, and I hope…”

But Inos did not wish to hear his gratitude. He was already at the door, hurrying before he regretted what he had done. His heart was not easy with the transaction, but he did not return to retrieve the stone.

As Tlan turned the crystal in his hands, it caught light from the fire as if it had a life of its own. It had a strangely empowering aura. His world was now vastly different; he knew that he had been played by the gods and then rewarded. He felt at ease.

He prepared the fire for the night and looked out the door once more to see the dazzling falling stars, and then he lay down, grasping in his hand the magic stone.

CHAPTER
~22~

TAGA WATCHED THE shower of meteors until dawn, noting that it was diminishing. The shooting stars still came from every direction; however, they had become more sporadic. He felt sad that the gods were ending this unbelievable spectacle, but the events of the night had influenced all the clan in a personal way when the rain of stars was given a link to their new Circle of Stones. So it had been a good thing. It had been an omen of good.

Turning to the door of his cave home and pushing aside the skin flaps, he built up the fire and warmed himself for a time before lying down. He was tired and sleepy; at the same time an excitement created by the shooting stars outside made him restless. He wondered briefly before he dozed off under his soft caribou skins whether the time had finally come for him to take his trip alone for the purpose of contemplating his new role as a shaman.

An inner voice confirmed this fact, and he understood at once and without question that the gods had spoken. He was called to go by himself, even at some risk, toward the mountains of the larch and birch forests where there were deep-flowing rivers. A picture came to him of himself holding up a fish in his hands, and he felt the cold water washing over his feet and the smooth stones of a river bed beneath him. And suddenly a deep sleep blotted it all out.

When Taga set out on his trip, he had pemmican in his bag and also an assortment of shaman supplies. Several of his best hunting weapons were stashed within easy reach. He was traveling light, bent on protecting himself and finding places for meditation on the way. Tlan had given him a kind of blessing, rubbing a line of red ocher onto his forehead. He had also given him a talisman to protect him – a necklace made of thin round slices of caribou horn strung on a thin strip of leather. Tlan explained that as the caribou was the totem of the clan, its horns would increase his sense of smell and give him strength and speed against an enemy.

Setting out in the cold air of early morning, he felt the darkness thinning and saw that all the shooting stars had disappeared. At first he was on the frozen tundra, but as the winter sun climbed in the sky, he climbed barren and rocky hills. Soon he observed that the valleys had the brown remains of grass and flowers along with shrubs. He knew that, besides the thickening vegetation, there were many more kinds of animals here, some for his supper and some whose wish would be to dine on him.

In a valley he surprised a hare. Whipping out a sling, he stopped the little brown and white creature in mid-hop and looked around for a camp site. It was getting late in the afternoon, and he would build a fire where he could sleep with some protection from animals. Straight ahead was a birch tree and just beyond was a large flat stone that formed a shelf where the next rise began.

The gray limestone looked solid and it was large enough for several people to sleep on comfortably. It was, however, not a big block of stone; examining it, he saw that it was more of a laminate plate resting upon a bed of small rocks and soil. It would do very well, he thought. His next action, then, was to gather the small dried cones under a larch tree and start a fire on one side of the stone shelf.

When the fire was blazing, he stepped to a small area of sand and skinned the rabbit, saving the hide and rolling it up; he cleaned the little heart and popped it into his mouth raw. Several other organs looked healthy and fresh, so he ate them at once. He fitted the carcass onto a temporary tripod of branches, which he set over the fire. With a sigh of satisfaction, he sank down near the fire, pleased with the prospect of supper and glad to rest by the warmth and cheerful little flames.

While he gnawed on the rabbit flesh and split the bones to suck the marrow, he looked around the hillside and the far valley. Nothing aroused his suspicion, and he felt ready to begin shortly his period of meditation. Wiping the grease from his lips and chin, he looked for a place to leave the bones. He stood up and looked at the ground below, a mixture of small rocks amid dried grasses. Suddenly he recoiled in shock. Many, many snakes were emerging from beneath the stone on which he was standing. The warmth of his fire had awakened them in their nest right underneath him. He knew in a moment that they were poisonous, and he could not cope with so many at once. With the sticks of the tripod he scattered the ashes of the fire; then, grabbing his belongings, he leapt off the far side of the stone shelf and scampered up the hill. As he ran, he could not help thinking that in another moment he would have been intent on contemplation, unaware of the silent danger of the snakes. It was a lesson the lonely traveler must always remember, and he must not forget. Because he could depend only on himself, he must not be lulled into complacency. Danger might be everywhere.

Soon darkness would come, and now he felt that it was imperative that he find a safe place for the night. As he started up a low mountain with a very, very flat plateau on top and no shrubs or trees, he happened to glance back. He caught just a flash of gray fur before the animal vanished. He was worried but resumed the climb, meanwhile arming himself with the slingshot. In one tremendous move he turned swiftly, found the wolf, and aimed so accurately that the stalking creature went down with his head pierced by the angular stone from Taga's weapon. He knew that he must determine if a pack of animals had followed him or if this lone animal had found the bones of the rabbit and picked up his trail. He waited quietly behind a tall rock, and soon he had reasoned for himself that only this one voracious, hungry creature had smelled his recent meal and hoped to catch him by surprise. The wolf did not move; it was certainly dead, with eyes staring open and fanged mouth agape. With much caution he approached it and drew his stone knife; he wanted a souvenir. Still wary, he kicked the carcass several times, and then he bent and deftly carved off an ear. To travel lightly, he could not carry more. Perhaps the ear of this wolf would join the pieces of caribou antler on the necklace, telling the history of his trip.

Because he did not wish other predators to find the wolf and pick up his human trail in the night, Taga dragged the long body to a hole and quickly covered it with rocks and pebbles that were nearby. Then he chose a spiral route upwards to the top of the flat mountain. With a flaming sunset lighting the large oval area, and in the distances inspiring views of the folding hills and mountains all around him, Taga knew that he had found a place to meditate. A rising moon later proved that the night would not be totally dark. The phosphorescent green orb overhead was compellingly bright.

He sat cross-legged, his robes wrapped closely around him, in the middle of the plateau. He did not feel the sweep of the northwest wind or the cold of the stone under him. What he knew with all his being was the depth and strength of this mountain amid its brother mountains of stone; he was one with their power and stability. He was one with the massive landscape, one with the enveloping sky and the rising, flooding moonlight. When he had left his own sense of human frailty, he felt the expansiveness of the world. He was transported above the loftiest mountains into the light itself, feeling as much as seeing the immense undulations in the dark below where flashes of silver marked the winding paths of rivers. Through the moments of the night he knew that he drew close and closer to the source of the spreading light, the moon itself. Then, he stood there briefly, on a terrain exactly like his mountain-top terrain of bare gray rock. Returning to his plateau on the earth, he saw his own body sitting there below him as he hovered in the air. The shining took hold of his heart and his deepest wish was to remain within its peace forever. Then he heard music, the three-note melody which Tlan often played on his flute. While its sounds grew tenuous and soft, the music began very gently to dissolve the shining light, and he gradually found himself at one with his body, seated on the moonlit plateau.

When dawn began to fill the eastern sky, he knew that he was free to go back home, for he had fulfilled his mission. He had expected to receive a message from the gods, some directive to change his life; instead, he had communed with the gods of the heavens and the earth, and they had granted him a special vision of light and peace.

CHAPTER
~23~

IT WAS LATE spring and the severe weather of the winter had ameliorated. The tundra bore some plants that were soon to flower as the constant west winds grew milder. Those of the clan who lived in caves began to put hides outside to air in the daylight, while the inhabitants of huts carefully examined their structures to find and repair the damage done by snow, ice, and strong winter winds. Being outside in the clean air was a joyful experience for the very young, who scampered around boulders and danced over the melting tundra from dawn to dusk, laughing and carefree.

The spring calving had increased the caribou herd by a third, as Gadu, keeper of the herd, gleefully reported. The herd now was too large to fit all of them into the walled pen, so it could be used only for those animals requiring special protection. Also, the tundra in the immediate vicinity of their cave community would be used up quickly with so many caribou grazing voraciously during the summer months. Gadu suggested that no fewer than a handful of strong men would be needed to follow the herd always, while he himself would stay near the leader of the herd, influencing thus the movement of the herd to circle around and return home after grass and moss had rejuvenated here. Both Tlan and Taga listened and agreed, grateful for the knowledge and energy Gadu displayed. Everyone depended upon these animals for meat and milk, as well as clothing, especially in winter; the animals ate plants with important and healthful ingredients, and the clan received the benefit of a green summer diet when they in turn ate the caribou who had eaten the plants and moss.

Tlan, Taga, and Gadu emerged from their meeting in Tlan's longhouse and stood for a time before the door in genial conversation. Taga, who had been gazing toward the Circle of Stones, pointed toward it and asked, "Who are those people gathered by the cairn in the circle? I think I have never seen them before. They certainly are wild-looking in comparison with our clan."

The three walked toward the strangers. With each step they were less impressed with the dirty, scraggly creatures who huddled at one spot, a few standing but most sprawled out. They all had long, unkempt dark hair that was so untidy that it was startling. The men had equally wild dark beards.

All of the group were very thin, as if they never had much to eat, and some looked ill. Tlan totaled their number and found two handful besides seven small children. One little girl with better facial features than the others had eyes of bright blue.

Taga arrived first at the group and addressed the nearest man. "I greet you. Where are you from?"

He frowned, contorted his mouth, looked puzzled and then apparently came to an understanding of the question. Without speaking, he raised an arm and pointed north and then moved the arm to point south. The man beside him stepped forward and spoke in a slurred, guttural tongue that Tlan was able to comprehend, although the accent made it too strange for Taga's ears. What Tlan heard was "We lived in north. Earthquake. Cold. We walk south and again south. Little food. Earthquake. We live on tundra and wander."

Tlan turned to his companions. "These are nomads who have survived at least two earthquakes. It is hard to tell where they came from.

Maybe north of here. They are hungry now. Gadu, will you prepare us a feast here in the Circle of Stones? Three caribou roasted will do. Their language is close enough to ours, and we shall soon be able to talk to all of them. Then we shall learn their background."

Several of the visitors had heard the words "caribou" and "feast." Their grins seemed more like leers, but their pleasure was evident, and they spoke in guttural tones to let their kinsmen know that they would eat. Several women uttered piercing wails of delight, an alarming reaction. Then they all gathered their tattered clothing close to them and sat in one long row, looking up expectantly.

Gadu departed, shaking his head. Now Taga and Tlan conferred at a distance. Where would they stay? Taga said in a very definite voice, "My wife will not welcome them in our cave; she would find it hard to get rid of the lice and diseases. They are filthy. Look!"

Tlan had seen the sores and the lice nits. "My Elar will help clean them up, but they could not stay in my long-house. In the coming days I will try to treat them for their illnesses. It is going to be costly to feed them if they stay long."

Approaching the group of strangers, Tlan spoke again to the man who had acted as their spokesman. "It will take time to roast the caribou. We shall have our clan to come here to the Circle of Stones, so that they can meet your clan. Do you have a camp nearby? If you don't, can you throw up a temporary one on the tundra?"

The man answered, "I am Puluk of clan of Urkluk. While we wait, we put up hut so we have fire tonight. We not like caves. We glad to meet your clan. We happy to eat feast of caribou." Saying this much seemed to strain him terribly, but this time Tlan and Taga understood fairly well. The difficulty was in the speech style of these people. Spoken carefully, their language was almost the same as that which Taga's clan used.

Taga called on some of his men to help the strangers get together a temporary shelter; this they did with some disdain when they saw the matted, wild hair and skinny bodies of this strange tribe. It was true that they did not see strangers often, and this encounter showed them how much better their clan lived under the benevolent leadership of the wise old Tlan. Tlan and Elar had both taught them much about being healthier; their wives had learned so much about making the family happy. The vicious behavior encouraged by the Great Tzan had been forgotten under the influence of Tlan and Taga. Taga's men were disgusted at the laziness and awkward unkindness of these strangers.

While the men worked on the temporary shelter, Elar and Tlan sat down among the women of the strangers and tried to draw out information. The close-up view of these women and children revealed disturbing abuse. Their coarseness in relationships was clearly pathetic. They spoke to each other rudely, often fiercely, and seemed itchy and ill at ease.

Elar was immediately drawn to the child with clear blue eyes, who was called Blun by a short, overbearing and unfriendly woman. Elar observed, as she went over to the child, how thin she was but how alertly she responded to everything, while remaining obedient and quiet.

Elar pointed to Blun and asked, "Who is mother?" They all understood her question. evidently, but each woman shook her head to say, "No." Nobody volunteered a direct answer, so Elar had to ask the child, "Who is your mother?"

Blun seemed to be about three years old but was so under-nourished that it was difficult to tell her age. She looked at her questioner searchingly for a very long time, until Elar was afraid she would not speak at all. Finally, with a sad expression, the little girl said, "No one. They found me."

Since the story was out and the kind woman was taking an interest in the child, everyone nearby wanted to talk about her, and suddenly a slurred chatter broke out, with some screams of anger at each other. Understanding nothing but that the crowd of women appeared raucous and near a fighting mood, Elar moved away from them. Tlan had turned his attention to this fuss and could interpret some of it, although what he heard was offensive and crude.

Tlan put an arm around his wife and told her, "As I understand them, this child was found by Urglun a day after their last robbery. He had killed her parents in the raid, and she followed him back to his camp. The clan is complaining now that she *is* an extra mouth to feed, and they wish to get rid of her." Then, seeing her reaction to this information, Tlan added, "Elar, your heart is too kind. If you take her, there might be trouble."

He saw that Elar had set her mouth in a stubborn straight line and that she would never swerve from her conviction that she could save this child's life by adopting her. He gave a resigned sigh and promised to find Urglun and talk to him. He did not like what he had heard about Urglun's habit of robbery, and he vowed to warn the men of his clan what might be expected if these people lingered. They were not only crude and dirty, but they were a band of thieves as well. What a misfortune their visit could be!

CHAPTER
~24~

As he walked slowly out onto the tundra to the site of the temporary camp his men were helping with, Tlan considered the implications of seeing his wife take another child to raise. This child, although scrawny, seemed about the same age as Oola. His long-house did not lack room enough for many more children, but Elar's kind heart might be her undoing, for she was no longer young. And he admitted to himself that another child would mean less attention to himself. He felt jealousy for the first time and was very surprised when he realized how much Elar had come to mean to him.

Taga had organized the work of construction, and the group was close to finishing a large hut with mammoth bone supports and a covering of hides contributed by members of the Caribou Clan. He came out of the gaping doorway and stood to look with satisfaction at the neat, strong building his men had put up so quickly. "Tlan," he said as the old man approached, "they are really lazy. Also, they are liars."

Tlan cut in witheringly, "And thieves too. The women just told on them. The small blue-eyed child is an orphan and Elar wants to adopt her. She was found by Urglun after he robbed and killed her parents. Which one is Urglun?"

"Urglun refused to work. He is the tallest and thinnest of the men. Shifty-eyed. He left before we went to get the big bones. Just walked off."

"Taga, tell our men to check their homes and see that their neighbors are all right, too. We must keep an eye on each of these people and hustle them out of here. They are dangerous."

Taga at once went inside, warning each of his men. As they hurriedly left, he told Puluk, who had been the first to act as spokesman for the strangers, "We have given you a building with strong supports and good covering. Your men can add the finishing touches now. I must go see about the food. By the way, where is Urglun? Our leader wants to speak to him."

"Don't have anything to do with that thief. Don't know where he went. We thank you for shelter. Best building we ever had. Big and clean." Puluk was overcome. "You kind to us. I warn you our clan all thieves and murderers. I like to live here. I good hunter and live right. Support family. My children now among bad people."

"I can't promise; all the members of my clan will have to agree that you may stay. Tell your men that the food will soon be ready; we will eat at the Circle of Stones." Taga was glad to be free to go to his cave in order to check on the safety of his family, and then he would give the Urkluk clan their fill of excellent caribou meat. After that, he knew that he would have to tell them to leave. They must go on their way. Their presence meant danger and corruption. Perhaps it would be unlucky in the future that one of their children would remain with Elar.

He found Maa and his two children contentedly resting after spending half the day cleaning and rearranging the furnishings in the cave; the two little boys had helped loyally until they really were tired. Taga retold the news he had heard from Tlan; Elar wanted to adopt the blue-eyed girl of the strangers; the man of their clan who had found the child was Urglun, a robber and murderer who right now might be ransacking some of the cave homes. After the feast, Taga would have to tell the Urkluk clan to leave at once; certainly Urglun would be banished forever from this area. However, one of the strangers, Puluk,had asked to join Taga's clan and live here with his wife Olun and three children. If the clan agreed to this, then Puluk's family might live in the temporary hut which was just finished. There might be others who were also fed up with their lives of hunger and conflict.

At his long-house, Tlan stood to bar Elar from entering. Elar held the hand of the blue-eyed child Blun, and Tlan had said that the child should be cleaned up before she came in. Elar fumed over his mandate, but she left the child outside while she came in for some foaming herbs, her bone comb, and a sharp knife. From somewhere in her storage bags she found a little garment made of the soft underside of a caribou. Then, still in a huff, Elar took the child's hand again and they left.

Tlan knew their destination; over in the next valley the spring from the cave in their community emerged briefly after traveling underground; because it had gained a lot of force running downhill, it produced a beautiful waterfall before once more seeking an underground path.

Elar led the girl, who followed obediently and without question, to the waterfall. As they walked, Elar gave only a little explanation. " I intend to give you a bath and cut your hair, Blun. Then I have a new garment for you to wear. You will be the prettiest girl at the feast."

Blun regarded her gravely, saying, "I think I have never had a bath or a haircut. I hope it does not hurt."

The small pool below the falls had warmed a little in the midday sun, so there Blun was soaped all over and also given a shampoo. She stepped out of the water rosy and clean. Wrapped in a warm hide, she sat perfectly still while Elar cut her light brown hair to a bob just below her ears. After she had put on the new caribou garment, Elar encouraged her to look at her reflection in the pool. Little Blun was fascinated; she was finding a new sense of self-worth, for nobody before had spent any time taking care of her. She smiled and danced around a bit, and Elar was vastly pleased, because the child in front of her was innocently charming and pretty. She would win the heart of old Tlan, too.

CHAPTER
~25~

TO DRAW TOGETHER the clan and all the newcomers, Taga brought out the shaman's drum. Tlan was excused from giving a performance on the flute; the action going on at his house was so important as to unnerve him completely for the time. Elar had proved her point; when she appeared with little Blun, who was exquisitely fresh and clean and on her best behavior, he had capitulated at once. Not only was this a pretty child; she spoke like an adult, with mental ability far beyond her years. Evidently her parents, whoever they were, had been remarkable people, for they had taught her a lot before they were brutally murdered by Urglun. Since she had followed Urglun to the Urkluk tribe, she had existed on the fringes of the group of children there. She had learned to be self-effacing, quiet and obedient, as much out-of-sight as possible, but still other children had beat her and the grownups had been even worse.

Blun was almost incredulous to see what a happy home Elar had and that she was to become a daughter in that home. At first she did not let Tlan come near her, and she was wary of the laughing little boy Oola. Gradually the two children felt at ease with each other, since nobody could help liking Oola. His sense of fun and companionship bridged the gap quickly, for Oola was generous in sharing his playthings and his space. She was very observant, however, and when she realized that this home was planned to revolve around the old man, his importance to Elar and Oola helped her to accept him.

The insistent beat of the drum was as hard to resist as the aroma of the roasting caribou. Taga had debated whether he should wear his shaman's mask, but then he had decided to appear less formal. The announcements which he would make after all had eaten would be harsh to the newcomers. He wished to make his earlier speeches simpler so that they could enjoy one very good meal as they had been promised. Then he knew that he must tell them to move on – to journey on to some other place. To Urglun he would firmly pronounce banishment on pain of death.

After Taga's brief, polite welcome, the food was brought out on stone trestles. The laden trays which were set down amid the strangers caused a riot. They had anticipated an ample feast, and Taga's clan had been generous; the caribou was so succulent that the shaggy-haired newcomers roared and fought for every handful. The children imitated their parents in a great free-for-all. Taga noted, however, that no morsel was wasted. No food got thrown aside; all bones were crunched and sucked noisily.

Meanwhile, the members of Taga's clan appreciatively ate with restraint, holding themselves aside in a manner Taga had not originally intended. This was not a feast of conviviality; all of Taga's people knew that they were sharing their food with a traveling band of thieves who could not be allowed to stay. In the background were a group of trusted and strong men led by Beros, who patrolled their homes to prevent looting as the strangers ate and departed. Urglun was in the center of his clan, eating earnestly, and they would escort him away later. They intended to search him to recover anything he had stolen.

At last the trestles were being licked by little children and the grownups were loudly belching and wiping their faces when Taga once again faced the members of the Urkluk tribe. "People of the Urkluks," he began, "you came to our camp hungry and tired. We have given you generously a good feast, and we hope you have enjoyed it. We ourselves do not eat this well often, but we wanted to honor you.

"Your own people have disclosed that you use your energy and wits to rob others as you travel, instead of working to supply food for your families. We frown on such behavior because we are honest with all people as our way of life. We do not steal. We are people of good will.

"Because we could not live safely with you among us, you must leave. Please take your own possessions and your families and go far out on the tundra. Urglun, you are banished for life from this area on penalty of death if you ever return.

"The temporary shelter which has been built will have a tenant; Puluk and his wife Olun, with their three children, will remain with us and live there. He has given his promise to work hard for his family and be a peaceable neighbor here. We can use a strong, trustworthy man and his family because a Great Wind took away our leader, the Great Tzan, and most of our tribe, while it leveled the buildings on this very spot. The Circle of Stones you see here is a memorial to the dead of that time.

"Beros and his men will give you escort as you leave now. Spend the night out on the tundra as you usually do and do not come back here. We say farewell."

CHAPTER
~26~

WHILE BEROS AND other men escorted the Urkluks a good distance away onto the tundra, Taga took part in the patrol that guarded the home community, lest the thieves come back at night. These strangers might be fierce fighters, but it was certain that their best weapon was surprise. There was no disturbance during the night after they left, but Beros sent two of his men to follow the Urkluks for many days.

On his first day with Taga's clan, Puluk came to Elar with a request; all his family wanted to be clean and to have haircuts. Elar graciously led them to the waterfall and its pool, bringing foaming plants to use for soap. They bathed and washed their hair; then one by one they sat for Elar to trim their shaggy hair with her very sharp stone knife. She combed each one's hair and had them admire themselves in the reflection from the pool. Puluk was surprised at how beautiful his family was, never having seen them in such good condition before. Olun's hair shone in the sun as Elar braided it and wrapped the braids around her head; when her husband complimented her, Olun wept with happiness.

Four others of the Urkluks had joined Puluk in the temporary shelter: his brother Romluk and his wife Asun and two children. They, too, asked at once to clean up and get haircuts. The change for all nine of these newcomers was profound; it was an inner cleansing as well as a change in appearances. In all, ten members of the Urkluks had been left behind by their clan, including little Blun, and they all became good members of their adopted clan.

Elar talked with Asun as she made her hair tidy and comely, and she learned that Asun had a terrible fear of earthquakes. "We alive but we had earthquakes twice," said Asun. "Last time our home a cave. My children not home when earth shake *so* bad. Everyone in cave killed. My mother, my sister, my brother, all killed. Cave fell in on them. No way to escape. We cried for them. Then we vowed to live out in open."

Elar thought deeply about this threat to cave-dwellers, for she had been a cave-dweller for many years without any worry at all. She resolved to talk with Tlan about earthquakes.

Elar found her chance to discuss earthquakes later in the day when Beros and Ino came to report on the departure of the Urkluks. They had caught a glimpse of Puluk and pretty Olun and were astonished at them. Romluk and Asun, too, had been transformed unbelievably. On hearing them tell their reactions, Elar brought Blun for them to see; they knew about her adoption. They marveled at Elar's ability to see the beauty inside others and her ability to bring it out. Having seen a lot of the Urkluk clan's sullen behavior, however, they did not think those who had left would even have wanted to wash or to comb their hair.

"We came near to a big fight with them, Elar," said Ino. "We have very few men to fight for us now. Great Tzan loved to have tough men around him, and he trained many men to be strong fighters. We are softies now. We are too kind."

"If fighting is needed, our clan will be strong," said Tlan, near the fire. "We are not cowards. You saw how forceful Taga was when he spoke to the Urkluks. Our watchful presence here kept them from stealing from us."

"We have just welcomed two young men and their families into the clan," said Elar. "They will add some strength in fighting or in hunting bigger game."

"They are living in the new shelter, aren't they?" Ino asked.

Elar gave a short laugh as she said, "The newcomers avoid caves completely; they have survived two disastrous earthquakes. In the last one Asun lost a mother, a brother, and a sister when their cave fell in on them. Asun says they were doomed because there was no way out of the cave. Her story makes me a little fearful now for Taga's family."

Beros quickly broke in. "You should not worry, Elar. Usually there is some warning, I think, when an earthquake is due. Your husband is smart enough to feel it in his bones."

Tlan lifted his eyebrows but said nothing in comment. In fact, he had given no thought to the possibility of an earthquake. What his wife had brought up was new to him, and he needed time to study the matter. It was true that those who lived in caves were vulnerable in case of a powerful earthquake. At such a time the open tundra would be safer.

Beros and Ino soon left to check on the home patrol, a group filling an entirely new role in the life of the community. Not since the death of the Great Tzan had this peaceful clan needed such protection for their own homes. The patrol group was functioning effectively and the men were loyal and purposeful; having had a long period of peace had not left them lazy and soft. The clan in its present state represented a very able group who valued their homes and families and were fully willing to defend them.

Elar said to her husband, "Tlan, how can we ask Taga and Maa to move out of their cave? They enjoy living there."

Tlan was thoughtful as he replied, "Give me a little time on this, Elar. It certainly is possible that such a calamity might hit us without any warning at all, and then it is also possible that some warning tremors or jolts could let us know to flee to the tundra where mountains would not fall on us. I think that this is a question for the gods. I must find a way to contact the spirit world where I can learn what the future holds for us."

There was silence around the fire for a while. Then Tlan bent over to search for something in his shaman's bag. He withdrew a large quartz crystal, a uniquely clear stone which attracted shimmering, sparkling light from the fire. Its elegance and purity caused Elar to cry out in awe. She had never seen so wonderful a stone. She could not take her eyes off its magic, but she was afraid to touch it.

"This marvelous stone was brought to me by Ino. He picked it up at the Red Cliffs. Taga did not know Ino had it, but on the night we dedicated the Circle of Stones, Ino came here in the night to hand it to me. His conscience had come alive when he thought about the dead we honored that night. He knew that a shaman can have a special need for such a stone. I was sure that the gods had sent it to me, with Ino as their messenger. Now this piece of crystal will focus my thoughts, and I will find the shaman's way into that other world."

CHAPTER ~27~

Taga sat just inside the door flap of Tlan's longhouse. He held the drum and on it he sounded a curiously monotonous pattern of beats. He used his hand to produce a soft, even rhythm; the tone of the drum had surprising depth, which made it enter into one's consciousness and become part of one. The hypnotic rhythm was intended to help Tlan to enter the world of the spirits; Tlan felt that the spirits wished to speak to him and tell him of the future. This event was of the utmost importance.

Tlan sat by the fire, holding the marvelous rock crystal given him by Ino. A broad facet of the stone, clear as spring water, caught the firelight, and Tlan gazed steadfastly into it as the drum worked its hypnotic spell. At first the stone told him nothing; it merely mirrored his own eye, enlarging it many times so that he saw the lashes and the iris. Gradually the entire room grew larger; then he thought he was out under the sky, which was immense with glittering stars. He looked down upon the long-house and saw within it the figure of Taga, who was still beating upon the drum with his hand, and he also saw the hunched figure of himself, an old man who stared with glassy eyes into the crystal he held.

Then he spun through the sky and through time itself, until he heard a voice very near his ear and producing an echo that was louder than thunder. It called his name, "TLAN!" At once he turned toward the voice, and it said harshly, "Do not look at me." Thereupon he was filled with terrible fear lest he make a mistake and lose his way through this exalted realm of the sky. The voice, deep and filled with authority, announced to him, "The future is open to your eyes at this moment, Tlan. What is it that you want to know?"

Aware that he was talking to a god, Tlan trembled as he answered, "My clan lives in caves where they are comfortable, but we are warned that earthquakes bring sudden chaos and death to cave-dwellers. Will we have an earthquake? I must warn my people."

Tlan was hit by a powerful gust of wind, a wind that seemed to be trying to tear his very soul out. There was nothing to cling to, nowhere to set his feet. Through the wind he heard the deep voice speak, "An earthquake will tear apart your hills and mountains. Your caves will disappear forever. Far out on the tundra your clan will be safe."

"When? How much time do we have to prepare?" Tlan was anxious.

"There is time to prepare. When the heat inside the earth becomes too much, the mountains will open up. It is necessary. Look to your clan and prepare. Tlan, your work is nearly over, you know."

"Has my time come, oh great god?" cried Tlan.

"Not yet, you foolish shaman. But you are old, and you must have another shaman ready to help your clan when your time comes."

Tlan found himself calling out into a windy silence, "There is more, oh great god. I need to know much more. Oh, hear me."

But it was over. The voice said no more. Tlan felt tired and old. It took all his moral strength to bring his soul back into the long-house, where he hovered for moments above the fire.

Taga had been watching the old man who sat beside the fire, as still as if he were in a coma. As time passed, he became more and more worried about Tlan. Since he was not strong, the old man might not be able to recapture his soul after his out-of-body experience. Something could go wrong. but he waited patiently to see Tlan show signs of coming back to life.

As Tlan uttered a sigh and set down the crystal he had been holding, Taga was bending over him. Tlan looked up, and his eyes were much deeper set than before, full of the exalting experience he had just undergone. He felt weak. “Let me sleep,” he said. And although Taga yearned to know what Tlan had learned from the spirit world of the gods, he had to wait longer while the old man pulled furs over himself and fell asleep at once.

After a time Taga heard a sound at the door and found Elar there, anxious to hear that Tlan would be all right. Taga put away his drum and sat down with Elar.

Elar began a conversation. “Taga, yesterday you were holding the stone eggs and looking at them in a very special manner. You treat them as if you are in awe of them. Where did you get them?”

Taga smiled appreciatively; this was a favorite subject. Taking the long way to the answer, he talked for some time about his home near Tlan’s hut and his happiness there with Maa and little Tuit. Then one spring as twilight neared, the three were walking toward home when it began to hail and the weather changed without warning. As they crouched down in a small cleft with an overhang to shelter them from the gigantic hail, the Great Wind blew over. At the time they did not know how immense that tornado was, for it was the one that demolished the village of Tzan and killed most of the people; a short time later Tzan himself died as a result of his injuries. When the Great Wind had passed, Taga and his family found that it was snowing heavily, and later they discovered that their hut, their home, had been blown away entirely by the Great Wind. Maa was in tears and frightened, so they returned to the little cave and they slept until morning under the rocky overhang. An amazingly bright sun woke Taga, and he looked around for the ptarmigan he had trapped the previous day. Instead of the two birds, he found two eggs of stone imbedded in the walls of their shelter. One egg had a small reptile head just emerging from the broken shell. Maa awoke as he set the eggs before him and stared at them, for the rays of the strong sunlight turned them to gold. Maa said, "East," a name for the sun-goddess. Tuit woke up and stepped out before them, lifting his hand high as he pointed toward the sun and said, "East," in a very authoritative voice, like a command. At that moment he too was gilded by the sun so that his parents felt very full of emotion at the splendor of the sun, the mystery of the eggs, and their surprise and happiness in their son. They felt it was a holy moment when they were especially blessed. Then Taga had said, "We will go east," a pathway that led to his dear uncle Tlan.

Taga ended with a retelling of how Tlan the wise, the shaman, had consecrated the eggs with red ocher a few days later, meaning that they were now holy relics for Taga's family to keep forever, for generation after generation.

This was such a remarkable story, and it presented Tuit in such a favorable way that Elar's eyes were shining when Taga finished. "East," she murmured, "is certainly one of the names of the Goddess of the Dawn, the sun."

"I have felt ever since that I am to lead my clan toward the east. It is a strange feeling that does not go away. There have been many new duties, however, since we left Tlan's home to the south. A very big responsibility has been my apprenticeship to Tlan while I learn from him the role of a shaman. It has been rewarding to sit at the feet of so learned a shaman, for he knows much about the heavens, the stars, the sun and the moon. He is a great healer, with a vast knowledge of herbs and spells. He is in intimate contact with the spirit world. He will be long remembered for his wisdom as a leader." Taga stopped, deep in thought.

"Taga, you are a remarkable young man yourself," said Elar. "You have proved that you have great qualities as a leader as well as a shaman. Tlan is aware that you will soon replace him. All the clan will recognize you as a real shaman, one called to the role and inheriting that role from a family member."

Taga, nursing that ambition in his heart, smiled and nodded assent. He had already been through a real out-of-body experience. He knew this was true.

When Tlan felt stronger, he recounted to Taga and his wife his experiences in out-of-body state. They trembled when Tlan, in great agitation and fear, remembered that the greatest god of gods had spoken, and his days as a shaman were numbered. He had been warned that another shaman must be ready to serve and to oversee the life of this clan. Also, in answer to Elar's sharp questioning, Tlan could respond that there undoubtedly was a chance of an earthquake at any time, and in the near future it would be a certainty.

"Then the Urkluks were right," she said. "We must soon get everyone out of the caves. Asun's story warned me. But tell me, Tlan, were you told that you will die? Is it as certain as that? Oh, Tlan, I think that I cannot bear it!" Elar buried her face in her hands, quite overcome with grief.

Tlan got up with effort and sat beside her, comforting her by cradling her in his arms. "Do not weep, Elar. I am here now. We are still together."

Her sobs subsided as she leaned her head against him and reached up her arm to stroke his head. It was such an intimate moment that Taga turned toward the door to leave them alone. As he went out into the cold, the wind rushed at him, but the sky above *was* clear and a deep, dark background for scintillating stars. He stepped into the open area where he could view all the sky and scanned the winter constellations, all familiar to him.

His attention was claimed by a shooting star in the east, just starting its arc across the heavens. He was certain that this star was for him; it was a sign that his ambitions found favor with the gods. As both shaman and leader of his clan, he would in the future lead the clan toward the east.

CHAPTER
~28~

TLAN SAT IN the sun, to the casual eye an old man deep in contemplation but once in a while letting his head dip down as he nodded off. He felt comfortable as the warmth of the spring sun soothed his bones and lessened the pain of winter-swollen joints.

He jerked to attention as Asun came up, hurrying as fast as a very pregnant woman could. "Oh, shaman, we got such whooping and coughing at our house. Both Puluk and my baby have terrible spring colds; they can't talk, so hoarse. You got some medicine, please?" In her anxiety she was still swinging her heavy body right and left.

"Just let me get my shaman's bag, my dear. Has the baby got the croup?" At her passionate nod, Tlan rose and went into the longhouse. Finding his wife busy by the fire, he spoke softly to tell her where he was going.

"And don't you bring back some terrible colds to your family, Tlan. We have children in our house, too." Elar spoke a bit sharply.

He did not answer but, picking up his bag, ambled out the door. He and Asun made an odd pair as he shuffled along after the swaying, puffing woman.

The two ex-Urkluk families still lived in the house put up for temporary quarters for the visiting clan. Before Tlan had come to the entrance, he was aware of the illness inside, for the coughing was fierce, in bass tones and in a child's voice. Tlan said softly, "Well, at least they can still cough and make a sound. It could be worse."

He bent over the feverish, restless child whose red face showed how much energy was being exerted in its painful spasms of coughs. For a few moments he observed, flinching and backing off at each violent outburst. He used his hand to pull back an eyelid and view the pupil. His flat hand rested briefly on the baby's forehead to gauge how hot the fever was, and at his gentle touch, the baby relaxed and was quieter. Then he reached into his bag and withdrew a ball of pine tar from a small leather pouch. Putting a tiny piece on his forefinger, Tlan rubbed the pine tar over the baby's tongue and inside its mouth. He said to the mother, Asun, "You must keep this baby's feet well covered; its feet are cold. The pine will cut the phlegm in its throat and the coughing will stop. Here, I will give it a potion that will make the baby sleep and give you some rest. This fine baby will be all right when he wakes up."

Next, he went over to the far side of the hut where Puluk, uncle of the sick baby, was coughing spasmodically with deep bass honks like a northern goose. After feeling the man's pulse and holding his forehead to ascertain the amount of fever, Tlan made a grimace, just for the benefit of Puluk, and said, "Bad cough. Really bad cough. We'll break that up while it's just in the throat and before your lungs get congested. Here, this is pine tar to open up your nose and throat and stop the cough. Let it dissolve in your mouth – slowly."

While Puluk did as he was told, Tlan conferred with Olun, Puluk's wife. "Make a hot tea with this potion and let him drink it all while it is hot. It will soothe the fever and let him sleep. He certainly is going to be all right."

Then, looking around the suddenly very quiet house, he called out, "Let them sleep. And you women look as if you need a rest too." Nodding at their duet of thank-yous, Tlan backed out of the house, giving a little cough himself to expel the foul air of the sick room.

As he trudged back toward his house, Tlan saw Yun running toward him from behind the next hill; his expression was wild and he gasped as he ran. “Where are the hunters? Ino! Beros! Puluk!” He ran past the old shaman, because he had seen Ino emerge from a nearby house. Shocked at being ignored, Tlan turned to hear what Yun’s emergency might be.

“Ino!” panted the young man. “Ino, the biggest animal in the world is on the other side of that hill! It is much larger than our caribou and has very shaggy hair hanging down. I’ve never seen anything like it. It was just standing there in the valley, looking dazed.”

“Shaggy? Long hair? Dumb looking? Hey, Yun, you’ve seen a bison. Don’t get too close to him, and he won’t hurt you, probably. I wonder what he’s doing here? He’s pretty far away from his pasture lands to the north. Let’s find as many hunters as we can and go for him. Come on. We’ll get Taga first.”

Tlan called out, “Puluk is sick. I’ve just been to see him and give him medicine. But don’t let that stop you. Hurry! A bison is a rich catch!”

Meanwhile Taga had just entered the valley where the bison was standing; he gasped when he saw the massive head with its short, curving horns and small, wicked eyes. Long brown and woolly hair covered its head and humped shoulders but not its oddly small hindquarters.

The animal grunted and made a sidling move toward a small patch of grass. As he turned, Taga saw that his coat was falling off in patches. Also, in profile the beast had a long, shaggy beard. From the hump sitting on his huge shoulders, his back sloped down to a tapering rump and short, tufted tail.

Suddenly the beast threw up his head, sniffing the wind. He had caught the scent of Taga and was alarmed. He wheeled around to a stance in which his head was lowered as he watched Taga with those small, evil eyes rolling. He was not too close yet, so Taga decided to sprint for a ragged clump of birches, the only green cover available in the sparse, stony valley.

The animal had been tasting the twigs and spring leaves of those birches, and he did not approve of Taga's move, so he also moved toward the small clump of trees, not too rapidly.

Taga, seeing this, dodged out into the open and headed toward a formation of huge rocks behind which he knew there was a narrow passage leading into another part of the valley. Here he stood for a few moments in front of the huge rocks, testing the possibility of using his slingshot. He decided that his chances of piercing that tough hide were small. His motions were antagonistic, however, and the animal was incensed. The bison lowered his head and charged at the man. He came swiftly, stirring dust and stones and gaining speed; his aim was straight for Taga.

Taga tensed and stood still until he realized that the animal's charge was a blinded rush; then, at the last moment, he dodged to the left and into the large fissure between the rocks. On and on Taga went until he could safely climb to higher ground and look down upon the scene he had left.

With a wild crash, the bison butted his lowered head into the rock wall; so tough was his bony forehead that it was almost like stone, and it had shattered the rock face. Taga saw the animal lying still. Was he dead? Or was he only dazed? If he was not dead, it would be a risky maneuver to get close enough to kill him with a stone knife.

At that moment he saw the gang of hunters from his clan, with Ino in the lead and all armed. They had a variety of weapons, including a long wooden stick held by one man. As they entered the valley, they caught sight of the huge brown shaggy beast lying motionless. Ino, who had started to chant a boastful and nasal hunting song, broke it off, and the hunters gathered in a group to reconsider their actions. They saw Taga on a cliff above the animal.

Taga climbed part of the way down from his perch above the fallen bison; from that height he could see blood spattered upon the face of the stone wall and a huge pool of blood issuing from the mouth and nostrils of the creature. Then he saw that a horn was gone, and another close look revealed that the impact had pushed the horn back into the bison's skull; whether this had killed him was still not certain, but the animal was severely wounded, at least. Evidently he had lowered his head and turned his head a little to one side in order to impale Taga on a horn, and this had left his horn vulnerable when he crashed on the rock face.

The beast had fallen on his left side; his great bloody head was at the foot of the stone face with which he had collided. His shaggy legs and sharp hoofs stuck out, revealing a soft underbelly now unprotected. Taga thought that the creature's nostrils, eyes, and mouth might be soft and vulnerable now, also, before he regained consciousness. Taga waved to the warriors to hold back, and he disappeared from sight as he came down behind the cliff.

As he emerged nearer to the hunters, he was greeted by Ino and his group, all very excited. They could not see yet what had happened to the bison; they only saw that he lay without moving and that he was very large. Taga warned them that if the animal stood up, infuriated, all of them would be in grave danger. He added, "There are several places on his head that seem soft enough for the stick to go in if it is sharp; there would be some protection in being a little distance away. Also, the underbelly and some part of the chest may have softer hide, but we might have only one chance to try to plunge the stick into his heart. We need to do something fast, while he is lying there unconscious."

Ino said, "Here, give me the stick. I am not afraid to go up to the beast. I am strong. One deep plunge of the stick into his head will be enough to kill him. I am not afraid."

At that he grabbed the stick and began to trot toward the bison; he went directly to the side of the animal, trying to determine first if the massive chest moved with the effort of breathing. He could not make out any movement, but some time had already passed, and he felt he had to act. The large head was so near to the rock that it was difficult for Ino to take aim properly at the nostrils or open mouth without getting perilously close. He edged nearer and nearer, balancing the stick in his right hand and planting his feet firmly for the throw. Then he let the weapon fly with all his strength and with accurate aim right at the open mouth. Just as the stick sailed into the mighty throat, Ino, now unbalanced by the force of his throw, saw one bloody red eye of the bison open and blink at him. Unnerved, he fell and was suddenly scrambling on the stony ground to get up and away; the bison was alive! He thus did not see the result of his throw, although his companions saw the great shaggy animal struggle to get up, falling and making another mighty effort to rise. When the bison stood, tottering, on four feet, the long stick protruded from his mouth; the beast roared and shook his head again and again to get rid of the stick. He lifted a shaggy leg and pawed at it with his hoof, moving around and around as he fought the painful thing piercing his mouth and throat.

Ino, trembling, had gained a safe distance from the enraged bull and now had hidden behind the clump of birches. The hunters looked around for shelter and retreated part way. All eyes were on the bison, which continued to move around in a circle and roar.

Suddenly, the beast stood still; it tottered a few steps forward and fell heavily with the stick still in his mouth. His body shook with spasms like an earthquake passing; then it was still. The hunters gave a loud shout. They shouted again and again, the chant ringing through the rocky hills.

By now, all in the village knew that the hunters were accomplishing a dangerous task; they were killing a huge beast that had wandered into the next valley. Soon the entire village would have a feast, cause for rejoicing. Even greater news was that there would be extra meat to be dried and a huge woolly hide; then other parts of the animal would be valuable. The women of the village knew that they would be needed soon to help in the task of cutting up the carcass and transporting the meat; they immediately got their tools together. When a runner appeared to call them, they were already prepared and excited about the opportunity for extra food.

As soon as he could approach the animal, which was surely dead now, Ino ran over and, with his sharp knife, cut off the tuft of a tail. By hunting rules of the clan, Ino now would get cuts of the choicest meat; second choice of the meat would go to Taga and his family. After that, every family would get a share, and the whole village would feast tonight while the meat was tasty and very fresh, in a communal roast held in the Circle of Stones. As the men cut back the tough, hairy skin, the women, on arriving, gave great cries at the sight of the deep redness of the exposed meat. It had little fat, and any veins of fat looked yellowish instead of white. They were eager to taste a meat that the youngest had never eaten. Men and women worked together with a hearty will throughout the rest of the day, sometimes breaking into nasal chants – happy work songs their mothers and fathers had known.

CHAPTER
~29~

It was a clear spring night with a multiplicity of stars overhead as the clan began to drift back to their homes after the feast at the Circle of Stones. There was still a happy sense of well-being and contentment because everyone had eaten so well, and they all knew that there was much more meat. The gathering had been full of good will, to the delight of Tlan, who fawned over the brave hunters, especially Ino and Taga.

Midway through the jovial dinner, there had come some alarm from Puluk's family when Asun, who had overeaten scandalously, suddenly had stood up with an "Oh!" Her pained expression caused women near her to look at each other meaningfully. Her time had come. Asun's child was going to be born.

Now the call went out to Elar, who came over to pat Asun a bit, ask a few questions, and assess the situation. Because of the sickness in their house, even though Puluk had become much better by the afternoon, Elar decided that the child could not be born in the same room; Asun must be taken to another house for the night. With two women who had volunteered earlier to attend her, Asun waddled off. Elar promised to go to them when the feast had ended; she knew that she had trained many of the village women to assist in child-birth and these women were very caring and alert.

Left alone after Elar went to check on Asun, Tlan sat looking at the stars. The birth of a baby to one of the newcomers was indeed a good sign. So was the capture of the huge bison. Although a chill was in the air, he lingered to savor the good emotions of the evening.

In the eastern sky a small and obscure star began to grow in size and brilliance; within a very short time its light outshone all the other lights in the sky. It was a supernova, a star that had exploded (although tens of thousands of years would pass before astronomers would understand this phenomenon. The core of a star had collapsed, its envelope interacting with the outward shock so that the envelope was ejected explosively into interstellar space, and suddenly when the photons reached the surface of the star, within several hours the surface of the star had brightened 100 million times.)

The spectacle in the heavens was fascinating; Tlan could not move as he saw the expanding light of the star. All his life he had waited to see this particular phenomenon, for seers had spoken of such exploding stars as magnificent signs, portending doom or great events. As he watched, it continued to grow in brightness at an amazing speed.

When Taga came searching for him, Tlan was stiff in the joints because he had leaned his head back for so long in one position. Taga, too, was amazed at how fast the star was growing; he did not know how to judge this sign from the heavens, but he agreed that this was an important event for the clan. In a dazed way he asked Tlan, "What is its meaning? Are we to take this as an omen of danger, or is it an encouraging sign of good in our future?" But Tlan was not ready to give an answer and so he shook his head and continued to stare.

The two did not move until Elar found them a long while later, when the star was an enormous brightness. She came to tell them that Asun's child had been born safely and both mother and daughter were well. The respect and attention the two men were paying to the unusually bright star aroused her protectiveness and she inquired, "Does this have to do with the child that was born tonight? Or is it an omen of an earthquake? Oh, tell me!"

But Tlan could only shake his head, for he was thinking at that moment of the prophecy the gods had given him that his days were now numbered. Was the star a sign just for him? He could not discern the meaning of this rare display in the heavens.

For two nights the star outshone other lights in the heavens; then on the third night, as swiftly as it had burst and grown, the star declined in power and thereafter was too dim to be seen. On the second night Tlan had a dream of falling stones; he was in a cave and the roof of it was falling in upon him. He had not been given any warning, and his terror was intolerable – fear for himself as well as for others. He choked from the dust of the falling debris and woke up coughing hysterically, only to find a calm, gray dawn.

Tlan, meditating on his dream of the cave falling in upon him, finally concluded that he was being given a warning, and the caves must be vacated at once. Taga agreed, although it would be hard for his family; Maa had made their cave such a cheerful environment, and his two sons loved living there. Safety was the first requirement, however.

The last of the bison meat was being worked on in preparation for drying, so it was not a good day for a meeting. Therefore, Taga scheduled a meeting of all villagers for the following morning at the Circle of Stones. Meanwhile he spoke to Maa about the necessity for moving out onto the tundra. She protested that they probably had a great many moons yet before any earthquake might come. Nothing was sure about this warning. It sounded to her like a trick to get them all away from their comfortable cave homes, perhaps a trick by the Urkluks.

Nevertheless, Taga went from cave to cave to discuss the problem and his fears with other cave dwellers. Almost all of them did not want to consider moving again into huts on the tundra. An earthquake seemed a vague fear; they dismissed it as a possibility. Taga, shrugging his shoulders, returned home almost skeptical himself.

On the day of the clan meeting Tlan was to preside. He wished to be forceful and order everyone to pack up and move. He needed no more persuasion to believe that every day was their last before the big earthquake came. Taga *was* more flexible on the subject; his wife was against moving. Elar, ever since her conversation with Asun about her fear of caves, had understood that there was danger. She was even afraid that they would not be safe out on the tundra; great cracks in the surface of the tundra could be dangerous.

Thus, Tlan asked Asun to speak to the clan. This was very hard for her, as she was recovering from childbirth and had her baby to think about first. She agreed, however, because she had faith in Tlan and knew what the threat of earthquakes meant.

Therefore Tlan convened the meeting when the sun had warmed the earth and the setting of the Circle of Stones was pleasant. All the clan appeared, but no one had smiles. Tlan would be talking about a complete disruption of their simple, comfortable lives.

Tlan told of his dream; to him it was full of meaning and substance; however, to the women and men of the clan for whom the caves had meant an ordered, happy way of life, it was easy to say it was only a dream. The young people of the clan had not even heard of an earthquake. "All the more reason to expect that one might happen," said Tlan.

Asun stood and repeated the story that she had told Elar about losing members of her family in an earthquake. "That is why we did not move into a cave here," she said, shifting her little baby in her arms.

Beros asked Puluk, "Can you prove that she is telling us the truth, Puluk?"

Puluk was warming himself in the sun and was caught by surprise; he spoke up in rather hoarse tones, "Certainly she is telling the truth. I saw the damage done by the earthquake."

Tlan felt that he was getting nowhere and must be sterner. "I appoint Beros and Taga to go today out on the tundra and find us a spot far enough away that we can rebuild our village and feel safe there." To those who demurred, he added, "This is preliminary so far; we must be ready for whatever happens."

Tlan faced a disgruntled group. The task of moving any part of their households would be overwhelming. Men, women and children would all have to carry a share of the furnishings of each house or cave, even if this meant making several trips to the new site. Gadu sat in a frowning mood: his task of moving the herd was perennial; out on the tundra the growing herd would soon eat up the lichen in any spot, necessitating a plan of keeping them moving all the time to make sure they always had food, no matter what the weather.

Finally Tlan said flatly, "This meeting has been held for your protection. I love the clan. We are doing so well as a community that we cannot do without any one person. My thoughts have been to give you the warning that the spirit world has let me know about. I hope, for your sakes, that you will heed my warning." He turned to go.

At that moment all in the clan were aware of a deep rumble from far beneath them, and the rock-strewn ground waved slightly so that those who were standing up had difficulty keeping their balance. Tlan was thrown down abruptly.

They had experienced a tremor; it was not a ruinous earthquake, for which all were grateful. It was convincing proof for Tlan's argument. He did not have to say anything more. They got up and went home quietly, shaking their heads at the task before them. Immediately they began the long effort of preparing to move, while Taga and Beros set off at once to the east to search for a place of relative safety.

CHAPTER ~30~

Elar saw Tlan fall and went to him. He seemed to have trouble getting up, however, and he favored his left side as he finally stood. She whispered, "Lean on me. I must get you home, Tlan." His left foot was dragging and he could not use his left arm, but with her support they walked slowly to their house nearby.

By the time he rested in his own bed, the left side of his mouth was drawn so that he could barely talk at all. Her face wet with tears, Elar wrapped him in skin coverings and sat by him. She reached out to warm his cold hands with her own vibrant, warm ones. She knew that if he needed the attention of a skilled shaman to survive, this man was himself the most skilled medicine man her clan had ever known. She waited for him to tell her what she must do to save his life.

Taga and Beros had already left on their search for a new site. To whom could she turn for help? Perhaps she could find Yun if the situation became more critical. Meanwhile, she kept her vigil, watching his skin grow grayer every minute and his hand more cold.

It was Maa who came in to check on her and Tlan, for she had seen the fall and the effort it took Tlan to get up. She was aghast at how feeble he had become in such a short time. Elar was almost helpless with grief and fear. Maa felt equally helpless, but her practical nature told her to stir up the fire and make a hot drink; it would be good for Elar, at least. Her own children and Elar's two children were still at a neighbor's house, where they had been kept while the grownups went to the meeting. She talked a bit, gently, as she busied herself with the herbs for the beverage, and Elar began to feel less alone.

Elar even thought of a stimulant herb that might bring some relief to her husband, and they both worked at using a bone ladle to pour some of it into his poor, twisted mouth. He smiled a one-sided smile at them, for they had chosen the right herb to stimulate the flow of blood into his cold, gray left side, but he was beyond speaking now. He knew that he had suffered a death blow, and he was having difficulty analyzing for himself how severe it was.

Tlan soon knew he had spoken his last words to lead the clan. He had no more to say. After the hot drink stirred his circulation, he relaxed and began the process of giving himself up to the darkness which was closing in. He recognized that the god had warned him that his time was near, and this was it. In a blurry way he felt tired and very old, but ready for the next adventure into the unknown.

When he opened his eyes, he saw that Yun had come in and had put his arms around Elar to comfort her. Maa had gone, but these two would be there to witness his last moments. Seeing him open his eyes, the two bent down close to Tlan, and Elar stroked his forehead lovingly. With a great effort, Tlan moved his right hand to the head of Yun and looked at him. It was evident that he was blessing Yun. The effect on the young man was deep, as Yun closed his eyes reverently. Then Tlan turned his gaze on Elar, in silent devotion, for a long, long moment before closing his eyes.

He did not open his eyes again. What wrestling his spirit was going through was not apparent, although his own spirit had often enough confronted the spirits from that other world. By degrees he slipped away and his breathing stopped.

Elar was inconsolable for a while. Yun let her weep, knowing that this was the time for it, because the clan faced an enormous upheaval and there would be little time for a burial, even for so famous a shaman.

CHAPTER
~31~

OUT ON THE tundra Taga had organized the move out of the caves in three stages. The main site he selected for their new homes was, he hoped, far enough away to give them a feeling of security. A few men would be dispatched to begin buildings - huts - to give the clan a sense of community there.

At the halfway point, Taga planned for the families to bring their possessions to this place so they could go back for second or third trips. Then, satisfied that they had brought enough of their belongings, the families could move them the remaining distance to the new village. Guards would be posted at the halfway point and at the new village to prevent any pilfering. Families would be warned that at least two families must walk together at all times, and no one was to go alone.

Having set up the plans for his village, Taga returned to his waiting family, leaving Beros to oversee the moving, starting at once. Along the way he noted the small piles of stones he had used to mark the way for others, each pile forming a symbol familiar to his clan – a fork pointing toward the rising sun.

As he neared the long-house of Tlan, on the outskirts of the Circle of Stones, Taga stopped short at the sound of low keening; a woman was spending her grief. He stepped into the house to see Tlan lying on his bed and Elar at his side, alternating periods of disconsolate sobbing with moments when she threw her head back with high whining and ululations. Yun stood at the head of the bed, not moving, but at the question on Tlan's face, he nodded assent.

The shock was so great that Taga went down on his knees, his head bowed down. For a few minutes he struggled with his sense of loss; the old shaman had been like a kind and wise father. Tlan had also been his mentor, his teacher. How would he cope with the present crisis without Tlan's guidance? The responsibilities now falling upon him were almost unbearable. In the midst of his grief, he sensed the voice of the old shaman soothing him and giving him directions. The cave that had belonged to Elar would be a good place for Tlan to rest, for it was there he had found his new love.

Yun came toward him with a concerned face and said, "He went very quickly, but he gave Elar a wonderful smile, and he let me know that I am to take care of Elar and the children for the future. It is his wish."

It was difficult for Taga to speak, but he managed to tell Yun, "He wanted to be buried in the old cave of Elar, and considering that families are beginning to move right now, it seems that tomorrow morning will be the only time to gather them for a burial."

He paused then added in a choked voice, "My wife and I will quickly get everything out of our cave. Will you see that the body is moved there?"

Then Taga went over to Elar and put his arm around her tenderly. He turned back to Yun to say, "While I stay here with Elar for a little while, why don't you find Lin and let her know what has happened?"

As Yun arrived, his wife was with a group of small children she had been caring for, and in another moment Maa entered with her sons, so Yun told them all, expecting wails of grief. Maa, her face marked with shock and dismay, asked to leave her sons and rushed off to her husband.

It was heartbreaking to see Elar's grief and that of Taga also, and Maa could only cling to them wordlessly, understanding their personal sense of loss. She knew that the greatest man her clan had ever known was now gone. How could they get through this crisis without Tlan's careful, insightful wisdom?

When Yun returned, he took charge of Elar while Taga and Maa went to prepare the burial cave; all their household goods had to be taken out at once and assembled for the trip to their new home. Meanwhile, the clan must be told of the death of Tlan and of the funeral the next morning, as well as the rules for their journey. Taga wondered how he would find time to plan a funeral impressive enough to honor such a great man. And even as this thought came to him, he was aware of Tlan's calm voice explaining how it was to be done. First, the cave was to be cleared out and the articles wrapped in skins; care must be taken with the new shaman's equipment and with the stone eggs. Then Taga and Maa would go from home to home, informing each person and answering questions.

At each threshold they found much confusion, to which their news of the death of the old shaman added distress. The people of the clan were very fond of their leader and shaman and also felt bereft of his wise leadership at this time of approaching crisis.

"We shall all be safer at the new village," Taga emphasized. They had felt the earth tremor and agreed. No rocks could fall on them if they were out on the tundra. Many families made the march to the halfway point to set down their burdens and then return to be present for the burial. Guards were on watch to keep their goods safe, so they did as they were told. They made the exodus as orderly as they could.

Taga, his heart torn with grief, completed his round of the homes of the Caribou Clan, and at last he came back to Elar's old cave, which would serve as the resting place for Tlan. The body lay within sight of the entrance, raised on a bier for those outside to have a good view of it.

Although it was summer, Tlan wore a flowing robe of soft caribou. Around his bier were some of his treasured belongings, such as the carved cups of bone. Someone had taken the time to find a few meadow flowers from a nearby valley and he held a bouquet in his hands. Outside the entrance a few men were piling up a small mountain of stones to be used later to seal the cave against animals and thieves. As all things were in good order, Taga sat down by the bier to consider the burial which he would preside over in the morning at sunrise.

CHAPTER ~32~

IN THE STILLNESS of a very early summer morning all the Caribou Clan had gathered below the ledge outside the burial cave. Only a few twitters and rustlings of birds in the nearby valley could be heard as the group in respectful silence looked up at the bier on which rested their leader and shaman, Tlan. A small fire burned on the ledge outside the cave.

Softly at first, there came from the cave the music of Tlan's bone flute. The melody floated in a familiar pattern: three notes up the diatonic scale followed by the gentle arching back by one note before an expressive pause, then the repeat. The clarity of the tones and the nuances that spoke of the emotions of the musician had their effect on the clan; Elar openly wept, tears tracing down among the new wrinkles on her cheeks. But the music did more than revive memories for the clan; it soothed and calmed the grief that it evoked. As it went on and on, it grew louder. Then an almost imperceptible accompaniment began on the drum, which continued through each pause with its steady, pounding beat and slowly grew louder. At the end of one such phrase, the drum halted and there came the loud punctuation of a rattle. As the music resumed, with the rattle again interrupting in its turn, the flute gradually faded out, leaving the percussion instruments to continue their pattern.

During a vigorous announcement by the rattle, Taga emerged from the cave wearing the tall painted mask. At Maa's suggestion he had painted red slash marks on his arms and legs, extending the ferocity of the mask's impression. As the drums and rattle gave him a rhythmic background, the shaman performed a slow, dignified dance, acting out in gestures, emotions and movements the life story of Tlan, the great leader and shaman. At a very dramatic moment for the members of the clan, midway in the performance, a tenor voice began a strong, nasal, wordless song. The accompaniment that continued to the end of the dance included the steady drum, the insistent rattle, and the soaring, nasal man's voice with its quavering emotional values.

In the silence after the music, Taga began to recite the ritual verse he had heard so many times from Tlan.

The people arose from the west.
They followed the caribou.
They moved over tundra and mountains.
Over the tundra and mountains, ice and snow,
The people followed the herds.
The people are strong in life and death.
The people move toward the new dawn.

There was much more to the recitation, more that Tlan had taught him, and it was received with rapt attention. As he then sat down by the fire, the funeral drum again started its heavy, hollow beat. The tenor voice was raised in its nasal, wordless lament, so deeply shared by the clan that, softly at first then swelling, they all lifted their voices in this song without words, imitating the first singer with their nasal tones. They threw back their heads and let their sorrow find release in this unison singing, somehow all finding together the same newly created melodic lines. When it seemed near an end, someone sang again with renewed vigor, and the clan sang thus for a long time.

Taga let the silence grow heavy before he rose and entered the cave to sift the red ocher into the ears, the nose, and eyes of the dead. While he did this, he pantomimed the spirit of the old shaman rising from the body. Throwing the rest of the red ocher upon the corpse, he went out to face the clan and asked, "Who has food for Tlan to eat in the afterlife?" The response was not surprising, for every woman wished to participate in this part of the ritual, and it took a long time to deposit all the wrapped offerings near the head of the bier. Taga asked, "Where are the weapons that will protect Tlan in the afterlife?" and all the men brought beautifully made stone axes to be placed by the right hand of the old shaman.

Taga went over to the fire; putting out the fire symbolized the ending of the burial, and he felt a reluctance to leave the remains of Tlan here. Beneath his robe he felt the weight of the large rock crystal that Ino had given to Tlan; when he had put it on the bier before the burial, Elar had insisted that it must be used again as it was intended, instead of resting in a tomb. He doused the fire and signaled for the stones to be set in front of the cave entrance.

The clan had already begun to stream toward the Circle of Stones, where the usual burial feast was waiting, this time an unusually generous meal to prepare everyone for the march eastward. The tantalizing smell of roast caribou filled the air, and they fell upon the meat vigorously. Most of the women and men realized as they enjoyed the feast that they were ending an era in the life of the Caribou Clan.

CHAPTER ~33~

The women were starting the cleanup operation as a few older members of the Caribou Clan lingered over their food. The gray arena surrounded by the stele had become a familiar center for the community, for many important events had been set here; thus, it was not easy to leave. Who could expect the harshness of a devastating earthquake on a summer day like this one?

Elar was in the middle of the group, still confronting her grief and her feeling of being alone. Beside her sat Yun, now dedicated to caring for Elar as well as his own family. Little Oola ran around carelessly, restless because he knew that they would soon leave.

Oola felt his feet slip under him as he passed one of the tall stones; in fact, the ground seemed to give way beneath him and he fell. Just at that moment the tall stone began to topple over as the toddler looked up in dismay. A deep rumble came from deep in the earth, like an incredibly great animal passing by. Oola cried out for help; then, understanding the direction in which the tall stone would crash, Oola rolled away from the heavy pillar. It came down with a shattering force that left a pile of stone rubble. Oola, still rolling, was safe beyond the Circle of Stones. He was, however, a very frightened little boy.

Yun reached him first and, gathering him up into his arms, delivered Oola to his mother. Elar soothed his crying even though she was more shaken than the boy. The other older people were alarmed by the rumbling of the earth and immediately headed out onto the tundra, where most of the clan had gathered. Elar, carrying her son, followed them, and with Oola's dramatic deliverance from danger, the clan began its exodus across the expanse of the flat tundra in a crowd, all following the markers placed earlier by Taga. There was fear in their eyes; they thought that the ground beneath them might open up at any moment, so they set a quick pace and urged the children to walk fast.

Taga had seen the burial cave sealed and had sent on ahead the men who carried the heaviest burdens. A group of men had helped him check the caves and huts for any stragglers, so that when the rumbling came, everything was ready for the march.

Ino lingered despite the danger, for he thought he had glimpsed Urglun, the villain of the Urkluk Clan, in the rock shadows. Ino had felt the earth tremors under his feet, and he knew that this was a terrible warning; he had heard all the stories circulated by Asun about her losing family members in an earthquake. To practical Ino, the danger presented by the thief and murderer Urglun was more real, more urgent. He felt that he had to corner Urglun to keep the Caribou Clan safe, for they were more vulnerable while they traveled toward their new home.

Taga was near the head of the long line of the clan as they walked fairly rapidly over the grassy, spongy trail. He kept his eye on his own family as he tried to set a brisk pace for everyone. There was incentive enough during the first steps to get away from the scene of the falling rocks, but as they reached marker after marker on the trail and burdens grew heavier, the clan needed to see Taga leading them.

The sky overhead became a pure blue as morning clouds faded and the weather warmed. Taga spoke to his wife encouragingly to point out the advantage of clear weather; he noted that his two small boys had settled into a steady gait after chasing each other playfully around the grownups. He was glad to see Beros catching up to him, for he could then get a report on the group of men who were acting as guards to ensure the safety of this venture. Beros and his brother Ino had been so important in their efforts that Taga wished to thank them for their leadership in guarding the clan; the strong men like them had made this move successful.

Beros was smiling as he drew near, for both men were watching as Tuit, leaving his place beside small Tor, walked beside a little girl with long waves of brown hair, and he occasionally tried to catch her hand in his. "That's your daughter, isn't it, Beros?" asked Taga.

"That's Sula, yes. If she seems disdainful, that is her nature. My wife Troz and I love her and she is a good daughter." They walked along in companionable silence for a while before Beros resumed thoughtfully. "She was born just after the time that you eloped with Maa. Tzan was still upset over your disappearance and did not know about her birth – fortunately. Sula is the daughter of Tzan and his wife Seldun. You remember that all his girl babies were supposed to be drowned. Well, Seldun would not have it that way with this one. She fell in love with this child and persuaded Ino, the warrior sent to take the child away, to spare her. My wife and I took Sula into our home to raise her; Seldun was able to visit her in my hut and it made her intensely happy. She rewarded Ino with great affection, too. She had a torrid affair with him. I think that is why Ino has not taken a wife. Who could equal a wife of the Great Tzan?"

Taga's amazement showed in his eyes. "Seldun had at least four sons for Tzan, didn't she? Then she perished in the big tornado along with those sons. I remember Bulun and Sanal; then Bugun was born, and the youngest was Mung. What a pity all those fine boys lost their lives at the same time. Seldun had her own hut for her family and kept her distance. She was a beautiful woman, and her daughter has the same wonderful appearance."

"My brother really has an eye for women. Did you know that he has had an affair going on with Olun, the wife of Puluk? I told him to be careful; those Urkluks have an unpredictable side to them. He may not know what he has been playing with."

"This does disturb me, Beros. I admit that Olun, once she got cleaned up and her hair groomed, was a pretty little woman. She turned the heads of many with her earthquake stories. Tell Ino to be watchful. Better, tell him to find a wife of his own. He's old enough to support a family."

They talked then of the guard duties which Beros had faithfully tended to. After he left, Taga walked on in deep thought. He was partly nostalgic with the memory of his first meeting with Maa and partly apprehensive over the news of Ino's interest in the Urkluk woman. Later, he fell in step with his wife to discuss both subjects in a soft, private voice.

Maa said, "So the Great Tzan has another living descendant, Taga. This one is his daughter, and she is going to be a beauty! Look, she is about the same age as our Tuit, and right now she is about as tall."

"I am very concerned about Ino's entanglement with Olun. She has a background among the Urkluk Clan, and that could spell trouble for us when we already need to be watchful as we travel so far." Taga's voice was serious.

As the Caribou Clan walked away from their old home, heading ever eastward, Ino was left far behind. He was sure that Urglun was skulking around among the abandoned caves, sly enough not to have been seen by the other guards of the Caribou Clan. Ino did not mind someone picking up useful objects left behind by householders, but he sensed that Urglun was after the more valuable items put into the burial cave of Tlan. This thought made him angry enough to hide and watch for the thief.

Certain that the entire Caribou Clan had now left, Urglun walked out into the open and stood with his hands on his hips as if appraising his own territory. His survey brought to his attention the recent wall of rocks built to - seal the burial cave, and he sauntered over to it. The task of dismantling even a part of this wall looked forbidding, but soon Urglun was removing the rocks one by one, starting at one corner. Evidently he thought he had all the time he needed to rob the cave.

Ino loaded his slingshot and took aim. Unfortunately, Urglun bent down just as the stone whizzed past his head and hit the wall of rocks with a sharp crack. At once he stepped back and melted into the shadows, from which he could watch for his enemy.

Ino remained motionless and quietly hidden. He hoped that he would soon be able to get another shot at the grave robber.

CHAPTER
~34~

As URGLUN LURKED in the empty darkness of the caves, aware that an enemy was watching for him, Ino waited for him to show up again near the burial site of Tlan. Unknown to either of them, a third man – tall, graceful, very handsome – had entered the area from the west. He was cautious because everything seemed changed. He last saw the Caribou Clan when he was eighteen years old, and now he was thirty-eight. It was Alun, the son of Passa, fourth wife of Tzan, and his father was Tlan, her lover. Tlan had long ago returned from the Himalayas thinking that Alun, his companion on that trip, was lost at the site of a glacier when a blinding snowstorm obscured the view. But Alun had survived and after having been gone for twenty years, he had returned with the hope of seeing his beautiful mother and his father. In his time the stalwart guards of the Great Tzan allowed no strangers to enter the area without due explanation, and Alun had expected to meet some tough opposition before being recognized. Indeed, it would have been hard to remember Alun as the bright and personable young man who left with Tlan for a great adventure in the high mountains to the west, for Alun's hair had turned nearly white. His step was lithe and he was slim and fit but Alun was already approaching old age.

Alun, on the high ground of the hills, looked for the long-houses of Tzan, but those had long ago been swept away by the great tornado. Far below he glimpsed an unfamiliar ring of tall stones around a flat area which he remembered as the village of the Caribou Clan. Nothing seemed as he once knew it. Worst of all, there were no humans about. Everything looked deserted. He wondered if this had to do with the earthquake tremors he had felt at intervals. He advanced toward the edge of the hill country and sought a path down to the tundra.

Suddenly below him he saw a drama unfolding. A tall, well-built man who looked like one of Tzan's guards was sitting by a large boulder, half in its shadow. On a low ledge above him there appeared a scrawny, very thin man with wild hair, who had a large rock uplifted in his hands. In the next moment the unkempt assassin hurled the stone down upon the man below him, splitting his skull. It was over quickly. The wild-looking man, glancing up, saw Alun on the hill above him and scrambled over a rocky path down toward the tundra.

Alun was transfixed. Just as he had convinced himself that the former site of the Caribou Clan's village was deserted, he had witnessed a murder. He had not recognized either of the two men, although the victim resembled the remarkably strong and healthy sons of the Great Tzan, while the murderer had a sly, dirty, evil appearance.

Alun hurried down to the fallen man, but he had died instantly without knowing what had happened. There was nothing that could be done for him. Alun examined the blood-covered countenance, but he did not know the man. He was sure, however, that this was a member of the Caribou Clan. How he wished that this man could speak to him and explain what had become of the clan.

He could not leave the body of one of his clan out in the open, so he dragged it over to a great pile of stones that seemed to cover up the mouth of a cave nearby. There he straightened out the arms and legs and covered the man with many stones to keep wild animals from devouring the body. And so, Ino the brave hunter/warrior shared a burial spot with Tlan, the great leader and shaman of the Caribou Clan.

Alun walked among the empty caves, understanding that they had been occupied only very recently. Here there was a stone cooking vessel and there he found the remnants of a ragged doll fashioned of straw. As he finally stood in the center of the Ring of Stones, admiring the precision of the planning and placement of the stones, he began to understand where all the people had gone when the earth beneath him began to rumble and he sank to his knees in the effort to stay upright. The ground swayed weirdly, incomprehensibly. Around him several of the magnificent tall stones toppled over. He knew, then, that the clan had gone to the tundra because they feared that a devastating earthquake would erupt.

Therefore, Alun followed the trail of the many passing footprints out onto the tundra; soon he began to find the familiar marker stones with arrows pointing in the direction the clan had taken. His heart beat fast as he realized that in a short time he would once again be among his kindred; he would be reunited with his Caribou Clan.

Taga watched as the members of the clan, having eaten a good evening meal at the halfway point, settled down for the night in family groups. He visited each family and was satisfied that everything was in order and that the adults knew that the move was out of necessity because a massive earthquake was due. They were much safer out on the tundra than they were in an area of falling rocks and cave-ins. Then Taga circled the camp, speaking with each of the guards, asking especially if anyone had seen Ino. Beros had come to him to ask him, for Beros had not seen his brother since the burial. There was no information about Ino from anyone. Then, as Taga went back to Maa, Tuit, and little Tor, everyone went to sleep under the stars while the moon passed through the wide sky overhead.

In the grayness before dawn Alun was halted by a guard on the western fringe of the Caribou camp. Alun told the guard that he was from the Caribou Clan but had been gone for a long time. The guard brought him to Taga, who woke hearing the name now almost forgotten; this stranger said that he was Alun. Taga knew that Alun was presumed to be dead. His father had just been buried. Alun was telling the guard that he had been raised as the son of Tzan; Taga alone knew the mystery that Alun was the son of Passa and Tlan, born of an illicit passion that began when Passa was brought to be the fourth wife of Tzan but was proclaimed too young by the other three wives.

Taga looked closely at the handsome, gray-haired man who stood before him, and he found a resemblance to Tlan in the refined intelligence in the eyes. Alun, despite the outward signs of age, was still thin, athletic and graceful. Taga, remembering the youth Alun who had been not much older than he himself, knew at once that this stranger was the true son, and the only real son, of Tlan. He first introduced himself; then he welcomed Alun with a great hug, full of emotion because he had to give the news that Alun was one day too late to see his father buried. It was a terrible blow, and so was the news that Passa had died in the great tornado that caused the death of Tzan.

There was much more to be told. Alun listened very seriously as Taga spoke of the rescue effort that Tlan and Taga's family made, and how it turned into a reorganization of the remnants of the clan under Tlan's wise, kind guidance. The Caribou Clan had prospered and grown since then, even though so many had perished in the awful windstorm.

CHAPTER
~35~

ALUN, TOO, HAD his story to tell. For a long time he was married to the sweet and lovely woman who had helped him to recover when he staggered up from the crevasse, half-dead and broken. When he was able finally to travel enough to look for Tlan, his father seemed to be gone from the area. Sweet and untiring Lara had died trying to give birth to their stillborn child, and Alun then began a long, long trek back to his beginnings, over mountains and great deserts and rivers.

His memory of Lara was veiled in the sorrow he had felt when she died. That delicately beautiful face, oval with a pointed chin and translucent, perfect skin; and her liquid brown eyes, mysterious yet mirroring her generous heart – these were pictures that swam into his dreams sometimes, but they were no longer real.

As his family began to stir, Taga proudly introduced them to Alun. Maa was very matronly and sweet-tempered, beautiful and capable, and the mother of two growing boys. Tuit tried to be mature to show that he was the older, but the shy grins of eager little Tor were heart-warming. Both boys made it evident that they had found a new hero, and Alun felt that he had found a warm new family.

A guard stopped by to report that all had gone well during the night, and he added that Beros had just returned, still looking for his brother and more concerned than ever. This reminded Alun of the murder he had witnessed back at the village of the Caribou; when he told of the wild-haired man who threw down a large stone onto the tall warrior/hunter, killing him, Taga, Maa, and the guard all knew at once that Urglun of the Urkluks had killed Ino of the Caribou Clan. They had no doubt that Urglun had been trying to pillage the tomb and that Ino had found out, with tragic results. The three men went to find Beros and to tell him that his brother Ino had been buried at the entrance to the burial cave of Tlan.

Beros, his wife Troz, and young Sula were full of grief, so Taga spoke of Ino's great loyalty and courage and how he would be missed much by the other warrior/guards who had looked up to him. The family tried to take comfort in their leader's praise.

Troz drew Taga aside to say, "I can tell you confidentially that since he had no wife of his own, he made eyes at Olun, wife of Puluk, who used to be with the Urkluks. Because Olun has been having an affair with Ino without Puluk suspecting, she needed someone to confide in. She told me. I was horrified and warned her to break it off. Puluk would be enraged and jealous." Troz dabbed at her red eyes, seeming very sad yet gossipy.

Taga turned red with embarrassment at this news. It partly explained why Urglun would have made Ino his target. Then Troz went on.

"Olun saw Urglun near our village just before the burial of Tlan, and she was very fearful for herself. We were heading for the burial cave when she told me that he spoke to her. She was really trembling with fear, but she said that all she had told him was that an earthquake was coming and that the clan was relocating, so he was in danger and should leave."

Taga replied, "So Urglun was spying on us all the time. And he is still out there on the tundra. He will be looking for any opportunity to get the advantage of us. Our clan is vulnerable while we are traveling, with our household goods spread out. This may be a hard day."

Beros, his face full of wrath, was preparing to leave. "I must hunt him down. This is my burden and I cannot rest until that dirty, sly animal is dead."

Amid cries from all the men of "Be careful, Beros," he left, walking back along the trail that led to the burials of his brother and the shaman.

Taga turned to face the others. "Today we must take care that all stay together. There could be an attack from the Urkluks, despite the threat of a big earthquake. They see that we will be strung out on the trail, and they may take this opportunity to pay us back for sending them away."

The stricken faces of the women showed that they were not ready for the harsh reality of a fight; for such a long time their way of life had been peaceful and prosperous under the leadership of Tlan. However, the men of the Caribou Clan could be counted on to fight bravely and skillfully if need be. As the clan prepared to leave, they realized that, for most of them, their entire stock of belongings was here in this halfway camp, and that someone in each family would have to make this trip once or maybe twice within the next few days. As this idea was brought to Taga, he frowned a bit at the thought that the very strong men he would count on to fight for them all might be needed to make trips back and forth to carry household goods to their final camp. If only he had some way to transport the goods, as on a sled, then all could go at once, with no second trips. It might be a little harder to pull a sled, but a sled could save so much time. He mused aloud about using sleds, and Alun and Yun, standing near, thought this would be brilliant. But, they asked, what material could be used for the sleds? The forests where wood was plentiful were far away. Yun mentioned the great stash of bones of giant ancient beasts not so far away.

Suddenly Maa had the right idea. She asked, "What do we have most plentifully? The hides and skins of our animals. If we pile our possessions on top of the hides and secure each hide as a sort of bag, we could pull the hides along the surface of the tundra. We could even cut a sort of handle to pull by. The children could give a hand, because two handles could be cut in a bag." She was really warming up to this idea, and it was getting better and better. Taga, with some surprise, remembered that it had been Maa's idea to use a sled when their family and Yun came to the rescue of the Caribou Clan after the great wind had killed so many. Also, he remembered that Tlan had been admiring that a woman could be so resourceful.

Everyone felt enthusiasm for Maa's wonderful idea, so each family put it into practice. Before long, the little caravan was organized with several people pulling each huge hide bag, with not too much effort. The families were better organized, too, walking closer together now. Maa beamed because her idea had worked so well, and many friends came to tell her it did. It was an especially nice moment when Alun applauded the idea and the spirit of cooperation among the Caribou Clan. In *his* experience in the long ago past, this clan had always worked together because they felt the power of Great Tzan and were afraid not to do as they were told. It was a strong comparison between the two leaders, Great Tzan and his brother Tlan. Tzan had wielded his power in a cruel but successful manner, but Tlan had cultivated kindness, creativity, orderly methods of work, and intelligent inquiry into problems. He had made the members of the clan proud of themselves and unwilling to behave badly toward others of the clan. Tlan had made them a social unit bound together by caring.

The summer sun had become hotter by afternoon, so the weary travelers were relieved to reach at last the place on the tundra which Taga had chosen for them. They were cheered to see a number of huts ready for occupancy; this made the whole clan feel better about moving away from their comfortable village. In a way, they were home again. Everyone waited only for the evening meal before lying down tiredly.

Alun had been introduced to Elar and her two children, Oola and Blun. He was much intrigued by the backgrounds of the children. It amused him to learn how Oola, son of Tzan, had survived only because of Elar, and Oola was becoming not only handsome but also so genial that he pleased everyone. Blue-eyed Blun, while not an Urkluk, had a puzzling origin, but under the tutelage of Elar, she was both poised and capricious, adult and other-worldly. This odd combination in her personality made for an unusual beauty. Alun was reassured that Elar and these children had made Tlan very happy.

Nowhere in all his travels had Alun chanced upon a group of people with such good will, such ability to care for others. Also, he began to understand that these descendants of Tzan were more intelligent than most of the humans he had encountered. While Tzan had developed his organizational skills to an exceptional degree, it was Tlan who had, in his lifetime, shown an amazing overall intelligence that made him outstanding.

Alun pondered the idea: the Caribou Clan were all physically strong and able as well as intelligent. He looked around and saw that they were all attractive and alert, clean cut and friendly. The descendants of Tzan were clearly leaders in this group because they had exceptional physical beauty and creative intelligence. He suddenly felt a surge of deep family pride in his Caribou Clan and he was glad to be home again.

When he learned about the Urkluks, Alun had a sudden fear that this unkempt, uncaring group of people might be able to erase from the earth the astonishing achievements of the Caribou Clan, leaving on the tundra only bones and little evidence of their happy existence. The Urkluks were only marauders and murderers, and Alun himself had seen an example of their cruelty. This was a time in the lives of the Caribou people when they were weakened temporarily. And who knew what catastrophe might be flung at them by a gigantic earthquake? The combination of the Urkluks and the natural calamity of an earthquake might mean an end to the Caribou people. These gloomy thoughts led him to vow that he would do all he could to protect his clan and preserve their way of life.

CHAPTER
~36~

IN THE MORNING everyone seemed refreshed, eager to explore the new area. A great need was to construct the remaining huts so that every family would have a home. Women and children helped and most of the homes were put up during that day by willing hands. A few remaining huts would go up on the next day, and the people who would work on them were assigned to that task. Yun pointed out a small stream as the source of water, but its location was not near enough for women or children to go there alone; a rule was made that water would be brought to the camp two times each day by a party of people and anyone could accompany this group. Otherwise, no one was to go out alone to the stream. It was pointed out that a member of the Urkluk Clan might endanger a smaller group.

In each home, work was going on to make individuals happy and comfortable. The women were busy settling into their huts.

Taga's design for his new village was a circular one. The homes were in a circle around a central area which contained two large long-houses, one of which was his. The other would serve for single men and visitors. In the future more elaborate plans could be made for playgrounds or outdoor assembly areas. There was certainly plenty of space here. A few low hills and a sparse copse or two of willows near the stream were all the landmarks to vary the wide, flat tundra. After one night here, in easy summer weather, Taga was pleased with his choice of location.

His morning reverie was interrupted by a guard who came to report that two of the Urkluk Clan had been seen near the stream when the guards had accompanied the early group of women bringing water back to their homes. This was really bad news. There had been no trouble getting all the Caribou people and all their belongings safely to the new village, and Taga had hoped that the Urkluks were gone. However, that was not in their nature, he realized. Their intention was robbery, and they would wait until the Caribou Clan had an unguarded moment.

Taga asked whether Beros had returned, and he was told that Beros had just come from the west and had gone immediately to his hut.

He found a sorrowing Beros telling his family about the bravery of Ino, who had remained behind at the caves despite the threat of an earthquake because he thought there might be grave robbers near. Ino had been watching the burial site of Tlan's cave when Urglun circled around and came from above, silently, throwing down a large stone upon Ino's head. According to Alun, who had witnessed this act, Ino's skull was split open and he died instantly. Seeing Alun on the hill above him, Urglun had run down the path to the tundra. Alun, recognizing the fallen warrior as a member of the Caribou Clan, had gone to Ino but could not do anything for him. Rather than leave the body to animal predators, Alun had buried Ino under the same stones used to seal the cave where Tlan was buried. On visiting the site, Beros was satisfied to leave Ino there, at the edge of the burial cave. When he concluded, Beros impressed upon his family that Ino had been to the end loyal and brave.

To this Taga added his own eulogy, for Ino had been an important leader of his guards as well as a friend. Taga added that the Caribou Clan would all like to be a part of the mourning and that he would plan with them for a gathering of the clan in the next few days. He also told Beros of the sighting of two Urkluks down by the stream this morning when the women went to get water. The enemy was lurking in the area, waiting for an opportunity to strike.

Beros was enraged that the Urkluks were near. His wife could not restrain him from declaring, "I'll stop them. I'll get even with them." She did get him calm enough to listen to her for a moment; she worried that he had not had food or sleep and would be at a disadvantage if he left at that moment without taking care of himself.

Taga announced that he was preparing a plan for defense of the village so that the women and children would know how to act if the Urkluks came. He invited Beros to come with him and help in the overall defense strategy planning, and then he left.

Guards not on duty were called to the meeting, and together with them, Taga put together a plan that called for women and children to come to the central long-houses if an attack occurred. He asked if they might have weapons to use in their defense, and he learned that every boy had his slingshot and practiced continually. Every wife had knives for preparing food.

Taga told the guards to spread the word that if an attack came, women and children should come to the central long-houses and bring their knives and slingshots. "With rocks for the slingshots," added one guardsman. Taga agreed.

Another plan had to be made; they would have to go out in armed groups to hunt for the Urkluks. Perhaps the Urkluks had a permanent sort of camp in the area. The Caribou needed to have more information on the movements and location of the enemy; spying would be safer at night. The stream seemed to be a point of contact right now, so an armed group might go there and look around.

Other advance planning was concerned with actual battle tactics when the enemy was confronted. "Hand to hand combat is hard work," said the same guard, "but that is what we have been training for. We know our business, and we are strong."

Taga planned further tactics. He knew the advantage of accurate slingshots. Older boys and a few hand-picked men made up a group who could operate at a distance when needed and could pick off some of the enemy. The men would act as leaders to curb poorly aimed or wasted shots.

Alun suggested that sharp poles would give an advantage, and a roundup revealed four of these among the huts, so a small group of men could be armed with them as well as standard large axes and knives. Seeing what his men had at their disposal, Taga devised a plan for battle if they faced the enemy. His men would form into two rows to advance. The first row would have men with long, sharp poles in between men wielding axes and knives. The orderly, firm advance would itself throw the Urkluks into panic, for they were cowards. In actual combat, the polemen would spear the front line of the enemy, while the other Caribou men would engage those who were left. A rain of rocks from the backup slingshots would further weaken the enemy's advance, and these shots would be used at any time in the battle.

By the time the men had given their opinions and received their orders, there was a good spirit of camaraderie. Nobody wanted to have close combat with those smelly, dirty rats, but if it became necessary, the Caribou men would not lose the battle.

Taga and a few men wearing double-hide armor went out to the stream to look around. It was close to noon, and the sun made them very hot, but Taga asked them to bear with the situation for a while. It *was* cooler by the stream; Taga pointed out the pattern of trees at the edge of the water. These could provide cover for the enemy. Keeping a sharp eye out for any Urkluks, Taga and his men followed the stream as it meandered away from the hills behind them, becoming smaller all the while. Looking out on the tundra, they could see far in the distance. The object of their reconnaissance was to find the camp of the Urkluks. They had gone along the stream, quietly and in single file, until the sun told them it was mid-afternoon; they became aware of a line of hills in the distance, low hills with rocky projections. The stream did not run through the hills, but its path was not far away from them.

Taga felt a prickling on the back of his neck. He knew that this location would be right for the Urkluks. No one could cross the open tundra here without being seen, so any further scouting would have to be done by night. He turned to his men. "Do you want to wait here for the protection of night before going to those hills? I think we have found the location of the Urkluks."

Beros spoke up. "Let me wait here. When darkness comes, I will cross the tundra and find their camp. Then I will go back to the Caribou Clan village and tell you. If we are lucky, we will be able to attack them in a surprise move. Take the rest of the men back for now, before we are seen."

Taga agreed, but he did not want to leave Beros alone on this mission. Yun could be counted on in every situation, so he left Yun with Beros in a small copse of willows and headed back to his village with the rest of the men.

CHAPTER
~37~

WHILE TAGA WAS away with his scouting party, a guard sounded an alarm. He had seen a party of Urkluks coming from the stream toward the village. He signaled that they looked threatening and that he had seen a double handful of men.

Inside the village the women and children, hearing the alarm, did as they had been told. Bringing slingshots (with stones to throw) and their kitchen knives, they went to the central long-houses.

The men who were left in the village needed leadership since Taga and Beros were both gone, and it was Alun who stepped in to lead the little army. They formed two ranks, or rows, with their sharp wood poles interspersed with armed men in the front row. In the third row were men and boys armed with slingshots. They were all stern and orderly, very much impressed with their importance. The Urkluks had never seen such an enemy force.

Alun gave the signal, a low bird call, and all the slingshots were fired at once. They hit some of the enemy and one man went down temporarily. Then the front row charged, catching the Urkluks between the stream and those long, sharp poles, to their complete dismay. Unaccustomed to such tactics of warfare, three of the enemy fell, stuck hard in vital parts and dying. Boys in the third row were thrilled and frightened at the red blood smearing the enemy. Sensing the hard reality of their situation, other Urkluks began scrambling around on the ground, trying to get away. Another fierce round of slingshot fire felled an Urkluk who was hit in the middle of his forehead with a stinging, fatal blow. Then the hand-to-hand combat began as the Caribou men closed in. Alun, locked in battle with a young Urkluk, knocked the man's axe out of his hands easily then felt a wave of nausea as violent body odors engulfed him. The heat of the afternoon as well as the heat of battle made his foe slippery with sweat. Alun grabbed the man's body and forced him down while swinging his own battle axe, crushing the nose. Another swing left the man's right arm limp, and after a few more blows the enemy crumpled, dead. At that, one of the Urkluks escaped from the melee to run back to the stream and jump in. He tried to hide under the water until he was pulled out, yelling and gasping, to meet a similar fate.

A cheer went up from the village; women and children were now watching and giving encouragement to the home guard. But the remaining four Urkluks wrested themselves out of the clutches of the Caribou fighters and ran toward the village. At this, all the women and children fell back, until a few rounds from the slingshots caused the Urkluks to veer away onto the tundra. They ran with unbelievable swiftness toward the south, until they disappeared.

The battle was over. The Caribou had won without losing a man. There were six ugly, smelly, contorted corpses lying on the battleground. Alun called for the men to help him clean up the area because it was near their water supply. The dead men were put on old hides and pulled out onto the tundra in the direction in which their more fortunate companions had run. They were left far, far out on the tundra. Someone who checked a few days later found that the bodies were gone.

CHAPTER
~38~

When taga arrived back with his scouting party, the villagers were distraught, afraid of another attack and sick at heart. Everyone talked at once, full of details about the battle they had seen. After he knew all the acts of strength and courage that the Caribou men had done, Taga could only say, "You see that the Caribou men are brave and we will protect all of you. We are your strength."

Elar stopped in front of him. "Where is Yun?" When she was told, she was shocked and angry that Yun was risking his life at that moment.

Taga realized that he could not deal with all the matters of war at the same time. He turned to his wife for help with Elar's outburst. He explained that Yun could be counted on to keep Beros under control so that both of them would return safely. Yun had been the most dependable person around, and his mission was critical.

Yun and Beros, meanwhile, passed the time trying to be inconspicuous. They did not talk much but kept a sharp watch on their surroundings so that they would not be caught off guard. Beros, a very good brother, truly mourned the passing of Ino in the vigor of his young manhood. In low tones, he said as much to Yun, whom he trusted absolutely. Yun found the right words, as usual, to say that Ino had been acting for all the clan and so was a hero. Urglun of the Urkluks had been watching and had seen that valuable pieces of Tlan's favorite property were buried with him. For that matter, robbing burial sites was no worse than what Urglun had done to Blun, for he had killed her parents and kidnapped her. Both Beros and Yun growled bitter epithets that applied to the Urkluks.

Having thus established a kinship of hatred for the Urkluks, they turned to the subjects of Ino's strength, his courage, his loyalty to the clan. Beros, with a short laugh, said that Ino was never married, but he certainly had great appeal to women. Yun, who knew all about Ino's affair with Seldun, agreed. He was, however, thinking mostly about a more recent affair that might explain why Urglun chose to end Ino's life. Yun asked, "Did you know that Ino has recently been having an affair with the wife of Puluk?"

Beros sucked in his breath.

They waited quietly then, though not without a sense of companionship, until dusk fell. Then they discussed their approach to the hills. Lookouts on the highest hills might be looking down on them. They might stand out against the dusty gray-green of the summer-eroded grasses. Ino cut willow branches, intending them for camouflage, and they began to crawl slowly from the stream by the narrowest way to the hills. They planned to circle the hills, looking for signs of a camp. This would give them information for a later attack. They would try to be back at the Caribou camp by daylight.

Reaching the rocky foot of the first outlying hill, they knew that their guess had been right when they saw a path well beaten down by animals and men. Yun suggested that they avoid it, lest they meet some Urkluks too soon. Their mission was to learn about the Urkluk camp so that Caribou warriors could attack it with success.

Beros wanted to get his revenge at once, but he saw that the price would be too high. They were outnumbered. So they climbed an adjacent hill from which they looked down from the protection of a great crag.

There, in a kind of glen with a few stunted trees was a straggling group of huts. There was no movement. It looked peaceful, as if the camp was already asleep. There were no fires.

Beros whispered, "Is the camp deserted? Have they all left?"

"We'll wait a while to see whether they are there," Yun replied.

After a long time they saw a little activity outside one hut. They looked at each other, convinced that their mission was almost completed.

They were careful on the trip back down the hill to the tundra. Yun insisted that they circle the hills for whatever they might discover to give advantage to the Caribou warriors. Already Yun had a plan to draw a sort of map of the hill area, marking each hut; he had memorized it all.

When they arrived home close to daybreak, a few birds were making cuddling noises in their nests by the stream. The two were welcomed as heroes. Elar was wild with joy.

Yun took a wide, flat piece of bone and inscribed his map on it; his keen observations enabled him to draw the layout of the hills and the Urkluk camp, with each hut marked very accurately. Taga was so pleased that he took care to let Elar know how important the map was to his plan of attack.

As Taga sat by his doorway, a serious frown on his forehead, he became aware of a commotion on the edge of the village. Gadu had appeared, alone, with no caribou. He looked sick at heart.

He came straight to Taga, who stood up to receive bad news, seeing that there were tears in Gadu's eyes. His story came out pitifully. At dawn the herd began to graze as Gadu and his four men watched. A large group of Urkluks came out of the mists that had hidden them. They slew two of his men and drove off the spooked caribou in the direction of the northeast. Stampeding, the herd went faster and faster until the tundra was bare except for the two bodies.

Gadu had been a target of violence, but he was not badly hurt. First he went to the fallen men, two dead and two wounded. Binding up the wounds, he and the others buried the dead men and started back home, Gadu going on ahead of the others. He hoped to get men to help him track the herd.

Taga had already resolved to strike the Urkluk camp during the coming night. He counted on surprise as a big factor in this raid. He wished to have the fighting over and to know that his clan was safe again. The news that Gadu had brought strengthened his resolve to wipe out the entire Urkluk Clan; they represented a serious danger to all the Caribou Clan. He could not deal with any other problem until the raid was over. As the shaman, he had arduous spiritual preparation to make for the coming work.

CHAPTER
~39~

BEFORE DUSK HAD become a very dark night, all the men said their goodbyes to their wives, collected their double hide armor, and gathered restively near the stream. They were eager for a rousing fight. There was no talking; surprise was an element to be worked for.

Taga demonstrated that each man was to cover his face with a thin layer of mud from the stream so that his skin would not betray him in the dark. Hands, arms, feet, legs were camouflaged. He led them down the stream and halted at the point chosen by Yun as nearest to the path to the Urkluk camp. His plan was to spread out among the hills above and behind that camp and come from all directions. At a single signal every Caribou man would burst into a hut assigned to him. The Urkluks would die. This raid was to end all enemy activity and make life peaceful again. The axes and knives held by the Caribou warriors would be red with blood.

Beros fondled his weapons, for his assignment was special. He was to find Urglun and dispatch him. He smiled grimly in the dark.

It was Taga who gave the signal, a bird call in the night. There was a flurry of movement, a quiet scurrying of footsteps from behind rocks and out into the open. Each man found a hut and crept in. There was to be no noise, no outcry. Throats were slit in the dark; not a person was left alive. The dirt floors, already scattered with trash of all kinds, grew slippery with blood. The fresh smell of the gore mingled with appallingly dirty odors already native to the huts. The disorder in which they had found the whole camp became a nightmare of bloodied hides, discarded bones from recent and past meals, debris, and riotously red death.

The signal to withdraw was another low bird call, and the men met at the foot of the hill before retreating to the stream. Beros, his face stern, nodded to Taga and, alone, went back toward the Urkluk camp. His nod meant that he had found *his* enemy. After all the Caribou fighters had left the area, it would be the task of Beros to set fire to all the Urkluk huts.

Along the stream, Taga spoke to his men. He affirmed that tonight's raid had been a terrible event. The Urkluk Clan would be no more. The raid had been necessary for the continued peaceful life of the Caribou Clan. There would be no more dirty robbers and murderers.

When they saw fires light up the hill behind them, the men could not restrain the victory chant that was inside them; it burst out passionately, affirming all that Taga had said to them. Their hated enemy was conquered. Wrong had been righted. Blood had been spilled but it was not their own blood. It had been a night none would forget.

When they fell silent, they began to wash off the mud and the scent of the Urkluk blood. The stream was red from their double hide armor, which they washed and laid on grass to dry. The men were now anxious to reach the comfort of their beds and the normality of their own homes as they hurried along in single file, occasionally looking back at the fires in the distance.

CHAPTER ~40~

OUTSIDE THE HUT of Puluk, Taga heard such heart-felt sobbing that he wondered if he should intervene. Ordinarily he would not do so, waiting for the man or wife to come to him with any problems in their marriage. He stood for a while, reviewing all he had heard about Olun, for it was she evidently who was weeping. Despite having a good marriage with Puluk, lately she had begun an affair with Ino, which had been disastrous to him. And it was reported that she had had a conversation with Urglun just before the burial of Tlan. This thought led to memories of Olun's arrival with Puluk when both were Urkluks. She had eagerly embraced new standards of cleanliness and behavior, and her husband had been astonished at her beauty after she bathed in the pool at the waterfall and got her hair done up. Taga remembered that they had three children at that time, but he did not remember their names. It was the sister-in-law, Asun, who had pointed out that the Urkluks did not live in caves because they feared earthquakes. Taga thought that the families of Olun and Asun must feel very afraid now that the big earthquake seemed inevitable. He decided that he would send Maa to talk with these women; she was better in this sort of situation.

Maa did pay a visit to the hut of Olun and found her red-eyed and trembling with emotion. With discreet inquiry, Maa found, to her own sorrow, that Olun wept for relatives who had died in the raid on the Urkluks. That is how Maa learned about the raid; everyone in the Urkluk Clan was killed and the huts were burned, consuming the dead. Worse, the Caribou Clan warriors had returned feeling no remorse.

Maa left with a sick feeling. It would be hard for her to discuss this with her husband, the leader of the night raid. It was under his direction that even the women and children had perished in their beds in the night.

Maa avoided her husband as long as she could, but finally Taga insisting on having her information about the source of Olun's grief. Maa would not look him straight in the eyes. She spoke plainly, "Olun had some relatives who were killed in the raid on the Urkluks. Women and children."

Taga gasped. Maa, still not looking at him, added, "That is why she was crying. If she cried also for the loss of Ino, she did not say." And Maa rushed off with tears in her eyes.

For Taga then the results of the raid took on a different light. He had been harsh in his judgment of the Urkluks as a group; wiping them all out had been his quick solution to their threat to his own clan. He had held the power of life or death for a group of people, and he had acted as he thought best at the time to keep his own people safe. It was done. Nothing could bring back any Urkluk children. He could not wish to do so. It was not in the interest of the Caribou Clan. But he was in deep inner conflict now. He wished he had the guidance of the good Tlan now. What would Tlan have done in this situation?

CHAPTER
~41~

THE CHILDREN HAD gathered around Alun out on the tundra; it was a fine, clear morning after the sun burned off some haziness, and Alun, sensing their restlessness, had asked the children to a story-telling session. Elar, hearing him, put down her work at once to follow. As she passed Maa sitting in the door of her long-house, Elar stopped to explain where they were going, and Maa joined the group too. Among the children were Tuit, Tor, Sula, Blun, and many others, as well as Oola. They all sat in a circle around Alun, looking up expectantly.

Alun had a fascinating personality; when he spoke, his firm, clear voice was that of a leader and teacher. He had traveled widely and seen much of their part of the earth; there were many adventures stored in his memory. Despite his air of having been born the son of a great family, he displayed great generosity and caring in his treatment of old and young alike. In his short time with the displaced Caribou Clan, he had earned respect and admiration.

Alun began by explaining that it was the great shaman, Tlan, who had become his close friend and had taken him on a trip to the highest mountains toward the setting sun, mountains that were forever capped with snow and ringed with clouds. The children responded with ecstatic wriggling and cries of "Aahh!"

When he described the snow leopard he had seen from a short distance, Alun moved in a graceful, feline slouch to show how the large cat had stalked his prey, an equally white deer-like creature. He had been glad to be part of a group of people moving slowly up the mountain, because alone he might have been a victim of the beautiful leopard.

Once in the highest part of the mountains, his caravan had met another group of heavily-wrapped people moving in the opposite direction. Both groups had stopped, and at once there began some bargaining as travelers brought out treasures they were willing to exchange for equally valuable objects. Exotic furs from animals Alun had never seen and had not even imagined were displayed. There were furs that were yellow and incredibly soft when handled. There were hides from great mammoths that each man coveted because these skins were so strong and impenetrable. One man had a small bunch of long feathers that were of many colors; each feather had a huge eye on it, staring at the startled travelers.

The beautiful stones carried by some travelers were not only lovely, but they had the merit of being easy to carry. Some stones were of a deep blue that mirrored a sky with approaching darkness; some stones shone with the brightest colors of a wonderful sunset that spoke of a windy morning to come.

Alun remembered especially a fine clear rock crystal that was very large, a crystal that Tlan had wished for. Alas, he had nothing with him that was valuable enough to exchange for the big crystal. The owner of the crystal had looked into the stone and said, "It will be yours; I do not know what will happen, but this stone will come to you, shaman. It has claimed you." As the two caravans moved on in opposite directions, Tlan had said wistfully, "With such a stone I would find it easy to break through the portal between this world and the other. I know that is a healing stone like none else."

Elar carefully chose her words as she broke into the story. "That is true. That stone came to him. It was his."

Blun got to her feet, her clear, deep blue eyes meeting the gray eyes of the story-teller. She said, "I am getting shivers as I listen to your stories. Were you only in the land of the snows?"

Alun looked long at the beautiful little creature who was facing him, as exotic as anything he had described for the children. He had heard that nobody knew what kind of family she had been snatched from by the villain Urglun. This delicate, lovely child was so sure of herself, even defiant., as if she knew the impression she made on adults. He answered her question with another.

"Would you like to hear of our adventure as we crossed the dry, sandy waste that lies near but beyond our western mountains?" As she nodded, he continued. "Again, we had become part of a group of travelers because to travel alone through a wasteland of sand means sure death. We walked with a leader who knew the area well, so that we found water at every day's end on our journey. Several times we heard the sands sing to us in strange, low tones. Sometimes the voice of the sands called us by our names, and the evil spirit within the sands spoke in alluring tones to entice us to come away into the hills of sand. But if we did, we would lose our way, and our lives also, so we stayed close to our guide and the others. At night we heard the song of the sands as a tramping of many, many feet, as if a great multitude of people were coming. Sometimes this was very frightening. We were glad to reach the edge of this cruel, sandy wasteland."

It was Tuit who caught Alun's eye; the boy's eyes were very large and bright, and he seemed to be looking far beyond the present moment and into a distant future. He was beginning to see himself as the man he wished to be, a man having wonderful, brave adventures just like those Alun had told about.

The women were enthralled; story-telling was their favorite entertainment, and Alun's past held deep interest for them. There had already been several gossip sessions about this unusually handsome addition to the clan; some remembered him from the past and could link him with his very beautiful mother, Passa. They did not, however, have any inkling what woman might have been romantically connected with him before his departure on his trip to the high mountains. They were eager to know whom he would pick, who of the present clan would become his newest love interest. Knowing looks were exchanged between Elar and Maa, with raised eyebrows and much shaking of their heads.

Suddenly, as the group sat there, safe and happy in the sunlight of a comfortable day, the earth beneath them began to roll and groan. Oola fell on his side, gasping a little as he could not control what was happening to him, and he could not stand up. Some of the children squealed with fear. Alun, who had been sitting, said later that he felt like a straw doll being thrown aside. All the group sensed, as the shockwave continued to roll them around, that the great earthquake had begun.

CHAPTER
~42~

No one in the group could get up as wave after wave came rolling through their piece of the tundra. Those glancing back could see their huts dancing, some falling as if a giant had smashed them playfully. The whole event had a weird, cock-eyed orientation; the ground played a whimsical game of chance, with many lives at stake. Who was in control? They had no time to consider this question; they could hardly cope with their soaring fears and the relentless antics of their own bodies. It seemed to last for a lifetime, but it really was over in the time it would take to chew up and swallow a piece of caribou meat.

As the ground steadied and each person stood up, Alun and the women checked the group to see if anyone was injured. The children had taken a tumble such as they themselves sometimes initiated; aside from their outsized fears of the moment, they were not really hurt. Alun saw that the women were a bit disarrayed but certainly unhurt also, and he was grateful that no harm had come to those under his leadership. However, the village scene behind them showed huts on their sides and some clan members still on the ground. Furthermore, there might be greater shockwaves coming; this might be just a beginning of the earthquake.

Women were rushing toward their children, who felt the same impulse and hugged their mothers. Then, at Alun's urging, they all ran toward the village to help pull away fragmented huts from victims inside them, or to help anyone who had fallen.

With a great roar, an immense convulsion underneath them dropped them to the ground again. As the horrible sound increased, they traced it to the edge of the tundra in the distance, back toward their former homes in the foothills. As they were being tossed around crazily, some of them saw, far away, the tundra itself begin to rise up to form new hills. The earth was changing itself. The adults knew that deep splits and chasms would accompany the birth of new hills in their terrain. They had been right to leave their caves.

This time the earthquake had delivered its mightiest impulse, and the little group of adults and children were still when the ground stopped moving. There were smudges of dirt on everyone, a lot of bruises and scratches, but no broken bones among them. Instead, their eyes held for a long time that absolute terror that had come upon them as they saw that new row of hills which had risen out of the flat tundra toward their previous home. Nobody had ever seen such a happening before, and they were confounded. They could not take their eyes off the newly shaped horizon. The children's eyes were wide with disbelief and their jaws were slack.

Elar's thoughts were all on the burial cave which must have been close to the upheaval in the distance. Perhaps Tlan would not know that his resting place had been so disrupted, that his final peace had been so loudly and desperately disturbed. Perhaps. She found herself in tears of dismay; then Oola slipped his hand into hers, for his thoughts were similar to those that had caused her to weep. Elar, however, thought of one of Tlan's treasures that had not perished forever; she was thinking of the beautiful rock crystal which she had insisted that Taga keep back for his own use as a shaman to the clan.

CHAPTER ~43~

BEROS APPEARED OUT of the tundra, dazed and bloody, early the next morning. He collapsed as he reached his half-wrecked hut. His wife, Troz, hearing a noise, came out to find him lying unconscious at the threshold. She ran for Taga and Elar; she did not know if he had died or not. Taga, who had been in the camp during the earthquake, had spent the day of the quake helping to clean up and checking on members of the clan who were not accounted for. Beros had been important among the missing. Acting as shaman, Taga helped Troz to get her husband into bed. Before he checked the tall hunter/warrior for wounds, he asked Troz to wash the face, neck and arms, where dirt and blood were caked. It was evident Beros had walked a long distance over the tundra despite serious injuries.

Using a soft rabbit skin dipped in water. Troz uncovered a scalp wound that was severe; then the left shoulder and arm revealed red scraping wounds and a long gash; the right wrist had been broken; across the stomach there was another long gaping gash; both legs showed scratch marks and the small red holes of puncture wounds. It was Taga's guess that Beros had fallen down a cliff onto sharp rocks. They worked quickly while he was still unconscious to set the broken wrist and bind it to a splint of caribou bone. The deeper wounds were washed carefully with a herb potion that Taga concocted, after which they were bound tightly with the edges held close together. Elar helped with a poultice for the smaller wounds when they had been cleansed. The potion and poultices were to ward off infection and to aid in healing. Finally, they saw that he was resting and out of immediate danger. At that point Troz began to cry.

Taga turned to her, saying, "You and Beros have both been lucky, so don't cry. He is a strong, brave man. Beros will soon be all right again."

"I'm crying with relief," she said. 'You don't know how hard it was yesterday when I didn't know where he was or if he was alive. I thought it possible that he had gone back to where his brother Ino was buried, but that was a very dangerous place to be when the earthquake hit us."

When Beros groaned and struggled to rise, Troz quickly and gently held him down, explaining to him where he *was.* Elar brought water for him to sip, saying soothingly, "You have been fortunate, Beros, this time. You look as if you have been in the jaws of the earthquake and have come back to us."

Beros was unable to explain at that time, but he had indeed been to Ino's grave and had just crossed the Circle of Stones to return to the new village when he first felt the ground begin to tremble. Later he was able to tell his story.

"I began to run, but the earth was doing a crazy roll underneath me. Then just ahead of me a small crack appeared as the ground parted. I stared as it grew into a bigger and bigger hole; when I tried to move backward and away, I lost my balance and teetered on the edge of a deep and rocky slope that had not been there before. Then I fell down, down, down." He shuddered.

"I came to after a long time; my body had lodged on a rock that caught me in my fall. It was not night but there was no sunlight around me. I was on a slope of fresh earth and below me I could not see the bottom. I thought of my family who were waiting for me. I almost gave up hope of returning. There seemed no way to get out of that awful place. It was the worst ever!"

Taga cried out, "You are telling us that a huge and deep crack formed in the earth near our Circle of Stones?"

"Wait. Wait. There is more," said Beros. "Yes, a deep, deep chasm opened up about there, yes. But as I clung to the rock that held me on the slope, the earth began to speak in a very low rumble once more. I trembled so that I don't know how I stayed there; it would have been so easy to slide on down into that bottomless split in the earth.

"Then another huge upheaval began. The earth below my rock began to rise up toward me. My heart was in my throat, and I called out a goodbye to my loved ones, because I was sure that I would die." His voice became labored, and he panted at the memory. "I was lifted up like a child's toy while the air around me grew brighter as I came out again at the top of the great hole and kept going up while a mountain grew under me." He looked around as if he did not expect the others to believe him; he hardly believed the story himself.

Taga spoke. "My wife saw a row of hills or mountains rise in the distance."

"I became unconscious at some point; I guess it was all too much for me to bear. When I woke up, I was in pain from all my bruises and a broken hand and some deep cuts, but I was lying on the ground some distance from the new mountain. Actually, there was a whole new chain of hills or mountains that had come up from under the tundra. When I looked around I found that deep hole still there, stretching for a very long distance. Taga, we shall never be able to go back there; the earthquake has barred our way forever."

The others looked dumbfounded; how could this be? But Taga had his own answer to that question; his conscience told him that the attack on the Urkluks had drawn this powerful punishment down on his clan. Suddenly his knees were weak as water.

CHAPTER ~44~

ALUN HAD HEARD part of the story Beros told, and now he had urgent information for Taga. He said, "The women who went for water just now have reported that our stream is drying up. They think the earthquake has blocked it or has diverted its course. I went down to see, and the women were right."

Taga frowned. He was in no mood for further disaster, but it was true that the clan must have a source of good water. "This could get critical soon," he said.

At that moment Gadu entered the hut. Taga understood at once that Gadu was impatient to start tracking the herd – a matter now delayed disastrously by both war and earthquake.

Taga looked as if his load of responsibility had grown too heavy.

Gadu saw the frown of frustration and said, "It's been too long. We have to go now. It will not be easy."

Taga nodded assent to him and then turned toward Alun. "Alun has just told me that our stream is drying up. What do you suggest, Alun?"

Alun hesitated, caught by surprise. Taga usually had all the answers ready. Then he spoke, "Don't you think it is risky to go further out eastward on the tundra if you are looking for water? There are strong rivers and tributaries to the north and northwest."

Taga needed that lead. He was sure as he spoke. "Then the clan must head north at once. Alun, you will lead the Caribou Clan on this move. They have half a day now to pack up and leave. You will go at the head, with Yun guarding the rear and making sure no one is left. Beros must be carried on a litter until he is stronger.

"Gadu, I will go with you and a group of hunter/ warriors." He shook his head and frowned again. "It is not good to divide the clan this way. We must find a camp near water, and also we must go after the herd. And there could be another fight."

And so it was that the Caribou Clan was on the move again. Alun assembled a small group of young men to act as guards and two women to carry Beros' litter. This time more items had to be discarded, but the tough hides that had borne many loads were put into use again to haul household goods. Yun was a tough one-man clean-up operation, and soon all the Caribous were following a trail of stone arrow symbols across the tundra, heading north.

At first they saw only rabbits and birds, but as they entered territory that had rain more consistently, there was grass underfoot. That meant that game like deer could be found more frequently in this steppe-like country. When they camped for the night, two young hunters each caught a deer which had been brought down with their bolas and slings. On the second day they reached a small tributary stream, but it was the plan of Alun to go on to the river that today is known as the Tuul. After allowing a day of rest, Alun brought them to the icy, tumbling Tuul, whose fish he remembered. Although the terrain was hilly, they found trees, lush grass, abundant fish, and sweet water.

It was Elar who expressed for all the emotions of the clan. "Alun, you have brought us from the dangers of the tundra to this land of plenty. We are eating so well that I shall grow fat!" And plump Elar laughed at this joke on herself. She and Alun were standing on the edge of a grove of larch and birch, looking out at the newest camp on a grassy hillside overlooking the rock-strewn river. Children played near the tidy new huts, and at the central gathering area a large banked fire betrayed the roasting venison feast underneath it. This feasting was a daily occurrence, and the local deer were supplemented by a variety of fish each day.

Tuit had become the master of the techniques needed to catch by hand the local trout-like and tasty fish; it took resourcefulness and patience, for the fish were crafty, but Tuit was an unusually skillful hunter. He was growing larger than other boys his age and much stronger. Maa marveled at his prowess and his powerful, tough young body. It was hard for her to find him still so that she could put her arms around him and smooth his dark hair. This restless, active youngster looked amazingly like his father and knew it.

Elar and Osun walked over, and Osun immediately got to the point of questions she had been asking. “Where are Taga and Gadu now? Has anyone heard from them? Did they find the herd?”

CHAPTER ~45~

GADU LED TAGA unerringly right to the spot where he and his men had been attacked by the Urkluks. To verify the location, he found the two graves on the tundra, covered with rocks, where two of his men were buried. Then, wily tracker that he was, he began at once to follow the herd that had been stolen from the Caribou Clan. The herd had been on a stampede, galloping wildly toward the northeast, and there still were plentiful signs along their passage. It was soon evident that the Urkluks had few skills in herding; all they knew was how to stampede a herd so that they could take advantage of the situation. When the ever-widening trail got very difficult, Gadu was beside himself with anger.

"The caribou are spreading out in all directions," he said. "The Urkluks cannot keep the herd together at all. They are too lazy. The trail we are following right now will lead to less than half the animals I used to tend. We are drawing close, and by morning we will see them. Are we ready for the fight?"

That was the very thought that had possessed Taga all day as they pushed for speed on their search across the tundra. What would it be like when they got to the caribou?

Two of the men in his search party had brought their poles, remembering how effective the sharp sticks had been in the earlier battle.

Everyone had brought their slings, too, for these weapons had been good against the cowards.

Taga found that he had two handfuls of brave, sturdy men with good fighting spirit. He did not know how many of the enemy would be with the thinning herd. It was certain that there would be a hot fight, probably amid the spooked caribou. Both sides might be dodging terrible branched horns as well as large stone axes.

Then Gadu called out for everyone to halt. In the lead, he had come upon a campfire, evidently the last one, of the Urkluks. He was examining the carelessly discarded remains of a large caribou eaten for the evening meal. He stood up with a terrible expression on his face and cried, "The fools have slaughtered my lead male. No wonder the herd has dispersed itself so badly; the animals have no leader now." Gadu was in tears and shock.

This news sent a wave of anger through the Caribou men, and they pressed forward. Gadu went at the tip of a formation like an arrow pointing now mostly eastward, and they spread apart as much as three caribou lengths so as to see a wider territory. At dark they huddled close together until the first glimmer of dawn; then they were on the trail as before but faster now. Suddenly Gadu stopped and held up his hand. Swiftly the men gathered around him.

"I see three men ahcad," said Gadu, breathing hard. "The herd is so thin it is hardly worthwhile to gather them. The men right now are together; it seems they are eating another meal. Probably breaking fast this morning. They have not seen us yet. Sit down on the tundra while Taga gives us orders for the fight."

Taga had been racking his brain for a battle plan; he had been working on it for a day and a night. Nothing seemed right except a free-for-all, beat-'em-up, no-holds-barred plan. After all, they greatly outnumbered the Urkluks and could not lose. Gadu proposed that they stoop down while running toward the enemy. He asked for one of the sharp poles to use and was given one. Then Taga gave the word to run into battle!

Crouching, stooping, yet covering ground swiftly, the Caribou warriors were surprisingly close before they were sighted. The Urkluks were too late in getting to their feet, too slow in setting off. Gadu, in the lead, sailed his wooden spear at the bare back of a leaping man who kept glancing behind him. The shaft went through his body and, when he fell heavily, pinned him to the tundra. The other two men went in opposite directions in wild flight. The ping of a slingshot was heard as one went down; a sharp stone had caught him a damaging but not fatal blow on the forehead. As he fell too near a bull caribou already skittishly prancing, he narrowly missed the razor-sharp hooves but sprawled on the turf in a vulnerable position, dazed. Two Caribou men pounced on him, their keen war axes in hand, and they disjointed and hacked him to pieces.

The third man was thin and faster; he soon set a pace that was hard to match, but there was a field of racers with set and angry faces following him, and he could not get away. A Caribou drew near enough to throw his battle axe with good aim, catching one thigh and bringing down the Urkluk. A handful of whooping warriors were on top of him instantly and his end was mercifully quick. His lacerated flesh was attacked again and again as all the warriors wanted a bit of revenge.

It was over on this remote tundra battlefield, except for the tradition the warriors could not forego. They had to chant a deep-throated, animal cry of triumph.

The wildness could have gotten out of hand at that point, but Taga knew that they were all hungry, and he said, "We are heroes. We deserve a caribou feast."

The triumph was a limited one. They had come for the herd, and without the slain leader, the caribou were skittish and uncertain. Gadu discovered soon an acceptable alternate leader of one group, and then he began his techniques of leading, enticing, and managing this leader so as to send his grouping in a northwesterly direction. They all supposed that Alun had led the clan toward the north, and thus the animals would intersect with the clan at some point. Gadu chose three men to stay with him on the tundra and follow the herd.

This freed the warriors to return to their families, and they were restless to leave at once. The tundra covered up the scene of violence all too quickly and soon the wasteland looked empty except for the rough, strong winds.

CHAPTER ~46~

Maa looked pensive as she sat on a flat and rugged gray rock beside the river, sometimes dipping her hand into the clear and icy water. "She is thinking about her husband. We have not heard from him at all," said Elar to Alun. "He does not know how well we are doing, and he is probably worrying about his family right now." She dug a little harder into the hide she was scraping.

Alun looked toward the drooping woman by the river and tried not to betray to Elar's perceptive eyes his deep interest in the wife of Taga. Maa stood out among the women in the Caribou Clan; her beauty and poise had struck him when he first met her, and he found no one else with her warmth and charm. That Maa had been so close to Tlan was another endearing reason that Alun enjoyed her company. He loved to talk about Tlan, for he had learned that Tlan was his real father and he felt bitter regret that his father had died before he got to see him again.

Alun walked down the slope to the river and called out to her, "You must not worry about our warriors; they are strong and brave. Your husband will be here in no time. It's a beautiful day, just right for a walk beside the river. Will you come with me?"

Maa hesitated only a bit; then she uncurled her legs and stood with a graceful motion. Alun caught her hand in his in a naturally friendly way that she could not refuse, and they walked by the river bank toward the merry sounds of children playing and fishing.

Elar glanced up the hill toward the hut of Beros, who was lying outside on a pallet of pine needles with a caribou skin cover. He looked much better, although he had found the trip northward a painful ordeal. Elar had tended him when he could not sleep at night; their temporary camps had little comfort to offer an invalid. Her soothing medicine had helped him; she knew how to use grease from the caribou in a wonderful massage that could reduce scars. Her poultices helped heal the painful, purple bruises; also, her herbal teas were strong enough to help him bear the discomfort of travel.

She rose now and went toward him, "How is my patient today, Beros? For a man who rode a mountain as it rose out of the ground, you look amazingly healthy. Are you getting enough to eat?"

The happy grin Beros had for her was sweet repayment for the care she had given him. He enjoyed her joke about his experience in the earthquake. "Enough? Between the fish and game here, I have been eating constantly. Sula is old enough to bring in birds and squirrels so fast that we are feeding other families on them. She found bramble berries yesterday and before Troz could stop her, she had filled every container in the hut. Now we have berries drying on a hide in the sun, for eating in the winter."

Elar caught sight of Oola running into her hut. "I must find out what my son is up to, Beros. Later I will come back." And she left in a hurry.

Oola almost ran into her as he came bustling out of her hut. He didn't stop but called out, "Tuit says his father is coming. I want to hear the warriors tell their story."

Elar knew where Maa was at that moment, but she did not know whether or not to send for her. The scene at the place where Maa and Alun had halted would not have pleased Taga, so it was well that Elar did not send. Alun had held onto Maa's hand in order to prevent her stumbling on the bank of the river. As they passed the children and went on, he walked closer and the touch of his hand became a light tingle that was new and pleasurable. She grew very aware of his nearness, and under the shade of a spreading tree, he drew her to him. When she would have protested, he simply helped her to sit, and they both leaned back against the thick trunk of the tree, his arm around her companionably. Her emotions somewhat aroused, Maa was reassured when this was as far as he went; he was comforting her and she was permissive to this point. It was soothing to have a man care when she was worried about Taga.

For Alun, this was a moment he had dreamed of, but he could be patient. The green canopy above, the lulling sound of the running water, and the warmth of her body close to him made a perfect setting. He had hoped for more, but for that moment it was enough. Although he had closed his eyes, he was beginning to feel his heart race, and he wondered what Maa was feeling. She was very quiet. But their peace was just then disturbed by the voice of Tuit calling as he ran, "Mother, Mother, the warriors are returning! Father is coming! Mother, where are you?"

They sprang up and Maa needed no help as she ran out first to the river bank and embraced Tuit joyfully. She and her son leaped bushes in their race to be with the heroes who had gone to battle and were returning safe. As she arrived at the camp, she was sobbing with relief and joy, and Alun was forgotten.

CHAPTER
~47~

On days that were cool or colder, Elar had many complaints against the cold wind. She bundled up too much, for her bones felt thin; even incessant cups of hot tea did not soothe her. The alternative was to spend the day languishing on her pallet, as Tlan had done so often. This woman who had been so energetic could not stay in bed, so she forced herself to rise. And complain. Yun and his wife, Lin, were sympathetic; they went to Taga.

Lin said sweetly, "Taga, would it be warmer if we moved toward the east or the south? On mild days she is still full of life, but when she is chilly, arthritis pains her so much. We always felt so bad when Tlan ached in his joints, and Elar's problem is getting worse."

Taga, very moved at Lin's loving plea, promised that he would find a warmer site. "The children and women have found such a wealth of nuts and grapes in the forests here, and the hunting and fishing have fed us well. But the plateau to the east might suit us better, with the caribou herd closer to us. Yun and I will travel there to look it over. We could go at once, Yun. Are you ready?"

They followed the river Tuul as it wound in a giant curve to the south and southeast, then northeast again, and found a campsite near the present-day city of Ulan Bator.

There, close to the stream and its copses of birch, they settled the

Caribou Clan, intending to stay a year.

To help ward off Elar's arthritic pains, a hut within a hut was built especially for her. The double walls kept out most of the chill that afflicted her. Inside her cozy inner hut she sat by the fire most of the winter, her fingers always busy creating useful garments or ornaments.

Oola was six years old and helpful. His warm, loving disposition still endeared him to the whole camp; he was generous and sociable. Older ones of the clan thought he looked much like the old Tzan but without the cruel eyes.

Blun, nearly as old, was precociously adult in her thinking, although she could be a capricious child at times. Both children were attentive to their mother, whose eyes lighted up when they were near.

Beros, completely healed of his wounds during the winter, welcomed the spring with renewed energy and delight in being alive. He felt a special joy in Sula, who was now nearing ten years old. She had inherited her mother Seldun's beauty and was just beginning to blossom. He would not let her marry for a few years, but he knew that she was looking at the young men who were available, and the best of them were too young. She would be desirable and eager to mate before Tuit, Oola, and Tor reached manhood. Beros did not even consider any other young men of the clan. The children of the Great Tzan were noble in appearance and action; she must somehow find for herself a mate who would be her equal in intelligence, distinction of physical beauty, and accomplishment.

As spring lit the hills with trees in bloom and the few cows in the caribou herd dropped their calves, the returning warmth and the freedom from an icy winter brought rejoicing to everyone. Taga, seeing that his clan was once more prospering, felt a lift to his spirits. He had a sudden longing for adventure. Gazing toward the northern mountains in the distance, shimmering in a mist that sunset turned into a ruddy cloud, he daydreamed. A voice at his elbow put into words his vague desires.

"It is said that the ancient, giant lake or inland sea to the north holds many wonders. One of them is the nerpa, a graceful silver seal that dives deeper than any other. I saw a woman wearing a silver cloak made of those skins, and her hair was also silver. It was unforgettable."

Taga turned, his fancy caught by the vision. Alun went on; he was once more telling his adventures. "There is also a little, oily fish that is transparent; it has no scales. You can only catch it at night, using a torch, or when storms wash them up on the shore. The oil in these fish is valuable as a medicine; it is a miraculous healer. I think it would be exactly what Elar needs." He ceased because Taga was captured by the idea of the little fish that healed. He had tried his spells and potions on Elar, but both he and Tlan had known that arthritis did not yield to spells. Taga's eyes spoke for him as a purpose dawned; he did not speak aloud and Alun moved away.

"But Alun has been there and has seen the miraculous tiny fish that would cure Elar. I would like to have oil from the little fish in my medicine bag, too, for others. It would be the adventure of a lifetime, and with a great purpose." Taga was pleading his case to his wife. Maa did not welcome such an absence; the thought filled her with dread. She did not know exactly why it made her fearful, but she did not want him to leave.

"How long would you be gone, and who would go with you?" She was trying to be practical and reasonable, but she inwardly felt terror, wild terror.

"A moon would be long enough; it is not a short journey. Beros would be pleased to undertake such a trip, I think; maybe he would suggest one or two companions. I will go to his hut now and talk."

As Maa supposed, Taga had omitted Alun from the list of companions because Alun would serve as leader of the clan while Taga was gone. Her inner terror turned to deep certainty that she could not handle the situation she would face shortly.

The four men started out on a frosty morning, wearing their travel furs; they would shed clothing as the day warmed up. Taga and Beros were in the lead, tall and bulky, followed by Arko and Buna, who were experienced warrior/hunters. Arko was short, tough and taciturn, a good marksman with the sling. Buna was sociable and talkative; he was young and unmarried as yet; he was very knowledgeable about animals, and Gadu was his father.

The men carried a kind of snow shoes to enable them to walk on top of snow as they traveled through the mountains ahead of them. Their packs were full of good dried meat and their hearts were light. It was a good beginning to a long vacation.

They headed due north for the first leg of their trip, for the ancient lake lay in that direction. Soon they had found the well-used migration trail animals had tramped out during millennia of seasonal movement. Since the bison and mammoth, the musk-ox and caribou all chose the easiest and most common-sense path through rugged terrain, it was good to find they could jog along at an easy pace on this trail.

Their destination was the lake called today Lake Baikal in modern Russia; it was formed because of movement of the earth's crust and the tension is still great enough today to cause 2,000 tremors each year in the region. Older people in the area have heard their families tell of a huge earthquake of the 19h century that reached magnitude 11, and in 1959 an earthquake occurred of magnitude 9.

This great stone bowl is nearly 400 miles long and 50 miles wide, big enough to hold a fourth of all the fresh water on this earth. It is at least 25 million years old. Some species of its teeming wildlife are unique to this lake due to its extreme depth and its age. It is today a mecca for tourists, scientists, and vacationers.

In the camp of the Caribou Clan by the Tuul, Alun kept the daily life running smoothly. Few problems were expected, especially as weather warmed up. Maa forgot her unease and spent much time with her two sons and with Elar. Tuit and Tor both excelled athletically, and their enthusiasms were exciting to their mother, whether the moments were spent in competing with the slingshot or discovering a lame songbird that let them nurse her back to flight condition. There was so much for them to learn about the natural world, and Maa learned also by being with them as they discovered. One week their hut had a marsh crane whose wing flapping was simply intolerable in the small space, but the boys were learning at first hand to know a fellow creature of singular beauty while its splinted wing and leg healed. When one session of violent protest by the bird resulted in the loss of several white and gray feathers, the boys actually studied the structure of the feathers. Then, when Alun found them sitting in front of the hut comparing the feathers, he spent a long while with them, looking at all the different kinds of feathers on their crane. Maa, too, became part of the learning as she helped to soothe the crane's restlessness at this inquiry.

CHAPTER ~48~

Day after lovely day passed with clear and moderate weather. Maa told herself that each day must be enjoyed before the hot winds and drought came. She loved spending time outdoors, and there were hills and small lakes near the camp that she had wanted to explore. The women always had a special purpose for such exploring: berry patches needed to be remembered; good sites for various roots must be revisited later, and edible plants might be picked at once while they were tender.

On a day when her sons were helping to build a new gathering place for the clan, Maa took a pine needle basket made by Elar and crossed a low hill to the south; she knew that there was a small lake there and its moisture would have made leafy plants and roots grow better. The view was pretty; the greenery around the lake included bushes and edible plants. She filled her basket and set it down, then found a spot to sit where she could look down into the clear and still water. Her musing was mostly about Taga. Where was he now on his journey? How long would it be before he got back? She worried a little about his safety, but today she did not feel any special loneliness without him.

Somehow it did not surprise her greatly when Alun appeared over the hill; he seemed to look into the distance as if searching for something. Then he saw her and with a smile walked toward her. She smiled at him in a completely natural way, willing to share the lovely lake and the sun.

She remained quiet, for the sun had flooded her senses and made her torpid, while the water mesmerized her. He sat down by her in a companionable silence, amused at her sleepy eyes. As the silence continued, he realized with a little shock how she had grown used to his being around her, near her and her sons. He said nothing, but seeing her nodding head, he moved a bit closer and cradled her head on his shoulder; her eyes closed and she dozed off. It was very natural and very comfortable for them both. He wondered if she was completely aware of the situation; *was* she feigning sleep? He kissed her cheek softly and realized that she was really asleep, a dead weight on his arm. Probably had lain awake at night worrying about her husband. He kissed her cheek again.

She turned her head drowsily toward him; he instinctively kissed her full on the lips and felt her kiss him back warmly but not passionately. It was his moment and he was afire with the possibilities.

She closed her eyes again dreamily, with a smile. He slowly leaned back with her until they were lying together with his arms around her, the opulent curve of her breast against his arm. He bent to kiss her lips again, with longing; then he softly kissed her neck and her ears. His lips were tasting a nipple when she awoke to the sensation of his body pinning her down while he buried his head in her breast with a shudder of exquisite pleasure. Her own body was tingling with a new delight, a different need to satisfy this man who was so loving, who had no other woman but who had chosen her. That was the terror she had felt – that she would not push him away if it happened.

His gentle hands brushed her stomach and her thighs, while new thrills shook her body. He wondered that she was yielding so completely, that suddenly he could do whatever he wished. He covered her face with kisses, then her body, while she yearned for more of this intense sweetness. She could only press into him, beseeching him to continue his caresses and to make her his.

Afterward, when he lay across her body, he could not stop kissing and caressing her. He felt that he would be forever hungry for her, for the feel of her soft flesh. She put a finger to his lips. She had been away too long and must return to her family.

She answered unspoken questions when she said slowly, "Taga must not know. I love him with all my heart. Go."

She made him leave her by the lake to ponder what had happened. But her inner turmoil did not exceed the vigor of the new emotions she felt. She was a new woman, with a new range of existence, responsible for her actions but aware that she could not have helped doing what she had done. When Alun offered his love, she could not have refused him. But she wished that Taga were at home.

CHAPTER ~49~

On his return from the ancient lake, Taga was renewed in spirit. The time away from pressing responsibilities had been as good for him as the exercise of mountain travel. He was fit and leaner than he had been; he looked wonderfully alive and handsome.

Among the many gifts he had brought back with him was a cloak for Elar made of silver sealskin. It matched her hair and made her look distinguished. The gift was incomparable. But for her he had another: the oil of a tiny fish that would cure her arthritis. She began applications at once, with strong faith in its powers, and she soon felt that the miracle had worked for her. She rubbed it on her skin each morning and night and drank it; immediately it made her skin younger and softer as it eased all pains. To the gratification of Taga, she told everyone about the miracle fish oil and how Taga had brought it to her.

Beros, Arko and Buna were happy to return home. For young Buna this trip had meant the chance to study wildlife that could be found nowhere else. His enthusiasm was immense, and Gadu took great pride in his son. He reminded Taga that Buna was the grandson of a shaman and thus had much intelligence and some education.

Gadu had returned to the village to report that out on the tundra there had been disturbing evidence that someone was pursuing his herd again. It was not an animal. He was certain on that point. He was almost sure it was an Urkluk, someone still alive and now an enemy with revenge on his mind.

Taga asked Beros if he would lead a small party to accompany Gadu back to the herd and investigate the problem. Although the herd was small, the clan depended on being able to have this source of food and clothing; it was the herd that had helped them survive on the tundra. Thus it was important to make sure that the herd was safe, as well as the men who tended it.

Gadu and Beros led the party out in the early morning. Some of the men who had fought the Urkluks twice already were hard-faced and grim.

Taga advised the camp that everyone should be cautious because it might be that a dangerous enemy was near the camp. When he said that it might be an Urkluk, there was a gasp from Olun.

On his recent trip, Taga had talked with strangers who also were going to visit the ancient lake, and he realized that many people chose not to live on the tundra. The Caribou Clan admired the surroundings of the camp on the Tuul River, and they had liked their first camp on the same river, where they were on the edge of a forest. When fresh water and plentiful game and fish were available, life was less complicated and there was time for a better quality of life.

This led him to think deeply about an idea he had first thought of after the great tornado. Why not move toward the east? There were rivers and grasslands to provide a new and rich environment. And now that Gadu thought there was an enemy lurking about the herd, Taga had another reason to wish to try a new location where they would be safe.

He asked Alun, Elar, Yun, and Maa to talk with him about this matter. Alun agreed that the land far to the east, beyond the tundra, was a rich and well-watered, though more rugged, terrain. Elar was too old for a change in her surroundings and kept quiet. Yun liked the prospects for the young people in the clan. Maa agreed with Yun that there were many young people who would soon become adults and they might find a better life.

Nothing was decided, but Taga felt free to look into this matter. At least they would get away from the enemy that Gadu had talked about. Taga had led his clan in two battles against this enemy, both of them cruel, merciless encounters. His conscience had been sharpened by his wife's opinion of the Urkluk massacre; she held him responsible for the killing of the wives and children. He did not want to have to explain another killing that made the clan safe.

For half a moon the clan was uneasy, waiting to hear from Gadu or the party led by Beros. Then one evening Beros strode in. He had bad news.

At night a lone enemy had stalked the herd of caribou and Gadu, alerted, had discovered him; in a desperate fight Gadu had been killed. At once Beros and his men had tracked the fleeing killer and had found him; the last of the Urkluk Clan then met a brutal death. Beros brought the body of Gadu back for burial as a hero.

CHAPTER
~50~

BUNA, SON OF Gadu, was seated by the fire in Taga's hut, discussing with the shaman the matter of his father's burial rites. There was little time, because the body had to be buried at once; he was a hero and deserved honor.

Taga said, "Your father could not ever be replaced, Buna; his attentiveness to duty and his love for the caribou were both remarkable; no one has ever known so much about animals before this. The clan feels the great loss we have suffered in his death. As a friend, I wish to tell you that I feel personal sorrow that you have lost your father. Your mother has been dead for some time. You are single. You have no sister or brother, as I recall. Please know that you can turn to me and my family at any time.

"The burial ceremony will be in our new gathering place at sunset today. We shall bury him beside the little lake in the next valley, just over the hill. It is a pretty place to rest."

Buna was still overcome by the tragedy of his loss. He spoke in low tones. "I used to spend all my time out on the tundra beside my father, but he felt I was missing some of the training of a hunter and warrior, so lately I have lived here at the camp. My trip with you to the ancient lake was my first great chance to prove myself as a man."

At that moment a young girl stood at the door of the hut, hesitant.

It was Sula, daughter of Beros, her head held high as usual. Despite her tumbled hair, her fresh morning beauty was disarming.

"My father has sent me to say that the burial site is ready, over by the small lake." Her eyes flashed as she took note of the young man.

Taga stood and walked over. "And he has sent his message by his beautiful daughter. Buna, you know Sula, don't you? She is the daughter of Beros and Troz. She has a great love for birds and animals." Taga turned to her. "Sula, he has learned about animals from his father's great knowledge."

The young man was red-faced but interested, so he spoke. "Gadu was my father. The burial is for him."

She was a little breathless. "I am sorry you have lost him. He was a real hero. I must go." And she left with a little flurry.

Taga felt that something unusual had just happened. Was Buna interested in the daughter of Beros?

"Buna, Sula's real father was the Great Tzan. Did you know? Her beautiful eyes come from her mother, who was lost in the great tornado." He paused. "She is still very young."

The young man found it hard to respond, and he tried to stammer out some appropriate thanks and a goodbye so that he could escape in confusion.

Taga's attention was soon entirely on the ceremony he would lead and the preparations for it. He found the shaman's drum, the rattle, a mask, the flute and set them before him.

CHAPTER
~51~

As the sun was low on the horizon, the clan began to drift toward the sound of the flute and drum just now starting their duet. Taga, with his flute, and Yun, on the drum, both wore tall painted masks and had red ocher, stripes in slanted parallel marks on their arms and bodies. A fire burned before them, defining an area for the performers that distanced them.

As shadows made outlying areas mysterious, the fire sparked and crackled while the masked figures grew more eerie and the music filled the gathering area – the familiar pattern of three notes up and one note back. The plaintive flute was hypnotic, and so was the drum's hollow, steady beat.

From the darkness behind the fire the clear, sweet voice of a young girl rose in a song without words, an elegy she made up as she went, in harmony with the flute but with an ever-changing, floating melody. It was so lovely and sad that the clan was electrified. She drew out the sorrow and let it soar over them, swelling and ebbing in waves of fullness and softness. After a long while a man's voice joined hers, a throbbing baritone that echoed the deep tone of the drum. Each singer was telling a separate grief, so they did not have the same melody and neither had words, but their emotion spoke eloquently to those who listened raptly.

The soprano voice ceased, then after a while the flute stopped; then the man's deep voice was gone, and only the drum's beat continued. Taga moved out of the shadows and into the light of the fire. With dignity and skill, he slowly danced the pantomime that revealed the life of Gadu: descendant of a shaman, great leader of the caribou herd, lover of all animals, companion of the caribou lead male that was slaughtered by the Urkluk, great warrior/ hunter, father of Buna. As Taga sat down, the drum ceased, and the members of the clan were silent, thinking about the life of Gadu and offering their grief.

A rattle sounded. A stretcher with pallet was brought in and set before the fire; Gadu lay on it: the red slashes on his body and one gaping red hole by his heart showed how he had died valiantly. To an eerie rattle, Taga went to sift red ocher dust into the eyes, nose, mouth and ears, then tossed the rest of the powder upon the body. He made a show of Gadu's spirit escaping the earthly body and soaring above, higher and higher, with the rattle sounding.

Taga turned to the clan and asked, "Who gives food for Gadu to eat in the afterlife?" The response was large; it took a long time to receive all the packets of food and put them near Gadu's head on the pallet. Taga asked, "Who brings weapons to guard Gadu in the afterlife?" It was Buna who brought the first large battle axe, which was placed by the right hand of the body; then many warriors brought axes, almost too many for the pallet.

Now the warriors who had brought axes were given torches and, as the pallet was raised by those who had brought it in, they formed a line on each side of the body to accompany it to the grave site. Taga symbolically stamped on the fire to put it out, and the stern, silent procession began.

Taga led them over the small hill, with the members of the clan following. Near the lake was a shallow grave, and into it the pallet was lowered. The men with torches stood on each side to light the event, but it was simple: dirt and stones were shoved over the body, then a small cairn of stones was built up over the burial site to protect it from wild animals. When it was finished, and the burial had been witnessed by all the clan, there was a general movement to disperse. A feast was waiting for them back at the new gathering place, so they did not linger.

CHAPTER
~51~

An unease came with the burial; clan members looked over their shoulders. Was there another Urkluk who might bring danger again? Life with plentiful fish and game was not enough; they had to find a place where everyone felt safer. After this winter, they might seek another home.

Taga sat by his fire with the large crystal quartz stone in his hand, hoping to find guidance from the spirit world. He had Yun beat softly on the drum with a steady beat to induce a trance, but he remained fully awake and even more alert. When he tried to make his mind blank, he always found his own troubled conscience within. He found no easy passage to the spirit world.

He paid visits to the grave of Gadu, who was a link to the Urkluks through his death. Since Gadu had been the son of a shaman, Taga felt that Gadu might speak to him with wisdom, as Tlan had done right after dying.

One afternoon he had been to Gadu's grave and then found a spot to sit gazing into the clear water of the lake. After a while in the sun he curled up and fell asleep. He had nodded off when he awoke to find a woman standing over him – his wife. He did not understand why she seemed so bewildered and in tears at finding him there.

Maa, from the top of the hill, had seen a man's back by the lake; she had assumed that it was Alun. When she ran breathlessly down the hill, her heart began to race at the memory of being with Alun. But tears of sharp disappointment sprang to her eyes when she reached Taga sprawled on a bit of grass behind some bushes, almost in the very place where she had been with Alun.

The tears did not last, because she realized that this could have been a disastrous day for her. She had been naive in the first place to yield to Alun; Taga was so faithful, and she loved him for the great man he was. As the wife of the clan leader and shaman, she must never again be unworthy of his trust.

Taga, unaware Taga, smiled and opened his arms to her. Hiding her confusion, she slipped down beside him and told him to go back to sleep. He put his head in her lap and he did sleep soundly.

The winter came fast, with deep snows and heavy ice. In her double hut, Elar was safe from the fierce winds that swept in polar cold. Except for the discomfort caused by the extremes of weather, the clan was in good spirits. Ice fishing at several lakes was good fun for the young and old; it was a new sport for many of the clan.

Sula reported to her close friend Buna that she had seen the first ptarmigan in its white feathers instead of its summer brown; its brilliant red crest stood out well against a background of snow. Buna, having done some bird trapping recently, agreed. They were together a lot of the time and found much in common.

Taga said to Beros, "Buna would make a good mate for your daughter. They are well-matched. He is the grandson of a shaman. It is better that he is not descended from Tzan. I like his friendliness, but he has a serious, mature side."

When Beros gave his approval, Buna moved into the hut of Beros and Troz, for Sula had dazzled her parents with her happiness. At once the two men began to enlarge the hut, where the family was somewhat too cozy when snows shut them in.

Taga, battling the worst of the ice, saw his future clearly as he observed the frozen world. The clan needed to find a path to the east and to a better climate in the sun.

CHAPTER ~53~

Making the rounds of the huts to see that everyone was healthy, Taga spent time in home after home where crying babies and complaining women created noisy confusion. When he came to the hut of Arko, he found a relaxed couple busy with handiwork by the light of the firehole in their roof and the embers of a dwindling fire. It was quiet.

He and Arko spent time remembering details of their journey to the northern lake, while Arko's wife listened avidly. Losun had pride in her husband's ability, and that trip had been his distinctive contribution to the clan. He was a well-traveled man now.

Arko had a reserve of common-sense, and during the conversation he remarked that when the ice on the river broke up, that would herald tremendous melting in the many mountain streams that fed into this one. The result would be widespread flooding, which would interfere with the hunting just as the weather warmed up. Taga recognized the value of this knowledge and promised the couple that he would heed their warning.

His next visit was to Alun, who agreed that Arko's advice was good; the Caribou Clan needed to avoid any flood basin that could be dangerous to them.

Within a few days Taga had asked a group consisting of Arko, Alun,

Yun, and Beros to make at least one day's journey eastward to find the next campsite for the Caribou Clan. They set out at once and after only half a day had found a setting they liked. It had pure, sweet water available and a sizeable forest nearby, and it was on a raised plateau overlooking the valleys that would flood.

They were barely able to get all their household goods to the site and begin the new village when very early and cold rains began. They were miserable until huts were all built and made sound. But thanks to the astuteness of Arko, the clan had escaped a devastating flood that caught many wild animals in raging waters choked with debris.

Taga praised Arko as he spoke to the clan in the small grassy clearing between the forest and the huts. The clan was no longer having big feasts because they had left their caribou herd behind. The rough terrain made it difficult to herd the animals, so they left the animals with three families that deserted them to stay at their camp on the Tuul River. Some of the Caribou Clan had had enough moving.

But Taga was now determined to continue to go eastward, far to the east. Alun, who had been to the east as far as the Great Water, gave encouragement to the idea.

As he addressed the clan, Taga put it this way: "We have an opportunity to find a new kind of life. We have left behind the life of the tundra, and our caribou are gone. You enjoyed life in the two camps beside the Tuul River, with flavorful fish from its cold waters and plenty of game for the hunters. But the winters were too harsh for us there, and we ran from a mighty flood. Let us take heart now and explore the land in front of us as we head toward the promises of the rising sun."

All the young people of the clan were enthusiastic about this compelling new view of the future. It was not surprising that the oldest men and women shook their heads in disagreement and dreaded the struggle that traveling meant for them.

The clan rested and hunted for a moon while the forest trees budded and bloomed, birds built their nests and sang about it, and other forest creatures sought to protect their newest offspring.

Taga sent out a party to find another site for a rest camp, and they chose a place that is the present city of Ondorhaan on the Kerulen River in Mongolia. The advance party sent a messenger/guide back and then built some temporary huts to welcome the clan when it arrived. This journey would not be too long or hard, but it established a pattern for the future wandering of the Caribou Clan.

After a moon of rest, the clan agreed to make the new journey, which was not too demanding and led by the Moron River for most of the way. They found perfect spring weather all the time and were on tundra most of the way. They were pleased to find huts already standing at the new camp.

While the clan rested, a new team of explorers was sent on ahead to find the next encampment site. They headed straight across the tundra to a range of mountains to the southeast. They discovered a pass through the mountainous country and two delicious lakes along the trail. Their camp was set up north of the present city of Buyant, near the foothills of the mountains. Again, they put up huts prior to the arrival of the clan.

The next advance group left Buyant and emerged from the mountains and hills to find themselves again on tundra, with sand dunes to their south. The way they chose, then, was a northeastern arc skirting the edge of the mountains encircling the area. It was a lonely trail.

The terrain became of great concern to Taga as they went through another pass and went by the area where today the modern cities of Dong Ujimqin Qi and Xi Ujimqin Qi are found, both a part of today's China. They followed a river now called Qagan Moron as it joined a larger one now known as Xar Moron into foothills and more mountains. To the south of this river were more sand dunes, so they took a route on its northern side until they arrived at the site of the present-day Chinese city of Dalin. It had been a rugged, mountainous trek, so Taga called a halt for rest and preparation for the coming winter.

More and more often Maa found that the man who walked beside her was not her husband; it was Alun, whose entertaining conversation made the walking easier for both of them. He was such good company that often Tor, who did not leave his mother much on the trail, was nearby, listening. Taga took notice but trusted his wife implicitly and took care not to show any jealousy. It had not occurred to him that Maa *was* appealing in the eyes of another man.

The advance party had discovered a grassy sward, and the river nearby was excellent for fishing. The hunters saw that the forests would hold many small deer. The clan had grown used to teepee-like huts that were easy to put up, for they consisted of a few poles joined at the top and covered with hides. The little temporary village each time was planned by Taga the same; this way the clan felt at home no matter where the camp was.

Little boys stamped down the grass around the huts and brought the women fresh-smelling pine branches to lay on the floors. In the afternoon Alun recruited children to help him catch the frisky fish in the cold stream; they found that they could indeed catch them in their hands and toss them out onto the sloping banks. They soon returned pleased with themselves because they had caught enough fish for all the clan to enjoy.

A group of women had found lots of edible roots in boggy areas near the river. Reeds were plentiful also, and they cut tall ones and began to weave them into buckets in which to steam both fish and vegetable roots. Troz, wife of Beros, was the teacher for this activity; coming from another clan, she had witnessed such cooking in her youth.

Tuit and Tor did some exploring of their own on the edge of the forest and found wild fruit. Their mouths were stained and they were nearly sated with the luscious fruit before they thought of the coming feast; then they ran back for a skin to fill so that everyone might enjoy this treat.

Beros emerged from the forest with a grin of triumph, and the four men who followed him carried two handsome buck deer. A cry went up from men and children who had gathered around fires in the common ground in the middle of the camp. It was impressive that members of the clan had assembled a good feast to celebrate their arrival.

There was some entertainment planned to follow the feasting. With their stomachs achingly full of fresh, wholesome food, everyone lingered around the fires with a great sense of companionship, relaxed and gregarious. Yun brought out his drum and Taga had his flute, to which they added the clear, birdlike voice of Blun, who created a melody without words, half humming, sometimes trilling. The music was harmonious, so pleasing that the clan wanted it to go on forever. The beautiful girl who danced before them and sang with infinite poise and grace created a kind of spell, so that after a long time of listening with deep appreciation, someone began to hum along. Others joined. Then everyone hummed wordlessly, anticipating the short melodic runs of the flute or the girl's voice. Men added deep tones to the lighter sounds of women and children. The world around the fires vibrated with the soothing sounds, and the hearts of the singers were joined to each other in a magical and happy moment.

Suddenly there was a shriek from a child near the edge of the crowd. Those near her turned to see a little girl dart forward to the safety of her mother. Behind the place where the child had stood was a row of strange people, all transfixed by the beautiful music. They did not leave. They apparently were waiting for more music. For a time the Caribou Clan faced the strangers, staring at them; the strangers were appraising the Caribous.

Their skin was bronzed by the sun of the summer that was passing, and they, too, wore the short, supple deerskin garments of early autumn.

They were well-built and beautiful people. One woman held a suckling baby; beside her was an older man; two young girls looked to be about twelve years old. Their sparkling, coal-black eyes were inquisitive.

The warrior/hunters who had stirred restlessly at first were apparently reassured that this group of strangers meant no harm. They had enjoyed the music.

Taga took the initiative and advanced toward them, threading his way among the clan members. When he asked, “Did you like our music?” they smiled but did not understand his words. He gestured for them to come and sit down by the fires of the Caribou, and this they did, without fear. The two girls of the strangers chose to sit by Blum, while the older man was seated between Alun and Taga. Maa was pleased to sit beside the young mother and child.

At first their communication was mostly through smiles, but as they exchanged first names, the staccato accents of the strangers grew more intelligible, and the men, especially, found it possible to comprehend some words.

Taga explained to the older man, Dong, that the Caribou clan was traveling east, toward the rising sun. They had come from the tundras far to the west after they had experienced a disastrous earthquake. Dong and his family had lived here by the river all their lives; his extended family here was numerous and they were spread out along the rivers.

The young girls were joined by Caribou youngsters, and twittering conversation arose easily. Blun soon was introducing Miti and Panni to others; obviously, real friendships were starting.

Taga felt expansive; he liked their new acquaintances and thought it would be useful to know them. He was pleased with the camp site and the resources of the area. He resolved to make this camp ready for the winter and to remain at least six moons for all to rest.

CHAPTER ~54~

ELAR, DURING THAT winter, was often sick. Yun and Taga both paid her much attention, but she herself declared that she was just growing old, too old for journeying. Oola was a great source of satisfaction, for his genial disposition made his household always pleasant. He had inherited good height and muscular stature, but he did carry a lot of weight. He was very handsome, another family trait, and this made him popular with the girls. He had a wonderful gift of talking and could persuade others to see things his way in life.

Taga thought about Oola's deep love for his adoptive mother and was worried because Elar seemed to be waning, and Oola would be devastated to see the woman who was the center of his life pass away. Yun would continue to take care of Oola, but life would never be the same for him.

Blun was older by at least two years; she was adept at cooking and housekeeping, so that Elar no longer had to work hard. Blun's love of music was a source of pleasure to her family, especially to Elar. Blun had made her own flute and often played it; Tlan had taught her, and they had made music together to the delight of Elar. When Blun began to sing her birdlike songs, the family was entranced; she was truly gifted.

When Blun saw Troz weaving baskets in which to cook vegetables and fish, Blun was enchanted and practiced the art of making baskets because there were lots of reeds growing near. She thought that she might make one that was water-tight; it would be so much lighter than the hides used to carry water. Maa, on seeing Blun's work, was pleased to show it off to the other women. Not everyone was successful at making a basket for carrying water and other liquids, but Blun blushed with pride over her achievement and made baskets at a furious rate as the weather grew warmer.

The native family who had joined them at the feast became good and helpful friends to the Caribou Clan. Miti and Panni were about the age of Blun, and the three were almost inseparable. Blun, visiting in their home, gained insight into the plentiful sources of food in the area. When the native girls gathered a type of crayfish from the smaller streams, Blun observed their method of preparing and cooking.

Taga was in conversation with Dong near the river and casually asked, "Whenever we leave in the spring, if we wish to follow this river, where will it lead us?"

Dong was at once full of enthusiasm about his native river and talked about it for a long time. "This river is very long," he said. "It travels all the way down to a bay which is connected to the Big Waters of the World. To the south this river accumulates many other rivers into it and also, as it nears the Big Water, forms many mouths, like a snake with many heads. In some seasons the mud makes travel by land very hard."

Taga had heard only Tlan and Alun speak of the Big Water to the east. He was intrigued to learn how Dong's relatives loved the environment on and by the river; they depended on the water for existence. They worshipped the river and had learned to "ride upon it" on rafts made of reeds they gathered beside the water. Just as the women had learned to weave reeds and rushes into baskets, the men had learned to weave together platforms that were water-tight so that they could ride upon them. Taga was eager to see these rafts, for his people had never heard of riding upon the water.

Following a wide path along the river bank, Taga and Dong arrived at a reed boat not far away. Dong's brother Koo, his wife, and many children with shiny black hair and bright eyes lived here in a house made of reeds tied together. Not wasting time, Dong led Taga to Koo's reed raft by the shore and motioned for them to get on the raft. He picked up two poles lying near; then Dong and Koo easily boarded the thickly woven craft. Taga, however, found it difficult to climb onto the raft because he did not trust it to hold them all up above the water.

He finally succeeded without tipping over the raft, and he imitated Dong by sitting down in the middle, while Koo took one pole and stood near the far end. Koo pushed the raft out into the stream by using his pole, and then he used it to guide the raft down the river.

Taga was fearful but thrilled as he soared upon the current at midstream, safe on the thickly woven and buoyant reed raft. They went only a short way down the river; then Koo handed one pole to his brother, and the two poled the raft back upstream against the current. They stayed fairly close to the bank and used the poles to push the raft along.

Taga wanted to know more and examined the craft with care. He discussed the skill required to operate the raft safely. He felt as if a new world had been opened before him and his clan. The experience of traveling freely and safely atop the river was exhilarating. When he returned to his clan, he could hardly speak because what he had experienced was so important.

To Alun and Tuit, he soon began to gush with great enthusiasm for this easy method of traveling. "You sit down upon this raft made of woven reeds, and the strong current of the river sweeps you along faster and faster. I have never gone so fast except when in an out-of-body experience. And this *was* like that."

When they smiled at his energetic description, he went on. "I could hardly believe what was happening to me. Just think. We could perhaps load our heavy supplies upon a raft and with almost no work get them to a place far downstream."

Tuit was excited, but he saw the problem ahead. "Some of our old people would never agree to ride upon the water. They would be terrified. They will insist upon walking with their feet upon firm ground." He spoke vehemently, but he wished it were otherwise. Tuit would be the most eager of them all to ride upon the rafts.

CHAPTER ~55~

THE WINTER WAS moist and cold, with a dampness that Elar felt to the bone. She longed for the dry, hard cold of her home on the tundra. She even felt homesick for the strong pulse of the winds forever blowing across the Gobi. There was a lot of snow, more than she had ever experienced and lasting for so long a period. Elar was often too ill to leave her pallet of skins. It was a winter of pain.

Dong explained that snow was important to the river. He said, "When the snow melts, all the streams might flood overnight, perhaps faster than that, and without warning. You must move your camp to higher ground. The area all around your camp might come to look like a great inland sea in the season of the floods. The mud of such a season will make walking so hazardous that you cannot begin a journey until the ground has dried up. Rafting will be dangerous because of the swirling eddies and floating debris in the river."

Taga took note and understood that they must decide where they would be safe during the floods. Also, they must be prepared to stay longer near this site on the river.

The young people of the Caribou Clan enjoyed visiting the native youths, with the result that two marriages were made before the winter ended. Taga worried about losing two young and promising warrior/hunters. The native girls discussed with their fathers the question of whether their husbands must remain with the river clan. The result was that Yin and her husband, Buno of the Caribou Clan, planned to stay with her parents, and he would learn all the skills of the river people. Lira and her husband, Biron of the Caribou Clan, wanted to go with the Caribou Clan when they left in the spring.

A group of young men, led by Yun, made rafts of reeds during the winter and learned to navigate them when the river was not frozen over. Four rafts were made ready to carry loads and passengers down the river to the place chosen each day for the night's camp. They were not large rafts, but with Dong's help they were made thick and strong.

When the spring floods began, the Caribou Clan were really not prepared to see how the spreading waters made the world so different. Dong had gone to his family's annual spring ceremony. His parents, brother, and cousins would greet the god of the river; they would try to appease their god, perhaps even by a sacrifice. The flood waters would then subside, leaving a fertile region with blossoming fruit trees and berries as well as lush root plants and the fat fish on which their clan depended.

Taga had earlier chosen a hillside beyond a small forest, but the move had not yet been made when the clan awoke to find water rising to their doorways. In a riotous, hasty flurry of packing up and getting to higher ground, some belongings were left, but no lives were lost. For a brief while Taga thought that Bumo and his bride, Yin, were missing, but his family reported that the pair had gone with Dong to the spring ceremony of the river people. Bumo's precise description of the three days of worship of the river god became a part of the stories and legends later retold around the clan campfires.

The flood vanished and the river became quiet; the weather grew mild; the forests were full of birdsong and flowering trees. Taga urged his clan to choose the heaviest household packages and bring them to the rafts, where eager young men were ready to oversee the loading. Only a few passengers were allowed for the first day of their journey.

Previously Alun and the clan's raftsmen had explored downstream and had found at least two camp sites they liked, so that two days of their travel were planned well. While the heaviest loads were on the rafts, the clan still walked beside the river on the well-defined path made by the river people. Good weather made the travel delightful, and when the raftsmen had pushed off with their loaded rafts, Taga led his clan south along the river that is today called the Liao River, toward the Bay of Korea.

During the summer they came near the mouth of the river. Scouts sent ahead reported marshlands which could not be navigated very well on foot, so Taga took the advice of Lira, the bride of Biron, and led the clan across the isthmus in an easterly direction. They were on a land route, so the raftsmen portaged their rafts, and householders assumed their heaviest burdens again.

They came out onto the great open area of the bay on the other side of the isthmus and were astonished to see how broad and clear the seashore was. Lira had visited this beach once before with her family, and now she showed them the wonderful shellfish from the rich waters of the bay. At an estuary to the south the men brought out of the tidal flats a variety of oysters, clams and crabs; using the rafts in deeper water, they netted shrimp. She showed them how to dive for scallops. The men had already discovered by this time how to bring in the curious fish called the flounder, which has its two eyes on one side of its head and is found in salt water. Sea trout and many other small and large fish were plentiful in the bay. When the men and boys assembled an exotic array of fish and shellfish, Lira taught the women how to cook them lightly to keep the flavors. As the women worked, Lira kept on describing dishes that could be prepared from these riches from the sea.

The Caribou Clan enjoyed this new diet so much that during the summer they circled the Korea Bay, never far from the cooling breezes and easy walking of the shoreline. The members of the clan were in awe of the new beauties they found in the landscape that was swept by salty breezes; cedar trees were wizened and stunted, and they bent away from the incessant wind, but they were wonderful in their beauty. Rock formations that punctuated the beach were indescribably picturesque. Women found on the beach shells of great beauty that had been washed up by storms, and these became prized because Taga and other men bored holes in them and made necklaces. Soon both men and women wore seashells around their necks. The children were more taken with the pebbles and small stones that were strewn on the shore: black, smooth and shiny, they were the product of centuries of the tumbling and rasping motion of the ocean.

They had reached a point on the western side of the long peninsula that is in the modern world called Korea, when a cloud of biting flies beset them in late summer. Lira looked toward distant mountains near today's city of Pyongyang and suggested that the clan seek the higher altitudes to get away from the insects. In the low hills northeast of modern Pyongyang a soothing wind from the west was pleasant, and they established a new village.

As they set up camp, Elar fell ill again. Oola had carried her on his back for days, and he declared that she must rest in her bed; her spirit was too weak to survive more of the torture of travel.

They remained here for months as Elar lingered, not recovering but unable to say goodbye to those she loved. She could no longer stand up, but the most tender care kept her alive. Tor took on the task of providing each day a handful of small birds to be made into nourishing soup. Blun combed the hills for nourishing seedpods and tender herbs to enrich the soup. Yun gave up all other duties to stay by her with a fan to cool her fevers. Oola and Blun were inconsolable.

Finally Elar weakened beyond their grasp, and she died here not far from present-day Pyongyang. Taga and Tuit both participated in the burial rites on a hillside overlooking a river. Blun's singing had a magical, unearthly quality as it throbbed with real grief. Taga played his flute, while Tuit gave a sensitive performance on the sacred drum. Such enthralling, heartfelt music had never been heard before in this part of the earth. The ground all around the area was strewn with flowers gathered on the hillsides and lovingly offered for her spirit.

CHAPTER ~56~

THE CLAN WAS heavy of heart and loath to leave behind them the remains of Elar, who had given so much of her spirit to teach everyone the secrets of harmony. In the spoken history of the Caribou Clan she became a goddess, a holy woman whose life had been lived for others and whose influence had always brought out the good in others. Maa pointed out to the young women of the clan that if they modeled their lives on generous Elar, they might become great also in the history of the Caribou Clan.

Taga and Yun were deeply affected by their loss, and the children were bereft. It was Maa who felt real loneliness because for most of her life Elar had been her constant friend and the person she confided in. While the others gradually got used to their grief, Maa did not. Her life was much diminished without Elar, her loving mentor. She was vulnerable because of this.

It had been only a moon after the burial of Elar when Alun planned a trip back down to the beach. It would not take too many days, and it would cheer up Elar's children and grandchildren. To play in the surf for a carefree day or two would be healthful fun. Who could resist such an opportunity?

Taga wanted to stay at the camp but thought it would be good for Maa, who seemed to be moping. The young people, Blun, Oola, Tuit, and Tor, were thrilled at the prospect of bathing in the ocean again. They promised to bring back some spectacular seafood. There was no reason to delay, so they gathered supplies for the journey and left at once in midmorning, a small party of travelers trying to find lighter hearts.

Once at the beach, two lean-to sheds were put up, one for Alun and the boys and one for Maa and Blun. That done, there was only resting in the sun and playing in the cool, delicious water. The youngsters invented games and raced down the beach, spending energy and tantalizing each other needlessly, but Maa found the rest she had needed as she lay in the sun or looked for shells by the shore.

Tor discovered the remains of a reed raft on the beach and was enchanted at the idea of repairing it and going out on the water. This kind of working with his hands had always appealed to him. Alun approved of his project, so he gathered reeds from a marsh nearby and summoned his work crew. Tuit declared bluntly that the old raft had decayed and would not be seaworthy despite patching. Tor yielded, so Tuit, Oola and Blun helped with a project of weaving a new raft that was sturdy and strong. The youngsters spent happy hours working together.

Maa gathered a matched set of shells for a necklace and went on down the beach until she was a distant figure by the edge of the water. Alun, seeing that the young people were happy at their raft, thought that she should not wander too far alone. He did not know whether she saw him following her as she walked slowly on and on.

When he caught up to her, she was laying out the seashells on the sand in the pattern of a necklace. They were among the prettiest he had seen, and they both stood back to admire them. He put his hand over her shoulder for a moment, then held her head to him as he kissed her forehead lightly. Suddenly the years of his desire for her rose within him. She felt the weight of his feeling as he swelled against her thigh, compelling and wondrous to her, and as she lifted her head he glimpsed in her eyes gratitude as well as surrender. He stepped in closer that he might enclose her in his arms, so she might know how desperate had been his need through all this time they had walked together on the trail without speaking of his love for her. He covered her with kisses on her face, her neck, her shoulders, her breasts, while she began to melt inside and burn with equal desire as she reached for him. She could not wait. This terrible sweetness of being one with Alun was what she had longed for and it was irresistible.

An incoming tide lapped at their feet; he still held his arms about her, unwilling to let her go after his passion had been spent. She was kissing his arms and chest to show her happiness at having shared that passion. They were in a smiling world completely theirs.

Alun, moved by a gentle fondness, kissed her lips and nose, a loving gesture. But he did not stop. The wonder of finally being close to her was so sweet that he covered her body with his mouth while waves of new desire arose in her with each kiss. His own arousal came sharply as he sensed her response and need to feel him within her again, a hunger beyond belief to him. When he could wait no longer, they came together with fierce energy and continued longing.

This time something had happened; a new light was in her eyes. She could not keep her hands off him. The very sweetness was unbearable. She clung to him. He understood and held her tight. This was only for today, no matter how deeply their bodies yearned for each other.

After a time he stood up. Her shells would be gone soon in the rising tide; he gathered them up and drew her to her feet, still clinging. She was not thinking now, as pure emotion kept sweeping through her. She let him guide her around a rock formation where they found a clear pocket of sand sheltered from the beach by the rock. Here she pulled him down and continued to hold her arms around him, to make him as close as possible. He acquiesced and cuddled her, kissing her to console her. He could not promise her tomorrow; he could only give her transcendent happiness today.

They were completely alone. Time after time as their passion rekindled they came together until their hunger was finally satisfied. They rested on the sand in a deep shadow cast now by the sun in the west shining on their rock.

He bent to kiss her again, but she pushed him away, slowly. Her body tingled with the light bruises from so many caresses, and she felt tired despite an inner energy that soared crazily. Although they had feasted on their passion, today's love-making would have to last for a long time. They would have to go back to the lean-to and the youngsters. She would go back to her loving husband.

CHAPTER ~57~

WHEN THE PARTY returned from the beach, they were all tanned and rested. Taga noted that Maa's moping and restlessness were gone, and she had new energy. The boys had brought back a new raft they had made.

Having talked again with young Lira about this area, Taga now knew that they were on a peninsula with a backbone of mountains running down it. It might be better if they crossed these mountains before winter came. On the other side they would find the Great Water, a magnificent wonder.

There were five rafts to portage now, along with the burdens of the household possessions. Taga followed the animal trails, as they had done before. Most of the way was not difficult, and they came out upon high ridges and began to wind down toward the coastal region.

Maa walked now beside her husband, Taga, who was usually in the lead. Tor still shadowed her everywhere, so he was near most of the time. Alun's companion often now was Blun, by her choice, but this meant that Tuit could be found near her, and thus Oola was close by. Often Yun was last, because he kept stragglers at a minimum.

They arrived just southwest of today's Hungdoki-dong, Korea, and looked out upon the Great Water. It was the modern Sea of Japan, an arm of the mighty Pacific Ocean.

The sight they saw was one our generation has never seen. The ice in the huge glaciers of their age was one mile deep in some northern regions of the earth, such as Canada. It had gathered so much water that the water levels of the great oceans had dropped three or four hundred feet, leaving wide dry beaches like tablelands fronting the ocean.

The Caribou Clan saw a flat, grassy carpet leading toward the northeast, and this great walkway edging the ocean was full of game among scattered trees. What the Caribou Clan did not know yet was that the wide walkway extended all the way around the northern Asian coast and on to Alaska via the Bering Land Bridge. For a time the animals and people of the Asian continent could walk across to the continents of the Americas on dry land, but when a later warming period began melting the ice, the Bering Sea again divided the two continents.

The Caribou Clan settled next to the ocean with the flat coast before them and gray cliffs towering behind them. Hunting on the beach was easy, so they ate game often. The fruits of the ocean were well appreciated by this time. Life by the sea was so enjoyable that Taga declared that the clan would settle down and build a permanent village near the shore. Apparently they had arrived at the east that was his destination. This site was southwest of present-day Hungdokidong, Korea. Taga's dream of arriving at the Great Water had been fulfilled.

The Caribou Clan remained in their village here for five years critical for the youngsters of the clan, for here they grew to the age of needing to mate. Tuit, born in 25,502 B.C., had been seven years old when the earthquake came in 25,495 B.C. In the year 25,490 B.C. when his clan arrived at the Pacific Ocean, having crossed the Asian continent from the Gobi Desert to Korea on foot, Tuit was twelve, near to thirteen. Blun, at least a year older, was probably thirteen. Tor, born in 25,499 B.C., was still only nine. Oola, born just prior to the disastrous tornado that claimed his parents' lives, was ten years old.

All the children soon became excellent swimmers and divers in the new environment. When they met two native families on the coast, they understood how the sea provides clothing as well as food, for they learned to hunt seals. When they wished to go out on the sea to hunt bigger fish, the natives laughed at their five rafts made of reeds and then taught them to make a new, one-man craft with pointed ends to meet the waves and slice through them. Thus the young people of the Caribou Clan grew adept at the survival skills of people who live by the sea.

CHAPTER ~58~

At first only Maa suspected that beautiful Blun had fallen in love with Alun. Alun's hair was very white and thinner now, for he had reached the age of 48. He was still athletic , slim, and active, and his advice and help were constantly sought by Taga and the youngsters. Seeing Blun so often by his side gave Maa a heartache that she would have denied. She thought privately that such a pairing was ridiculous. Really ridiculous.

Because Blun had no mother now, and she had always been stubborn about obtaining whatever she wanted deeply, for her there simply were no rules to this newest game. She resolved to trap the man of her choice. She knew that she was talented as well as beautiful; friends often complimented her on her startlingly blue eyes. Alun might be old, but he was easily the most handsome man around, and he had no woman.

At thirteen Blun thought she knew how to catch the attention of a man. She confided in nobody; the details were her own inventions. When she found Alun alone, Blun began sitting close to him, sometimes holding his hand until he withdrew it, as he always did. He had always been a loving uncle to the children and grandchildren of Tzan, and his joy in their achievements gave him the right to a brief kiss or caress as part of his congratulations, just as their parents did.

It completely disarmed him when Blun was not satisfied with a brief hug and kiss but threw her arms around him and clung to him.

Blun's behavior began to disturb Alun; then he shook his head and thought that he was attaching too much importance to her exaggerated fondness; Blun had always been a bit capricious. Soon Blun would choose a husband.

Blun hung around the hut set aside for single men, where Alun had his pallet bed. When he arose in the morning, she greeted him at the door. All day she was as near him as she could get. She escorted him at night back home.

Tuit said to his mother, "Blun is acting so strangely, mother. I never get to see her. Mother, I always thought that I would marry Blun, but she doesn't care for me."

What could Maa say to her son? She soothed him, saying, "Blun lost her mother such a short time ago. She may be lonely."

Then Blun did an extraordinary thing. She was desperate to have her way. At midnight she left her hut, careless of anything but her desire to see Alun. She entered the silent hut of the single men.

She caught her breath as she moved through the semidarkness; only one pallet seemed to have a sleeping man on it. By his snowy hair she knew that it was Alun. Her heart stopped. Had she made a mistake in coming inside? But no one would know.

Alun awoke drowsily to find that he was not alone in his bed; a girl was pressing the flesh of her body against his body as she wept and tried to kiss him. He was startled, but he knew it was Blun. Dear capricious Blun. He did not have to be told what her recent behavior had meant; the girl had taken a great liberty now to assert her goal. She wanted him.

He knew he must handle this situation carefully without hurting her feelings. This behavior could not be tolerated, however. He wondered if he had encouraged her, but he felt blameless.

"Little Blun," he said softly. "Blun, stop crying and talk to me. Is something wrong? What do you mean by this bizarre behavior?" He wanted to give her a hug and dry her tears, but Blun knew what she wanted and could not turn back now.

The girl kissed him on the mouth while she held him down; it was a wet, wild kiss of love and longing that was terribly sweet. She pulled his hand to her breast while her lips lingered on his, and she relished his reaction when he found how full and round it was. She wanted him to know that she was no longer a child, and that she needed a lover, him.

He was full of shock and knew that he must calm her down so they could talk. He knew how far she was prepared to go when her hand reached down to his stomach and caressed it. The hand was slyly moving downward and he felt his own rising response. She felt it, too, and relaxed into his arms. Her tears were over, and now she was to know if she had dared too much.

He tried to sit up, but she pushed him back and covered him with hot kisses while she maneuvered one of his hands to touch her body. Her tears were falling again, and suddenly it was too much for him.

"Blun, if you want me, this is not the way to do it."

"But I love you so, Alun. I want you so." Louder sobs indicated that a temper tantrum might follow.

"Here, here, you are a sweet and lovely girl, but you cannot hit me with such a blow. I did not expect it. Now lie still and let me talk to you. All right, now, tell me about it."

He held her in his arms as she let the tears flow, sometimes hiding her head against him. Gradually the fact that he had his arms around her was calming, and she stopped weeping but was restless.

"Don't send me away, oh Alun. Please." She was letting him know that he had won; she would apologize soon.

"Dear Blum, I will hold you tight and I will let you stay. How could

I have known? You beautiful creature!"

"Alun, marry me. Let me be this close to you for the rest of my life."

In the darkness she could not see a stunned expression cloud his face; this was too new for him.

"Blun, I love all my family tenderly, and you most especially, but I have never spoken to you as a lover. Isn't that true?"

Blun perceived that she was losing a little ground, so the tears started once more. He held her close but made no other move to console her.

She broke free and pounded on his chest as she exclaimed, "Alun, you pitiful fool. This is Blun! I am your Blun!"

As he gathered her into his arms again, he said into her ear, "All right, Blun. You may stay here in my arms for a little while more tonight. Tomorrow I will speak to Yun so that he will not be so surprised, and if you love me, we will share a bed. I will build a hut and marry you. You are a sweet prize, and I am an old man. It might not work out very well. What do you say?"

She was stunned. He did not know what her silence meant. Did she regret her rashness tonight?

Blun could not believe that she had won. When he held her to him tenderly, she could feel his questioning still. Why had she chosen him?

He gently kissed her forehead, her nose, her lips. When he kissed her neck and then her nipple, he was not prepared for the shock that went through her. She began breathing faster, and he held himself back. He could not believe his good fortune; he loved her, of course; now he was excited by her beyond measure.

CHAPTER ~59~

He was still awake when a rustling of birds told him that dawn was near. He had spent the whole night thinking of their future. Today their hut would be built. He would have her to himself after one more day. He could not wait.

He kissed her ear and spoke into it. "Blun. Little Blun. You must get up and go at once to your hut before daybreak. We shall talk this morning with Yun and he will go to Taga. Then our hut will be built before tonight."

"I cannot believe it! Is it true?" Languidly she put out a finger and traced his lips. Then she rolled over onto him so that all his exciting thoughts during the night of her newly blossoming figure and the sweetness of her hot love for him almost made him forget what he had said.

"Blun, dear, get up. This must be done right. Go."

So she stood up.

He gathered her into his arms and kissed her on the lips, nose, and neck gently and lovingly. Then he gave her a little push and she was gone, but he felt he could not wait for this night.

They talked with Yun and his wife, Lin. They said that they had found love together. They wanted a blessing on their marriage. Yun must go to Taga, and a hut must be built today.

"You know that she is looking for a father." Yun pointed out the obvious problem. "Her parents are dead and she wants a father."

Blun teared up. "I fell in love with him long, long ago. I love him passionately. I must have him."

"I will take care of her tenderly and love her the rest of my life," said Alun. "She needs someone to look after her. I want to care for her."

Blun was sobbing. "He's all I ever wanted. He is going to marry me."

Yun went to see Taga and the hut was begun at once. The day became a day of rejoicing and feasting. Blun put on her best costume and sat near the hut that was rising while her friends stopped by. They said, "May the goddess of the hearth bless your hut. May your hearth fire never go out."

All the men helped make the hut in the neat design of the Caribou Clan, and by mid-afternoon it was finished. Merriment and feasting continued while the flute and drum occasionally were heard.

Blun moved her clothing into the new hut. When she found that friends and family had showered her with new cooking bowls of stone and two carved bone cups – elegant treasures, she cried with pleasure.

Everyone pretended not to notice when the couple disappeared, for the fun went on. Tuit had left the village at noon, and Maa saw that he was sick at heart. He could not know that his mother felt something of the same aching in her heart as she saw the way Alun looked at his fresh young bride. Maa knew that Alun would never turn to her again. Already he had been besotten with longing for the night ahead.

He fastened the door flap and looked around the darkened hut for her. Perhaps she had not left the feasting yet. Ever since their morning leave-taking, he had felt a yearning to hold her again, an ache in his depths to satisfy the girl who kissed him so hotly and wetly. He was glad they had waited and were doing the right thing, but now the waiting would be over. He breathed harder.

"Alun? Oh, Alun! It was so hard to wait all day." She had a wet kiss for him that missed and caught his ear. He thought to himself how young she was; probably all nerves by this time.

He kissed her full on the mouth with a passion as fierce as that she had shown last night, a demanding, long kiss that reminded her that she was not playing a game now, however capricious she might feel. This night she was a woman, a married woman. She had said she needed him, her husband, and he intended to satisfy her.

CHAPTER
~60~

A BOWL OF FOOD was placed outside the new hut so that the bride would not have to cook and might stay in seclusion if she wished. It was morning and Blun had not slept for a second night, so she was walking in a dream as she retrieved the bowl. Alun was asleep, but her hunger now was for food. She found the fresh fruit refreshing and held the bowl near Alun's nose as she woke him. "Look what we have to eat. Come, let's eat together."

His eyes opened. He saw her seated on the pallet near him, and as memory of the night came back to him, he took the bowl and set it aside. His arms went around her, pulling her down to him again. He tasted the fruit on her lips.

The clan whispered and walked by the new hut. They were glad that the two had found a happy pairing. Blun had found the mate she wanted, and Alun would certainly take good care of her. Love sometimes comes as a surprise.

Soon the clan was used to seeing them together everywhere, clinging to each other. Alun was indeed besotted with her and indulgent. Blun was a fine cook and housekeeper; her teacher had been Elar, the best. Their marriage was full of happiness, beyond harmony, absolute bliss.

Tuit took Oola and Tor on hunting trips to absent himself from the village. His mother had her own silent grief, but she had the good sense to double her efforts to make Taga happy. Tuit, however, had no other woman to turn to; he loved Blun still. He said to Maa, "Mother, I shall never get married. When I am a shaman and leader, I shall serve the clan without a mate."

Her response was generalized. "We shall see."

Five years passed as the clan enjoyed their site looking out on the Great Water, the Pacific Ocean. The older generation remained fit, but they were feeling the weight of the years. Taga had been born in 25,519 B.C. so he was now past his mid-forties. Maa was a year younger than her husband. Alun, in his fifties, had become a very old man with a stunningly beautiful and very young wife. Blun was attentive to him and still happy.

Yun heard from the natives who lived closest that a saber-toothed tiger had been seen in the lower part of their peninsula; it hunted and killed at will. Yun went at once to Taga, who knew from the spoken legends of the tribe that this was a menace they would find hardest to deal with. What protection would they have from this cunning, strong beast?

Their huts offered little protection from such a terrible wild animal. Hunters did not have weapons that could kill it; their weapons were good only in close combat.

Taga ordered the hunters to make long, sharpened poles. Bolas and slings would not be effective. The only way to catch such an animal was to dig a pit for it to fall into; the trap could be baited with a deer. But a strong cat like this one might spring out of the trap and kill its trappers.

Taga had grown masterful, a larger than life leader who gave wise and cool guidance to the clan. But he could find no solution to this problem. To sit and wait for the cat to find them was intolerable. But what else? On checking with the natives again, he found them preparing to leave. They were afraid and were getting out.

Another bit of information on the cat was brought to them: it was getting closer. It was sauntering northward along the coast.

Tuit came up with a solution. Many of the young men were very much at home on the sea; the clan had five rafts that were well made of woven reeds.

At first Taga would not hear of it. Then he gave it some thought. He gave an order for more poles; this time he needed poles to guide the rafts. Tuit had a better idea; the poles for the rafts needed to be wider in the water, but small enough at one end to fit the hand. That is, some of the poles should be shaped like that. The small, narrow boats the boys used in the sea also needed wider poles with narrow, rounded ends. The youths of the clan already had six such boats.

When Taga ordered that household goods – only essential ones – should be sent to the rafts to be lashed onto them, everyone responded obediently. But the thought of launching out into the sea left them weak and cowardly. They saw to food supplies and water; Taga made a plan of the occupants of the boats and the rafts. The rafts would be buoyant, but if waves tossed them around, occupants would have a hard time staying on. Perhaps the people had to be lashed onto the rafts also.

The sea was still; the weather was good. The time had come, and the rafts were filled with reluctant voyagers. The commander of each raft memorized his passenger list and would be responsible for each person aboard. The six boats each held one person. Each raft had about six people on it. Those who were passengers, with no duties of using the poles, were lashed together and to the raft. This was more and more scary. The rafts were lifted into the sea and given a push to float them; then the six boatmen pushed off from the shore. The little flotilla had some trouble getting off; rafts butted into each other until they began to feel the current carrying them out into the Sea of Japan.

Many heroic tales were remembered later by the members of the clan who made this voyage. Fair weather and a strong current favored them as they went north and then curved to the east, roughly following a shoreline that looked rocky. They lost sight of land and were in open sea, with choppy waves and a stiff breeze, but the current carried them on. Most of the rafts and boats were within sight, all in the grasp of the water's flow. For four days and nights they held on bravely, encouraging each other. Then a gale wind sprang up, signifying that a storm was approaching. They were all doused with the salt water from higher waves just as the weather grew chilly and the sky darkened.

The men steering the rafts saw a promontory in the misty distance and huge rocks jutting out of the water. It was difficult to avoid the rocks with the clumsy rafts, but none spilled its load. Once around the promontory, they saw a cove where there might be some shelter. Hailing other rafts, the steersmen strained to reach the shore. The boats circled among the rafts, shouting directions as they all headed for the land. The five rafts got close enough for the passengers to wade ashore then help pull the loaded rafts onto the beach. Six boats nudged the shore and the boatmen stepped out into the water. Boats and rafts were far apart, all up and down the pebbled beach.

Out on the sea shafts of lightning streaked across the sky and then rain pummeled them all as they huddled on the beach in groups, miserable in condition but very relieved to have arrived somewhere on land. Amid the storm, Taga made his way up and down the beach, making certain that every raft had landed and that everyone was safe even if wet. As night fell the rain was lighter; groups wrapped their skins around them and slept on the pebbles or leaned against each other and slept.

CHAPTER
~61~

WITH A CLEAR dawn spirits rose; friends and family found each other safe, many weeping, whether in gratitude or in memory of the rough voyage. Taga drew them all together and announced that through great skill and courage all the boats and rafts had come through the sea with not one loss. At that a warrior/hunter felt so strongly about his battle with the sea that he broke into a war chant of victory; everyone joined him, some hysterically, as the loud, rhythmic chant echoed around the beach.

The rafts were raised on one end to form five shelters that were really less sheltering than they were centers at which families could gather. There was food enough, but the feeling of displacement made women and children cling to each other with a real hunger for home.

Wondering at the good fortune of his clan's having brought everyone to shore, Taga sent a scouting party inland to look for prospects of food and for a setting appropriate to a new camp. Some boys were sent up the coast to look for reeds or rushes, or for trees to be used for building huts. A third team was sent to work to find food by the shore – shellfish or fish. Women soon realized that they needed to dry out clothing for their families. Soon everyone found work.

Maa voiced the question for the whole clan, "Where are we, Taga?" But Taga had no idea where they had landed. They had crossed a sea, he knew, so they were separated from the land of their origin by more than mountains or tundra.

Actually, the Caribou Clan had been swept to the island of Hokkaido, which is northern Japan today, and they had landed on the western side of that island in a place near present-day Otaru.

The scouting party went across the island to the eastern side, where they found a broad grassy plain fronting the Pacific Ocean. The plain, of course, was caused by the receding oceans of their Ice Age.

The Caribou Clan adjusted again to new conditions and built another temporary village. Their diet from hunting and fishing was more than adequate. The young people had learned the survival skills needed for life by the ocean and soon wore sealskin and sharkskin while fishing, as an alternate to caribou. When one area was hunted out, the clan moved on along the wide beach on the eastern side of the island and made a new camp.

With a sensible, resilient leader such as Taga had become, and with the skills they had learned from experience and from clans they had met while traveling, the Caribou Clan adapted well to new conditions as necessary. They were following the animals which they hunted, along the shoreline passage heading toward the northeast.

In another year the Caribou Clan discovered a solid stretch of dry land leading from Hokkaido to the northeast; today it is an island chain called the Kuril Islands. Much of the land area traversed by the Caribou Clan has now gone under the water. They walked across this area to the peninsula of Kamchatka, following the game on the extended grassy plain by the sea. Climate changes were gradual, and food remained available from both hunting and fishing.

Finding the eastern side of Kamchatka mountainous, they followed its western side until mountains got in their way again. Here, just beyond today's city of Palana on Kamchatka, they crossed to the eastern side of the peninsula, seeing once more the grassy strip by the shoreline during the short summer months. The sea they faced at this point was the Bering Sea.

The shoreline extension was severely cold in winter, when a moderate amount of snow fell in this region, and the sea was iced over for the long winters, then the clan dug in and sometimes made houses of ice or went underground for warmer shelter. In summer the walking was easy and the grass attracted grazing animals of all sizes. Behind the shoreline loomed rugged mountains where hunting parties found new game. Both animals and humans of that time needed stamina for the long journey, but food was no problem in summer, and the Caribou Clan knew how to survive severe cold.

CHAPTER
~62~

TWO YEARS FURTHER into their journey around the northeastern coastline of Asia, as they wintered on the eastern side of Kamchatka, the men of the clan prepared for a seal hunt. It was not necessary to use their boats, for scouts had reported in detail on a nearby seal colony; it was near rocky terrain but accessible.

Alun, now aging decidedly, insisted on going along on this trek, to get a few skins for mitten hand-coverings. Hunting once again became an obsession. Blun went with him, even though she was pregnant with their first child. They were constantly together, sharing the thrill of encountering danger as well as the tedium of long winter nights. As she reached the fifth month of her pregnancy, Blun became awkward but not too much so, and her natural good health allowed her to feel very normal. They were both intensely happy over the coming child.

The party of seal hunters traveled by foot over a path stamped out early in the season by both fishers and hunters; it led around a cove that was under thick ice. From a cliff the hunters could see in the middle of the cove a dark streak of open water, but the shores were frozen as hard as rock.

They heard the seals before they saw them, and the humans fell silent. This group of hunters had agreed upon a plan of driving the seals straight toward a rock wall and clubbing them one by one as the animals were hemmed in. This would be efficient and quick.

Blun watched from a safe place as the men crept toward the graceful dark shapes on the ice. As the men drew near, they brandished their sticks and stone axes and yelled at the retreating shapes. To her horror, Blun saw Alun run over the ice toward a thin black line; he did not look down as he concentrated on the seal closest to him. As he reached the black line, it swallowed him. One moment he was running and the next moment he had disappeared.

Blun's terror was so enormous that she was stunned. When she began her agonized screaming, the other hunters looked toward her and understood what had happened. A slit, a small crack in the shore ice, had widened and Alun had fallen into the water and was under the ice. They rushed to crowd around the spot but found fragile edges by the small black streak that marked the crack in the ice. The men knew instantly that there was nothing they could do. Either the frigid water had already stopped his heart or he had drowned. In one instant Alun was gone forever. His body was never found. Blun had to be carried home; she was helpless, unable to speak.

It was Tuit who lifted her and carried her carefully, tenderly to her hut. He sent for his mother, but he did not leave Blun alone. For three days she did not open her eyes, while Tuit sat beside her pallet. Maa, too, attended the beautiful girl who looked so pale that she might have been dead also. Someone had to be there to keep out the many members of the clan who were eager to see her, to try to do something to help her. But it was important to let her rest, in the quiet gloom of her own hut, while her mind slowly began to look upon the unthinkable thing that had happened.

Finally she opened her eyes in a blank stare full of emptiness, for her world had become empty of her great love. Maa was in the room, by the door, and Tuit sat close by the bed, watchful. Blun could not speak, although she struggled for a moment to say something. Tuit saw the effort she was making, and he said it for her, "Rest, Blun; we are with you. You do not need to speak. Alun is gone, but I will take care of you."

She closed her eyes again and slept quietly. Maa thought that she should eat when she woke again, and she said so. Then she began to prepare a soft gruel made of grains she had gathered during the autumn.

Disconcertingly, when she became fully awake, Blun was unable to feed herself or speak. Moreover, she did not seem to be able to care to do so. Tuit moved into her house, feeding her and making her comfortable, talking to her as if she would respond. But she had no response to anyone. The world had ceased to exist for her.

Maa was amazed at the change she saw in her oldest son. He was quieter, but also taller, stronger. That part of him which had seemed fragmented, uncentered, had now become whole. Blun had become his whole life, and he was bent upon restoring her to activity and to acceptance of his love.

There came the day that she emerged to sit in a weak noonday sun, bundled up in beautiful furs, her shining red-blonde hair carefully plaited and wrapped around her head. Tuit was close by, attentive that she did not tire of all the attention from people who stopped by to speak. Blun still had not recovered the power of speech, although she now could stand and walk; she recognized some of the friends who spoke to her warmly, but she had no smile for anyone yet. It was too soon.

For Maa there was a terrible moment when she admitted to herself that Blun's bulging stomach evidenced Alun's child. She was stricken with the cruel ache of jealousy, and although she knew it was an unworthy emotion, she was wild for a day or two, absenting herself from both Tuit and Blun with excuses that covered years of loss. When she was able to trust herself once more, she had reconciled herself to the past and now looked forward to the wonderful gift of being the grandmother to Alun's child.

As spring drew near, Tuit described to Blun what was happening to the world outside their door. He reported on the arrival of the doves, the first swelling of buds on the wild cherry trees, the frail peeping of frogs.

Her first spoken word filled him with joy: "Dooid." She was trying to say his name. She was somehow expressing her gratitude for all he was doing for her each day. And she allowed him to hold her at night now, seeking comfort from his loving embrace in the long sleepless, dark hours.

"Mother, I am growing closer to her. She is slowly beginning to respond. Mother, someday she will love me as I love her." Tuit was almost breathing a prayer as he said this to Maa. And Maa made her own appeal to the gods who blessed happy households. She added a special plea to the goddess of child-bearing that all would go well.

A huge late snowfall deluged the village; few of the clan braved the wind-whipped and icy pellets that filled the air. After one trip to his mother's home, Tuit knew that he would not want to go out again. He began a task of applying deer grease to an old slingshot which he wished to make more pliable so that he might bring down a few rabbits still clad in white fur. The fire was warm and the task was not too demanding; he was content that the woman he loved lay nearby on her pallet. He glanced often at her round form under the soft skins.

She moaned. When she suddenly sat upright, her eyes were wide with fear and pain. Tuit knew instantly what was wrong; it was time for the baby. He needed his mother. In this blizzard he must go for Maa, at once.

Putting his arms around Blum, he explained to her that he was going to get the midwife, his mother. He sat her down by the fire and, pulling on his heavy furs, he plunged into the swirling snow.

The delivery took many hours, lasting from mid-afternoon until nearly daybreak. With the sun's first rays over the quiet, white world outside, a baby's cry broke the stillness. Blun had borne a son, a healthy, blue-eyed, and handsome boy. Maa at once saw his father's features in the child, despite his amazingly blue eyes. This, her first grandchild, would be beloved.

The birth of the child marked Blun's cure from her inability to speak; from the moment Maa brought the baby, bound in a soft rabbit skin, to be suckled, Blun was able to coo over him.

It was only a few days later that Taga made a public announcement, followed by a bountiful feasting, that his son Tuit was now the husband of the beautiful widow Blun, and that they would share the joy of raising her son, whom they had named Tlan. His own happiness was apparent, and the clan, too, rejoiced that such good had come of the sorrows of the past.

The Caribou Clan, a few years later, in one good summer season of following the big game, passed the Diomede while crossing the place we today call the Bering Strait but for them was merely part of the continuous journey over dry land. They did not realize, as our travelers came onto the Seward Peninsula, that they had reached an area that today is Alaska. From its start in the Asia of the Gobi Desert, the Caribou Clan had traveled to the continent of North America.

APPENDIX NO. 1 GEOGRAPHY OF THE NOVEL - TAGA AND MAA

1. **25,500 B.C.**
   Location in Gobi Desert somewhere south of present-day Ulan Bator where Taga has a hut and Tlan lives in a cave with hut attached. A rocky little stream is close by, and there is a line of low hills near. However, the tundra basically surrounds them.

2. **25,499-25,500**
   The site of the village of Tzan, which was destroyed by an immense tornado, and the new village founded by Tlan to replace it is somewhere near the present - day city of Arvayheer, where both hills and the edge of the tundra may be found. The hills here have a cave with a spring inside; the overflow of its water makes a waterfall and a small stream which goes back underground.

3. **25, 495**
   Five years after its founding, this village is destroyed by an earthquake which creates a great chasm between the hills and the tundra, while it raises a new line of hills also. This area on the present-day map is near the river Ongi, which curves out eastward then southward then again westward, making a big curve which ends in the Lake Ulaan Nuur.

4. **25,495**
   Fleeing from the imminent earthquake, Taga leads the clan out onto the tundra a distance of two days journey by foot. This new village is temporary, and it is near a small stream with a few trees,

Downstream an hour's journey by foot one finds a small line of hills, where the wicked Urkluk clan has its dirty village of huts. Surrounding these landmarks is the wide tundra. Taga's new temporary village is near the present-day city of Tavin, south-southwest of present-day Ulan Bator. (Please note that Mongolia has two cities with the same name; the other Tavin is due north of Ulan Bator.)

5. **25, 495 B.C.**

It very soon becomes necessary for the Caribou Clan to move again, because it is evident that the earthquake to the west has moved the small stream on which they depended. They have to relocate to be near a water supply. Taga leads them north toward the present-day river Tuul, which has its origin in the mountains northwest of Ulan Bator; there it branches off the Orthon River, which branches off the Selenge River and has origins on the southeast side of Lake Baikal.

6. **25,495 - 25, 494**

They follow the river Tuul to the site of present-day Ulan Bator (capital of Mongolia). From here to the east there are many rivers and there is more grass. They head east, crossing three rivers, to the river Tsenher and follow it to its juncture with a larger river, the Kerulen River. At a spot where three rivers meet at once (near the present-day city of Ondorhaan), they strike out to the southeast.

7. **25,494 - 25,493**

They meet a chain of mountains, which they cross near the present-day city of Buyant, at the narrowest point of these mountains. They find two lakes on their trail across the mountains. After Buyant they are once again on tundra, but it is grassy. To the south there are sand dunes, so they take a northeastern route around the edge of the mountains. They find it lonely and fairly barren here.

8. **25, 493**

They find a pass through the mountains near present-day Dong Ujimqin Qi and go through it to present-day Xi Ujimqin Qi, located on a short river.

9. 25,493 - 25,492

They hit a river now called Qagan Moron and follow it as it joins the river Xar Moron (which is much larger) into foothills and more mountains. To the south are sand dunes, so they take the northern side of this river to the present-day Dalin (now in China). This has been a rugged, mountainous route.

10. 25,492-25,491

At Dalin they meet natives who give them advice; there is a massive chain of mountains to the east and they must go south to the Big Water. They follow the Liao River south to the present-day Shenyang, and then continue south to the delta mouth of the Liao located on the northern part of the Yellow Sea. They are near the Pacific Ocean.

11. 25,491-25,490

They take a land route around the peninsula (Liaodong Bandao) to the present-day Korean Bay to a spot near Pyongyang, then across mountains to the Sea of Japan at Hungdoki-dong on the Pacific Ocean. They have reached the wide sea. They have spent five years going from the middle of Mongolia to the Pacific Ocean on foot.

12. 25,490-25,485

The Pacific Ocean has receded 300-400 feet, leaving a wide area of beach and regrowth that is fairly flat and which extends out into the present-day edge of the ocean. This wide edge of the ocean extends all the way around the northern Asian coast to Kamchatka and to Alaska; it is called today the Bering Bridge, leading from Asia to the American continent via land. The weary travelers settle down at Hungdoki-dong and meet natives who teach them what a rich diet the ocean can provide. They learn how to swim well, how to fish in the ocean, and how to make and use boats and rafts to navigate the water. The sea can provide clothing as well as food, just as their caribou used to do. They remain there for five years, and what they learn will make it possible for them to survive as they continue their voyage on land around the edge of the Asian continent to Alaska.

13. 24,485 B.C. 24,475

The Caribou Clan again starts to journey, going on the wide beach-land most of the time, to Kimch'aek on the coast, then up to Ch'ongjin (in present-day Russia). (The area near present Vladivostok was far different from its appearance today, due to the 300-400 recession of the ocean.) From Vladivostok and Nahodka (present-day names) they head up the coast but at Dal'negorsk they are shown how to raft across to present-day Otaru on today's Island of Hokkaido. They are able then to walk on dry land from there to today's Kamchatka Peninsula (where islands exist now). They follow the edge of the sea up Kamchatka to the present-day city of Kavaca and on to the present-day Bering Strait, where they find no waters dividing the northern continents. They walk on around the Peninsula to the present-day town of Nunjamo, then walk across the Diomede in the Alaska of today.

14. 24,475-24,465

Facing them is today's Brooks Mountain, and there are other mountain chains in the interior, so the Caribou Clan continue on the coastal route. This leads around today's Norton Sound and Pastol Bay, past the delta where the Yukon River of today empties into the Pacific. Still on the wide land strip bordering the Ocean, they go past today's Sheldon Point, Scammon Bay, Cape Romanzo, and Hooper Bay, and on to the present-day area of Toksook Bay. Here they halt, because Taga has fallen ill. This is the place where Taga, their leader and their shaman, dies, near Cape Vancouver, in 25,465 B.C. at the age of 53.

APPENDIX NO. 2

TIME FRAME OF NOVEL - 35 YEARS

25,500 B. C . . . . .25,465 B.C. (35 yrs.)

Taga . . . . .53 at death in Alaska
Born 25,517
B. C.16 when he eloped with Maa

Maa . . . . Still alive in Alaska

Tuit . . . . .37 yrs. old
Born 25, 502 B. C.
5 yrs. older than bro. Tor
When Taga dies, Tuit leads clan.

Tor . . . . .32 years old
Born 25, 497

Tlan . . . . Died in 25, 495 at age 55
Born 25,548 B.C.
Leader of clan and shaman

Elar . . . . Died at Pyongyang en route
Wife of Tlan

Oola . . . . .35 years old
Born 25,500, son of Tzan
Adopted by Elar

Blun . . . . Ca. 37 years old
Born ca. 25, 502 B.C.

Kidnapped by Urglun, adopted by Elar

Alun . . . . 63 years old
Born son of Tlan and Passa
38 years old at time of earthquake
on his return to clan

Beros. . . . . 57 if he lives
22 or so in 25,498 on
trip to Red Cliffs

Sula . . . . 37 years old
Dau. of Tzan and Seldun
born 2 yrs. before tornado
Adopted by Beros

Yun . . . . 45 years old
Born in 25,510 B.C.

www.ingramcontent.com/pod-product-compliance
Ingram Content Group UK Ltd.
Pitfield, Milton Keynes, MK11 3LW, UK
UKHW020144250726
13967UKWH00002B/856